ROCK STEP, TRIPLE HOMICIDE

An Introduction to Lindy Hop...
<u>And</u> a Murder Mystery

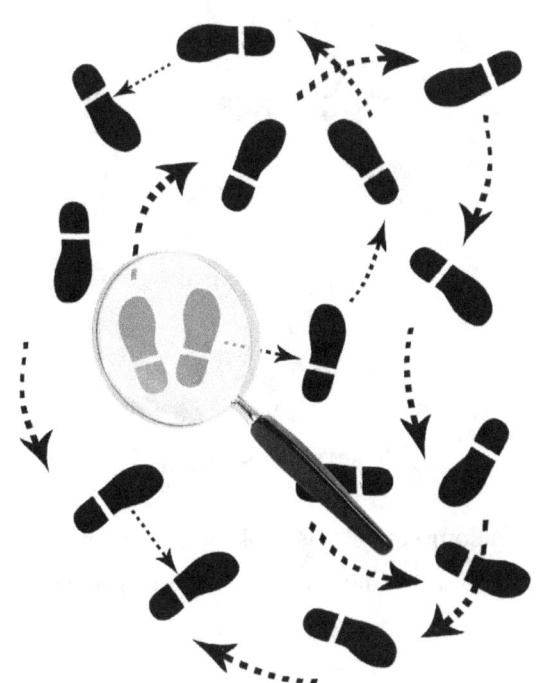

Also By Doug Dorsey

NEVER ALONE

•

BROKEN HERO

•

THE DECEPTION

•

THE RED LEDGER

•

THE BETRAYAL

•

KICK BALL SLAY

For a complete list of books available from
Studio 15 Publishing, visit www.studio15inc.com

ROCK STEP, TRIPLE HOMICIDE

A NOVEL BY DOUG DORSEY

STUDIO 15 PUBLISHING, INC.

Ponte Vedra, Florida

Printed in the United States of America
First published as a Studio 15 Publishing paperback in 2023

For information about permission to reproduce selections from this book, visit our website www.studio15inc.com or contact us at (904)874-4856.

The Library of Congress catalogue of the paperback edition is as follows:

Dorsey, Doug (Douglas A.)
Rock Step, Triple Homicide / Doug Dorsey - 1st ed.
ISBN - 13: 979-8-9856953-5-9
ISBN 10: 8-9856953-5-9

Edited by Robyn Zomorodian.
Short Story Contribution by Madison Dorsey.
Promotional Items by Phoenix & Sunrise.

Studio 15 Publishing, Inc.
Ponte Vedra, Florida
www.studio15inc.com

PRINTED IN THE UNITED STATES OF AMERICA

1 3 5 7 9 10 8 6 4 2

Limited/Debut Edition

This book is dedicated to William, Natalie and Oliva.
Three AMAZING kids, whose unique talents,
creativity and overall kindness are an inspiration.
-1 Corinthians 12:7-11

With appreciation to Robyn Zomorodian
who is a brilliant editor,
helps me to together write sentences proper,
and works tirelessly to ensure that these novels
don't have a single tipo in them.

BOOK 2 IN THE ADVENTURES OF DETECTIVE EVANN MYRICK

CHAPTER ONE
Dance Can Be A Great Escape

Raven's heart was beating wildly, tears streaming down her face, as she fled along the darkened, rain-soaked alleyway. "Why?" she muttered, barely able to catch her breath. "Why did you kill her, Frank? She was my friend, dammit!"

Sickened by the realization that Frank had taken the life of yet another human being, Raven was on the verge of passing out and could carry on no longer. She spotted a pile of discarded trash nearby, hurried over to it and then immediately began to vomit, her stomach in knots over what she'd just witnessed.

It was then, as she crouched over, that Raven noticed a sliver of blood on her hand. *How had it gotten there? Maybe from defending Brigette from Frank's attack. Or maybe afterward when I accidentally brushed my hand near the bloody 'X' shape carved into Brigette's neckline?* she thought. Regardless, just seeing the reddish smear caused Raven's body to tremble, and she was hit with a flood of emotions, aware that *none* of this would have happened if she hadn't first introduced her friend - Brigette Jackson - to Frank.

Worse, nobody knew Frank as well as Raven. She'd trusted him. Maybe she was a fool, but she'd seen the good in him. She'd *believed* he could be redeemed.

Of course, she also knew better than anyone how violent he could be. Frank, she'd come to realize, became unpredictable when set on edge - rabid, like an animal on the scent of its prey. Now he'd killed again, only this time he'd chosen someone close to Raven, someone whom she'd cared deeply for, and the death of Brigette was leaving her shocked and in disbelief.

For Raven, that was what made this killing particularly impossible to fathom, she *had* known better. She could've prevented this one, simply with wiser judgment. Of course, it didn't help that Brigette was the type to speak her mind, making some ill-considered comments about Frank, insinuating that he needed psychological counseling and that he was struggling with a mental disorder.

Raven didn't disagree with Brigette's assessment of Frank. She did, however, think Brigette could have used far more discretion in her delivery of the advice. *I told you not to piss him off like that*, Raven shook her head, as if somehow Brigette could hear her thoughts from beyond the grave.

The rest of what had happened earlier was nothing more than a blur to Raven. Frank had struck faster - and with more savagery - than Raven could even fathom, taking Brigette's life without any apparent regard for what he was doing. And Raven, unfortunately, didn't have the strength to stop him.

After the horrible crime had been carried out, screaming obscenities at Frank for what he'd done, Raven had done the only thing left that she'd known to do, propping Brigette's lifeless body up against the alley wall, doing her best to make her deceased friend appear presentable, so that Brigette could at least be found in a dignified manner.

Clomp, Clomp. Raven heard the sound of heavy-soled shoes approaching from the distance. It could be *anyone*. There were several homeless who'd found shelter from the rain in that alley. But it could also be Frank. And since she'd run from him, Raven couldn't be certain he wasn't about to turn his anger on her now, feeling betrayed.

But for now Raven had a more pressing issue, still panicked and short of breath. She was starting to hyperventilate. Hastily reaching inside her jacket pocket, she fished out a plastic bag, which she'd stuffed in there earlier that evening after buying a snack at a convenience store, and then placed the open end of it to her mouth, using it to regulate her breathing, restoring some of the lost carbon dioxide to her body. After a few tense seconds, the trick worked and Raven was somewhat calmed down.

Now was the time to find somewhere to hide out, at least until she could get a better feel for how dire her circumstances might actually be. Hurrying down the corridor, she came upon one of the few places still open - an old dive bar. Despite the late hour, the Edison bulbs on the weathered metal marquee were lit, indicating it was still open for business. Seizing on the opportunity, Raven pulled on the heavy door, which creaked audibly, and then quickly disappeared into the darkened threshold.

The establishment was dimly lit and almost entirely empty, save for a few inebriated regulars drinking at the far end of a long bar. Glancing around furtively, Raven spotted a side area with a sign that read, "RESTROOMS" and hurried stealthily over to it. Pulling on the handle of the women's room door, she then slipped inside, grateful that no one else was apparently around.

In front of her was a sink with an old, grimy mirror. Raven walked over to it, slowly sizing up her countenance in the mirror as she did so. It scared her instantly how much of Frank she could now see in herself. *Was she becoming like him? Was she a monster now also, simply by association?* The thought was terrifying. Raven understood that she needed desperately to get away from Frank, *no matter what sacrifices that might entail along the way.*

Running her hands through her long jet-black hair, Raven could see that she appeared flushed, dark circles evident under her eyes from lack of sleep. She decided to pull herself together fast and before anyone else saw her and grew suspicious.

Turning the water faucet to the left, she ran her hand under the stream of cold water, then cupped some of it in her palms and splashed it on her face. The startling feeling of the cool water worked, instantly jolting her senses so that she was thinking more clearly. Next, she dried her face with a paper towel from a nearby dispenser, did her best to straighten her shirt and then composed herself before emerging from the women's room.

She was so distracted by her troubled thoughts that she practically bumped into another patron just about to walk in. The woman gave her a surprised, dirty look, more so than was called for under the circumstances. Fortunately, though, Raven was in control of her emotions now, and easily dismissed the rude woman, wisely avoiding a scene.

From there, Raven wasn't sure what to do next. *She could venture back outside into the misty cold. But how wise was that with nowhere safe to go?* She couldn't head home for fear that her nosy neighbor in the apartment downstairs would hear her footsteps along the creaky wooden floor, a fact she'd eagerly volunteer to police if questioned later on.

Deciding it would be best to take a step back and assess things before making any rash decisions, Raven went over to the bar and ordered a drink.

After watching the bartender pour the blood-orange Vodka Martini, she hammered it down, then sank her teeth into one of the three green olives on a toothpick that had been placed along the side of the glass. Her nerves still a wreck, she swiveled in her barstool, lost in thought, searching for a way out of the mess Frank had caused.

It was then that she saw a quaint dance floor nearby. She hadn't noticed it when she first walked in, tucked off to the side and at the far end of a lounge area, hidden behind a row of dingy leather couches. In fact, she only spotted it now because there were two people on the floor - a couple - and they appeared to be accomplished dancers.

When the song ended, Raven watched curiously as the two dancers kissed briefly, then held hands as they walked off the parquet floor, seemingly in the direction of where Raven was sitting.

"I'm pretty sure I left my purse over there, Paul," Raven heard the woman speak, pointing toward the bar area.

"Okay, babe. I'm gonna hit the restroom real quick and then we can head out," Raven heard Paul reply, as the couple split up to go in separate directions.

Now alone, the woman made her way directly over to where Raven was sitting, practically looking right at her as she did. Then the woman began to speak and it was instantly clear her words were directed at Raven.

"Excuse me, I believe, um- that I left my purse on the floor just to the side of your bar stool. I'm sorry about that," the woman motioned as she smiled and began searching an area only inches away from Raven's feet. She then spotted a red leather handbag and picked it up.

"That was East Coast Swing you were doing, wasn't it?" Raven asked, intrigued.

"It was. Do you dance also?" the woman asked, pleasantly making conversation, but also aware she needed to kill some time while her boyfriend was in the restroom.

"I do. Or at least I *used* to. ECS was my thing back in the day."

"Oh, well then. Nice to meet a fellow dancer," the woman offered up a welcoming smile, almost as if she'd run into an old friend. "I'm Carrie by the way."

"Morgan," Raven lied convincingly.

"Nice to meet you," said Carrie. "That was my boyfriend Paul. We're not from here. Just passing through and decided to get a night of dancing in while we're in the area."

Raven was instantly relieved that the couple didn't reside in Oakland. "Where are you from then?"

"Seattle," Carrie explained. "I'm on the way to a work conference in Carlsbad," Carrie explained. "Paul's tagging along because there's a cruise out of San Diego that he'll be going on. Timing just worked out nicely."

"Sounds like your boyfriend… Paul… lucked out."

"Sort of. I think he's a little disappointed I'm not going with him. It's a dance-themed cruise. Lindy Hop. We'd never been on one before, but Paul found out about it online. He probably won't know anyone there but... then again, Paul has no problem fitting in *wherever* he goes. I'm sure he'll be in his element," Carrie laughed.

"It's a Lindy Hop event, huh? East Coast originated out of Lindy, actually."

"Impressive that you know the history of it," said Carrie, surprised.

"Just something I did a lot of in a prior life," said Raven. "It actually helped me work through some issues. Funny how dance can do that. "

"Most of us feel that way," Carrie agreed. "Maybe you should get back into it again. Once a dancer, *always* one. You never really get rid of the bug. Might want to look into going to a conference one day. Perhaps even one of those type cruises like Paul is going on."

"Hmmm, I might just do that."

"Hey, we gotta get going," a voice called out from the other side of the bar. Carrie then looked over to see Paul standing by the exit door, hands crossed about his chest, car keys dangling from his fingertips. "It's late. Long drive tomorrow."

"Coming now," Carrie called back, sliding the strap of her purse over her arm, then turning to Raven. "Okay, well, so um- nice to meet you..." Carrie said cordially, trying to remember her new friend's name.

"Morgan," Raven lied again, convincingly.

"Yeah, nice to meet you, Morgan."

"Likewise, Carrie," Raven replied with a smile, the right side of her mouth rising up to an equal measure with the left, giving her face an ominous appearance in the low light of the bar.

Their brief conversation now over, Carrie scurried over to Paul and the two walked out of the cozy establishment and into the haziness of the night, ready to return to their hotel, unaware of the person they'd just encountered or the violent act that'd taken place not far away.

Meanwhile, Raven began to formulate an idea - a particularly clever one - although her only potential hitch in it was if Frank found out and decided to tag along. Raven decided she would just have to find out some way to keep that from happening this time around.

*****

Evann Myrick was enjoying the scenery as he sped along the coast, navigating the winding roads of the Pacific Coast Highway. The weather was gorgeous, not a cloud in the sky. The seas were calm too, which Myrick was glad to observe as he was on his way to the port of San Diego. He'd been talked into going on his first ever cruise by a stunning redhead who he found it almost impossible to say no to and who he couldn't wait to be spending time with again.

Retirement had turned out better than Myrick had anticipated. For twenty years, he'd put everything he'd had into solving crimes. He was dedicated to law enforcement and he'd become a legend in the Department during that time, proving that he excelled at uncovering the culprits behind some of the most intricate of crimes.

But after so many years of chasing down criminals, it'd taken an immeasurable toll on him and it was time to find out what *other* adventures were out there. The cruise was a great investment of his hard-earned pension money. So was the decision to purchase the cherry red, completely restored 1958 Chevy Roadster, which he was currently cruising down the PCH in, listening to an endless array of rockabilly-era songs. Myrick, as it turned out, was an old soul, with a disposition suited more for a bygone era than the current fast-paced one.

He'd become a detective after growing up enamored by the adventures of private investigators portrayed during the golden age of film and who skillfully and methodically caught elusive suspects. Modern TV shows, meanwhile, drove Myrick crazy, giving the unrealistic impression that cases could be solved in mere hours, solved quickly with near-instantaneous forensic results (*which was entirely counter to how painstakingly long the real process took.*)

A no-nonsense detective, he'd oftentimes felt caught in the wrong time period, frustrated by politics which increasingly infiltrated police work. Fortunately, he had a keen mind and was well suited for that particular vocation regardless of generational changes. In fact, it had been a tremendous blow to the Police Department when he'd decided to hang up the badge. There was no replacing an officer like Evann Myrick, and even the Chief himself had choked up recounting war stories at the retirement ceremony.

A few weeks later, when Victoria Monroe called to ask how retirement was going and suggested that they meet up sometime soon, Myrick leapt at the opportunity. He offered to come to New York City, but Victoria had an even better idea, slyly hinting that there was a dance cruise departing from a port in San Diego - *and* that they should go on it.

Victoria knew that Myrick was in the process of opening his own private investigative firm, but she also thought it would be wonderful for the two of them to take a trip before he dove headlong into that new line of work. Myrick was instantly on board as she explained to him her novel idea, which just happened to guarantee them some alone time as well, free of distractions.

The cruise was scheduled to last five days, taking passengers down Mexico's Yucatan peninsula and culminating with a stop at the port of Cabo San Lucas. She'd found out about it from some friends in the Lindy Hop community, who'd organized a large group to go, getting a significant off-season discount from the cruise line in return. The cruise would even have many of the same aspects as the West Coast Swing dance conferences they'd gone to, including workshops and socials.

As if destined to happen, Victoria and Myrick had grown to love dancing together. The two had undeniable chemistry so having the opportunity to get to do so while also enjoying uninterrupted vacation time only made the opportunity sound even more enticing. Victoria also wisely pointed out another quirky and fun aspect to traveling with the Lindy crowd - they routinely dressed in dapper 1930/1940s era attire. It would be like going back in time, and she subtly hinted that it'd be nice if Myrick packed a few vintage outfits *just in case* they decided to join in some of the more lively themed events.

Myrick kept to himself the fact that he had just that type of clothing in his wardrobe already, and wouldn't actually have to spend much supplementing it for the trip. He then packed up his suitcase and decided to hit the road a few days early, traversing the long stretch of highway that took him through the painted desert of Arizona and finally detouring toward Santa Barbara so that he could catch as much of the coastline as possible.

His goal that particular morning was to be in San Diego just in time to pick up Victoria at the airport. The two of them would then head straight to the dock and in plenty of time to board the ocean liner as it left port promptly at 4:00 that afternoon. Glancing at the clock, Myrick could see that the time was 10:45 AM and that he would be hitting the Los Angeles area well before any serious traffic, allowing him to make it to San Diego right on time.

The wind blew through Myrick's unkempt salt and pepper hair, as he listened to *Great Balls of Fire*, doing his best Jerry Lee Lewis impression, fortunate that no one else could hear him over the din of the car's 348-cid V8 engine. Eventually, he'd sung himself hoarse and laughed through a cough as he changed the station, completely switching gears to public radio instead. He particularly enjoyed listening to political talk, especially when he disagreed with the discussion points of the commentator, vocalizing his impassioned counterpoints to the voice transmitting over the radio. It definitely helped the time pass by.

Yet, almost as soon as the host had gotten into a controversial topic, the station cut to a commercial break and then to a local news update. The top story revolved around a number of murders over the past few weeks in the Northern California area. Shockingly, there had even been yet another one the previous night.

The victim, Brigette Jackson, was a 31 year old female from Oakland. She'd been found deceased in a back alley. Police were in search of any information that might help catch the killer. They also put out a warning to the public, as it was necessary to be particularly vigilant walking alone late at night while police continued their hunt for the perpetrator.

As always, details were sparse, but they did mention that the manner of death was suffocation and that there were significant indicators that the same culprit (or *culprits*) were responsible for the heinous crimes. If that proved true, Brigette Jackson was victim number <u>six</u> in the brutal killing spree.

Despite having been in retirement for nearly four months, Myrick was finding it nearly impossible to completely transition away from his innately investigative nature. He'd been trained well and had been solving crimes most his life; it was essentially all he knew. So as the local news story played over the radio and brief details were revealed regarding the other murders, Myrick formulated his own theories about who could potentially be responsible, noting some peculiar characteristics in the way the murders were carried out.

In particular, two facts stood out to Myrick. **Fact One:** that the manner of death of all six victims was determined to be suffocation, which would've been difficult to pull off without the element of surprise. **Fact Two:** there was mention that all the victims were found, post-death, in a neat and orderly fashion, as if positioned that way, and with an 'X' shape marking carved into each of their necklines.

Taken in conjunction together, Myrick supposed the killer or killers were something of an oxymoron - capable of being cold and calculated at times but suffering a sense of remorse about what was taking place as well. And indeed, if there were two killers working in tandem that was certainly a rarity in serial murders.

Perhaps a Leopold and Loeb-type duo? Myrick wondered.

But when he was a mere thirty minutes out of the San Diego Airport, Myrick's focus quickly changed. He'd gone into cruise control, lost in thought, and was suddenly driving at a snail's pace. Now noticing the time - and how late it'd become - he sped along the highway, faster than he should've been going, the blue waters along the California coastline whirring past as Myrick attempted to make up for lost time.

As he turned onto the airport road, he almost instantly spotted a police car running a speed trap. Luckily, he'd been caught behind another vehicle, and - grateful for that bit of timing - he evaded the otherwise highly likely ticket. That was good, as the next sight he caught was of the arrival lane and a lone woman perched atop a luggage bag along the curb. It was Victoria, and she seemed rather amused as he pulled to a stop, tapping her finger humorously on a silver-banded watch.

"I'm so sorry," said Myrick as soon as he stepped out of the car and into the cool midday air, immediately reaching for Victoria's mid-sized bag so that he could throw it into the trunk for her.

But before he could even pick it up, Victoria tossed her arms around his neck and embraced him in a hug, a smile that reached from one side of the fair features of her cheeks to the other crept across her face instantly.

"I've missed you so much," she explained, her arms wrapping around his sturdy frame, and she couldn't help but notice almost immediately how toned his arms had gotten. "You've been working out, I see," she spoke again, impressed as she let go of the embrace.

"I have more free time these days," Myrick explained. He then stared into Victoria's eyes, the first time he'd gotten to do so in what felt like forever. She had a radiant smile and stunning blue eyes, and Myrick's next words betrayed just how lost he'd gotten in them in that moment, "You, um… so you, um, look amazing too."

"Thank you," said Victoria, simply smiling at the compliment, amused that she could make the seemingly unflappable detective fumble his words.

"Well, I say we head straight to the port," said Myrick, getting his act slowly together. He then reached down and picked up Victoria's luggage so that he could place it in the convertible. There was a light fall breeze that cut across the overhang, and it blew through Victoria's soft reddish hair, which only added to the pleasant atmosphere.

"Sure. Might be fun to get our bearings on the ship before it departs," Victoria answered back as she slipped into the sleek passenger seat of the sports car, glancing around at how stylish it was. "I absolutely *love* this car," she said, watching as Myrick hurried over to the driver's side. He then put the car into gear using the stick shift, pulling away from the curb so that they could set off on their long-awaited, whimsical adventure together.

"This is what a midlife crisis looks like," Myrick admitted, a sly look in his brown eyes, still completely fine with the rationale behind the decision to purchase the classic vehicle.

Victoria laughed, happy to see that Myrick was up for such a fun new chapter in his life, regardless of how he referred to it - midlife crisis or just a chance to finally experience many of the things he'd long put on hold. It was, after all, particularly nice to get to see this side of Myrick as well. Victoria had gotten glimpses of it on the dance floor, a playful aspect to the otherwise prim and proper detective.

He was more brilliant than any man she'd ever met, which could be intimidating at times, as he could see and sense things in other people that no one else could. So for him to be so willing to venture outside his comfort zone, setting off on an impromptu cruise at her behest, told Victoria that Myrick had a spontaneous side also, willing to simply follow along wherever chance took him.

For the first few minutes of the car trip, very few words were spoken, as just being in each other's company again was enough for both of them. There was an understood comfort, even if the two had been apart for some time.

Glancing over at Myrick, Victoria could see that he was wearing his wool flat cap; the one she found suited his personality perfectly. It was tilted down along his forehead, partially concealing his eyes. She also noticed his hand tap on the steering wheel, three times exactly, which Victoria found endearing, knowing that was his telltale sign that he was lost in thought. She secretly hoped it was about *her*.

"So, um, what's on your mind there, handsome?" she finally pressed, curious.

"That I can't wait to get to spend five days with you on the ship. *And* that I'm looking forward to getting a few dances in with you again."

"Same here. Wait until you see the vintage red flapper dress I bought," Victoria winked seductively. "It's perfect for Lindy Hop."

"Kinda forgot that was the theme of the cruise," Myrick returned, a resigned expression on his distinguished, interesting face. "You know I don't actually know any Lindy. I'm pretty certain it's that bouncy dance they do. But, um, that's not really me-"

"Oh, you'll see… it's incredibly fun… and it's not that hard of a dance. If you can West Coast, you can Lindy," Victoria explained. "But regardless, like I told you on the phone, they'll be playing a variety of music at the various clubs… and we can West Coast to most of it. Whatever makes you comfortable."

"This," Myrick smiled. "*This*, makes me comfortable."

"Good," Victoria's heart secretly leapt at Myrick's answer. "I promise to make sure you have the best time."

"Okay, but I don't want you thinking you have to chase me down the entire cruise just to keep me entertained. I can take care of myself. I hear there's shuffleboard on the ship… and I'm kind of a big deal at that."

"I totally believe you are," Victoria replied. "Everything comes easy to you."

"Not dance."

"You have fun doing it, right?"

"Of course."

"Well, that's what's most important."

"I'll never be able to compete like you do," Myrick expressed a concern that he'd secretly harbored. "I'll never be the dancer so many of your friends are. You know that."

"I don't care. And besides, I don't enjoy dancing with them nearly as much as I do with you. That's what matters most."

"As long as you're okay with that, then I'll give Lindy a shot also. There'll be workshops on the cruise, right?"

"Several of them. Just remember though this is a vacation. It shouldn't feel like work."

"How could I not have a good time? It's an entire week of wearing short-sleeve sweater vests, pleated trousers, plaid socks and penny loafers, dancing to Glen Miller songs and quoting Marlon Brando."

"Um, okay sure. I guess *something* like that."

"You know, uh-" Myrick began then purposefully paused, channeling his best Brando, his cheeks puffed out and his voice gravelly, like he'd swallowed a bug. "A lot of us dancers... we, uh, we like to appear the part, you see."

"Oh dear," Victoria chuckled, rolling her eyes.

"What, not impressed?"

"No, of course... it's just maybe you've got more of a future in shuffleboard than performing character impressions," Victoria chuckled.

Myrick offered up a stern look that quickly became a laugh at his own expense.

"Well then," deciding to call Victoria's bluff. "I guess good luck pulling me away from shuffleboard or any of the other cruise activities. I may just have to leave the dancing up to you."

"Oh, I'll get you out on the dance floor. You'll see."

Myrick glanced over and smiled, knowing that Victoria was probably right.

Victoria meanwhile pulled up a song list on her phone. "I created this *just* for you."

"Oh really."

"Yes, now listen and I'll help you find the Lindy beat," Victoria replied, as she chose a song with a lively cadence - *Stray Cat Strut*.

"You hear that?" she asked after allowing a few refrains to play.

"Nope," Myrick laughed.

"Listen, silly. Rock step..." Victoria called out in perfect rhythm to the music. "Triple step..." she continued, repeating the same phrases over and over again. "Rock step... triple step, triple step." She then explained in different terms, "1, 2... 3 and 4... 5 and 6." Pausing to see if what she was demonstrating was sinking in for Myrick also, she finally asked, "Not much different than West Coast timing, right?"

"Faster cadence," Myrick replied. "*Much* faster."

Victoria, meanwhile, noticed that Myrick was simultaneously tapping the steering wheel a deliberate three times as was his habit, only this time she remarked to herself that his three taps also fit the triple-step beat perfectly, as if that number had a new meaning for him. Despite his statements to the contrary, she could see that his timing was actually perfect as well.

"You never cease to amaze me, you know that," she remarked.

"And I'm never going to stop trying."

The rest of the car ride was spent between listening to music and the two close friends catching up on lost time. Victoria had created a playlist for them, and she selected a new

Lindy song she'd found - *Holy Roller Swing*. Once it began to play, she pushed Myrick for details on how his private investigative firm was coming along, instantly impressed with how much progress he'd made with it and the connections that he'd parlayed in law enforcement, building up a respectable clientele already.

In turn, Myrick enjoyed hearing about the growth of Victoria's dance studio, which had become the largest in the New York City area. He'd been able to keep up with much of it just by following the growth of Victoria's dance community on social media. His favorite part was that she'd even created a specific night for teens from a local church in Queens to come and learn for free.

The situation did, however, make him wistful as well, disappointed that they lived so far apart and that he couldn't simply travel to be there for Victoria's events. He was going to have to come up with some sort of realistic solution to that problem.

For now, things were nearer perfection than Myrick could ever remember. He didn't seem to have a care in the world. Meanwhile, the next song cued up on Victoria's playlist - *DC-10*. Myrick had never heard it, but liked the beat, oblivious to the irony of a song about the unpredictable nature of life - and the *shocking* ways a person can die.

CHAPTER TWO
Develop A Spatial Relationship With Your Partner

"I see you have an interior cabin. Your room number is 331. Elevators to all the entertainment decks will be located forward of Stateroom 349," the cruise ship receptionist noted, first glancing at the passport in her hand that read 'Paul Granger,' and then confirming the details on the reservation.

"Okay, thank you," Paul responded. He had on a faded ball cap, pulled down low over his weary face, as if the seven hour drive over from Oakland had left him completely spent.

He was standing in the atrium of a massive terminal, glass windows all around. Through those windows he caught a glimpse of the impressive 17 deck ocean liner he'd be boarding shortly - and he couldn't wait for the voyage to begin.

"Wonderful, well I promise you'll enjoy this excursion. This is the newest ship in our fleet - *The Savoy of the Seas*. It features two observation decks where you can catch breathtaking views of the ocean, a platform walkway that spans the entire circumference of the ship, a spa and Turkish Bath, a state-of-the-art pantheon theater featuring Broadway shows, a casino and - of course - our renowned infinity pool, which is housed in glass and extends out just below the navigation bridge, providing an exceptional view of the open ocean." The pleasant receptionist beamed proudly, her almond-shaped eyes wide in wonder as if the ship was her own prized-possession. "I see you're also booked at the reduced dance group rate. Our porter will go ahead and take your luggage up to your cabin while you get familiar with the ship."

"No need for luggage service actually. I didn't bring much," Paul patted the backpack tossed over his shoulder for emphasis. He was a light packer, always had been.

"Oh-okay, well, I have you completely checked in now. Food and drinks are all-inclusive. Your only real expenses are the duty-free shops located on Decks 5 and 6. I do need to let you know that the dance group discount doesn't include specialty cocktail drinks so if you order those at any of the bars, you'll be responsible for that as well," the receptionist explained. She was lovely with soft blonde hair and dimpled cheeks that gave her a certain appeal. She had Paul's passport in her hand and presented it back to him, just as Paul had fished his credit card out of his wallet.

"I can charge things on the ship, right?" he asked, flipping the light blue card around in his hand and turning it so that it faced in her direction.

"Yes, in fact most of the bars are cashless on the ship," the receptionist responded, her thin lips inching upward toward a welcoming smile, her lipstick a shade of red-orange like a carnelian stone. "Are you familiar with the dance itinerary this weekend? Your group has several events and workshops planned. My understanding is that there's a check-in station for your group set up at the center ship pool cabanas on Deck 14, which is the main pool and where most activities take place. You can't miss it... your group is dressed in 1940s beach attire," the receptionist chuckled. "So fun. Makes me wish I could be a part of the excitement also."

"Great, I'll head up there first thing then."

"And how many keys will you need?"

"Just the one... my significant other couldn't make this trip with me, unfortunately."

"Shame," the receptionist batted her eyes at Paul, then handed him the lone key.

Paul took the key, making brief eye contact with her as well. He then turned and made a beeline along a lengthy gangway that brought passengers up to the ship.

Almost immediately, he was taken aback by the stunning decor of the atrium inside the massive 17-deck cruise liner. To both sides were winding staircases, adorned with sparkling crystals that were practically blinding in their brilliance. Accentuating the imposing entrance hall was exquisite furniture and artwork throughout. The entire setting was magical and Paul couldn't believe his journey was going to begin soon.

The ship's ornate elevators were on the far end of the atrium so Paul headed in that direction, intending to take one up to the pool deck. As he did, he passed several other passengers and he could tell that most of them must've been part of the Lindy crowd, as the men were decked out in knitted bowling-style polos and the women in flared skirts. In fact, the entire ship was frolicsome, reminiscent of simpler times.

Once the elevator reached Deck 14, the doors opened to a stunning view of the outside midsection pool area. Curious, Paul walked over to a seaside railing along the ship, facing away from the port and allowing him an unfettered view of the open water. The weather was ideal and the view stunning with the sun reflecting off what felt like an endless ocean, as if it had been painted to perfection by a Master Sculptor.

Impossible to miss, there was also a tall pull-up banner just off to the side of the pool deck. Paul walked over to it, realizing it had the entire schedule of times for the various Lindy events over the weekend. He noted that there were workshops scheduled to kick off almost as soon as the ship embarked on its voyage to Cabo San Lucas.

The various classes took place every hour and most were located in the *Red Lotus Lounge.* In addition, starting at 7:00 PM, there was social dancing at *Club Deception* featuring a big band era orchestra. And to cap off the perfect evening, the event organizers had set up a social event at a jazzy dueling-piano bar - *The Phoenix & Dragon.*

Checking his watch, Paul could see that it was nearing 3:30 PM. The ship departed in approximately thirty minutes. He figured he could get checked in at the dance table and still have time to get up to his room, unpack and then maybe even get a workshop or two in, as he definitely needed a refresher course on Lindy, not wanting to make a fool of himself on the social floor. After the long drive, he couldn't wait to get his legs moving and seaworthy as well.

"Here's your event band," the helpful volunteer explained once Paul got to the check-in table, scrolling through the typed list and finding his name. "This will get you into all of the dance-related activities. There are approximately 4000 passengers on this ship. About a third are here for the Lindy event… so keep this on for verification that you're with our group."

"Thank you," Paul took the purple band and affixed it to his left wrist.

"I don't think I've seen you at any of our events before. First time?"

"First time ever being on a cruise," Paul announced. "I've always wanted to travel on one. This was the perfect excuse to come."

"Oh, then you're in for a real treat. *LSS* is an absolute blast," the volunteer referred to *Lindy Set-Sail* by its initials. "We pull out all the stops for our event attendees."

"In that case, we'll try to take advantage of all the fun things to do."

"I have no doubt you will. Tonight's schedule is posted on the banner. Tomorrow morning there will be comps, including a pro show. And then, starting at 8:00 that evening, there'll be outdoor dancing on the 17th deck by the infinity pool, complete with live entertainment. You've never experienced anything like dancing under the moon and stars, nothing around for miles but the vast ocean. Weather is supposed to be gorgeous tomorrow also. Calm seas. Tonight there's a social mixer at the dueling piano bar, located on the 6th floor. And of course there's workshops set up throughout the day in the *Red Lotus Lounge* - Lindy, Balboa, East Coast, Charleston… we've got it all on this cruise. Anything else I can help with?"

"Nope, I'm good."

"Save a dance for me," the volunteer smiled and used a common refrain which Paul had heard many times before.

"Definitely. You too. If I see you out on the dance floor, I'll come track you down."

"That'd be wonderful."

Paul fiddled with the band around his wrist, which was a little loose, but he preferred it that way over having it affixed too snug. He now had everything he needed and was in the mindset to enjoy the five day adventure.

As he turned around, he suddenly collided with another dancer, who happened to not be paying attention and bumped right into him.

"Be careful there, bud!" exclaimed the man who'd collided into Paul.

Paul didn't respond, but instead took a minute to size the stranger up. He could see that the irritated man had a drink in his hand and had barely missed spilling some of it on his solid red henley shirt.

"Hi, Talon," the volunteer who'd just checked in Paul called out. "Close one!"

"It was," Talon commented, collecting himself and then proceeding past Paul as though Paul didn't exist. He then immediately went into conversation with the volunteer, leaving Paul confounded at the man's rude behavior.

Paul shrugged his shoulders and was about to walk away, when he spotted a woman proceed over to Talon and tap him on the shoulder. She was beautiful with long strawberry blonde hair and eyes blue like the sea. She also had a very confident air about her.

"Apologize to the gentleman, Talon," she spoke as she got his attention.

"Nice to see you too, Victoria," Talon returned after recognizing the face of the vivacious redhead.

"Hi, Talon," Victoria answered, this time smirking. She then hugged him, but soon returned to her serious expression. "*Now* can you apologize to him."

Talon turned to Paul, who was still standing there, more perplexed than ever.

"Hey, I'm sorry, man. That was my bad. Just, uh, got a ton on my mind."

"No worries," said Paul. His eyes then drifted over in Victoria's direction.

"That fiery one is Victoria Monroe by the way," Talon added, seeing where Paul's attention was now focused.

"I am," Victoria interjected. "And it's nice to meet you." She extended a hand out to greet Paul.

"Likewise," Paul responded, offering a grateful smile.

"This is his first Lindy cruise," the considerate volunteer added helpfully.

"Oh good. Well, now you've made some new friends already. Talon and I," Victoria laughed and nudged Talon's shoulder as she spoke. "And this," she turned her attention to a person standing next to her, "is Evann Myrick."

"Nice to meet you all. I'd heard how welcoming the people were at Lindy events. Seems like that's proving true already."

"Yep, and we're working on Talon," Victoria jested at Talon's expense.

"You didn't always feel that way about me," Talon returned. "There was a time-"

Victoria cut him off mid-sentence, placing her hand over his mouth in jest, as if what he was about to say was comically forbidden.

Myrick noted a hint of playfulness in Victoria's words and actions that he wasn't entirely expecting. It then occurred to him that Victoria and Talon knew each other pretty well, maybe even had a past. He wasn't a particularly jealous person, although the exchange caught him a bit off guard, reminding him that he was *still* somewhat of an outsider in this environment.

"Are you going to the social mixer tonight?" Victoria redirected the conversation back to Paul.

"I was planning to. 10:00 in the piano bar, right?"

"I believe so. Myrick, here… and I," Victoria slid her arm around Myrick's. "We're planning to get a few workshops in. After that, we'll likely head over to the social."

"Which reminds me of the question I had and why I came up here to begin with," Talon cut into the conversation, his attention now turning to the accommodating volunteer. "You gave me a purple band, but I'm pretty sure that one doesn't include cocktails. Aren't the pros supposed to have *all* expenses comped on this trip? That's what I thought was explained to me."

"Well, not entirely," the volunteer explained. Only pros that are going to be teaching workshops during the excursion get the all-expense paid package. It's noted on the roster that you received the standard cruise ticket as a perk of winning the All-Star Classic at the International Lindy Hop Championships… but I don't see that you're on the teaching roster as well."

"Then put me down on the schedule somewhere. I can wing it."

"Oh," the volunteer returned, confused. She then began shuffling through a stack of paperwork. "Well, I do see that we need a couple of instructors for a potential 8:00 tomorrow morning. It was only penciled in as 'tentative'… but we can lock you in for that."

"Great, who will I be teaching with?"

"Well, actually right now it'd just be you."

"Go ahead and put Victoria down on there also," Talon grinned as he glanced back at Victoria, who didn't seem nearly as amused. "I'm sure she'll be happy to assist." He winked at her. "She's got a thing for rescuing guys in need."

The volunteer wasn't sure what to do so she looked over at Victoria for confirmation, an awkward moment of silence lingering in the air.

Meanwhile, Victoria shrugged her shoulders and sighed, her wide-set eyes rolling in abject surrender. "Sure, put me down to teach the 8:00 with Talon."

"Oh wonderful. That'll be a nice surprise for our cruise guests. I'll start getting the word out. It'll take place in the *Red Lotus* tomorrow morning," the volunteer informed them, then began to search around until she found a small bag. Unzipping it, she pulled out two gold colored plastic bands. "Here ya go," she said as she handed one to Talon. "This will get you drinks during the duration of the cruise. And," she turned to Victoria to speak, "Here's one for you as well."

"No, that's okay. You keep it. I'm sure Talon will buy me a drink or two to thank me for teaching with him." Victoria winked at the volunteer, deviously.

"Oh okay," the volunteer replied, placing the gold band back in the bag, simultaneously noticing a look of concern on Talon's face as she did.

"Well, again, really nice to meet all three of you," Paul interjected, not wanting to be entirely rude to his new friends and just walking off, but also spent after his long drive. "Hope to see you all at the social."

"Looking forward to it," said Victoria.

Paul immediately felt better as he decided to head down to his interior cabin to unpack and maybe get a quick nap in. He'd already made a few new friends, proving Carrie right that it was a good idea to go on the cruise - or at least so far.

*****

As soon as the music began to play, Victoria had Myrick out on the floor, insisting that the song was one of her favorites. Of course, Myrick was wise to her plan, aware that Victoria wanted to get him dancing before he undoubtedly began overthinking things. They could've played the theme to *The Muppets* and Victoria would have been ecstatic to dance Lindy to it with Myrick.

The expansive room was set up to mimic a 1940s era dance hall, complete with a live jazz band playing on stage - *Danny O'Neal and the Six*. All around them, dancers were attired in fabulous vintage styled clothing. Victoria and Myrick looked the part as well. Victoria had on a stunning red and black halter pinup dress, the color of the straps a darker shade of red than her hair, which was currently styled in a playful bandana updo.

Myrick, in turn, looked dashing in a casual striped shirt, suspenders, two tone Oxfords and tweed cap. Around his neck, he wore a bowtie, striped in alternating brown and off-white colors. Victoria particularly liked the look, thinking that Myrick not only appeared the part of a swing dancer, but also a rogue detective - an inimitable mix of Humphrey Bogart and Fred Astaire. Meanwhile, Victoria was determined to be his Ingrid Bergman, at least for the duration of their cruise together.

"Remember," she whispered into his ear as they found a spot in the center of the hardwood floor amidst the multitude of lively faces. "We're just here to have fun. No one else is watching us."

As she spoke, Myrick briefly glanced around. Then, his eyes returned to Victoria, simultaneously taking her right hand and holding it in his left. His own right hand he placed just above the waistline of Victoria's halter dress so that his arm reached from one side of her body to the other, securing her but not too tightly.

In turn, a playful grin came over Victoria's face and Myrick found himself lost in her presence, as he always did when he was this close to her. It was almost as if no one else was in the room, a feeling that he knew was unique and happened the instant she was in his arms. Sparks flew, even if they weren't yet spoken aloud.

"Here we go," he smiled and rocked from side to side to catch the rhythm, trying to remember the basic moves that he'd garnered from the workshops they'd gotten in earlier that evening.

Once he had the beat, Myrick led Victoria in a rock-step backwards, his movement surprisingly bouncy and natural. It felt instantly fluid, triple stepping forward and then triple stepping once more backward, while leading Victoria into a basic swing out.

Next, Myrick managed to lead Victoria on a couple of side passes and spins, all to six-count timing, sticking to that rather than the more complex eight-count ones. They were clumsily executed by him, but Victoria turned them into something more, and the two of them laughed as Myrick awkwardly pushed through the moves, somehow staying in step with the music.

"You're back-leading me, aren't you?" Myrick smiled knowingly, halfway through the song.

"Never," Victoria replied. She then back-led him so that she set herself up for a very seductive twirl, spinning around in a 360 and then practically sliding into his arms once she was facing him again.

Myrick was so caught off guard that his feet froze, Victoria pressing closer to his chest.

"Don't stop," she laughed. "You know the rules. *Always* keep moving."

"I know, I know." Myrick tried to get his feet in motion again. The brief hesitation had been a huge mistake though, and he was having a hard time getting back in the rhythm, even with Victoria's help.

The second half of the dance was clearly off time, but Victoria didn't seem to care. She was laughing and smiling and spinning in the most breathtaking fashion; her execution *beyond* impressive. Myrick had long since been dazzled by Victoria's ability to dance West Coast Swing. Now, she was doing it once again in a completely different style of dance. Her talent was unsurpassed, if also at times intimidating as well.

"Thank you for the lovely dance, baby," Victoria hugged Myrick as the song came to an end.

"Right back at you, doll-face," Myrick grinned slyly back, offering up his best hardened-detective impression.

Victoria giggled, a magical moment existing between the two of them, as if they were caught up in their dreamlike surroundings. Meanwhile, another song had started, a more romantic one. Myrick suddenly found himself overcome with Victoria's beauty. He took a step toward her, the dim ambient light creating an enchanting orangish glow around the locks of her hair.

"Can I have this next dance?" a voice suddenly cut in, a sturdy finger simultaneously tapping Victoria on her shoulder.

Startled, Victoria turned around to see Talon, having not even noticed his approach.

"Um," she stumbled with her words, "I mean, I was already about to-"

"It's okay," Myrick chimed in. "*Everyone* in here has to be dying for a dance with you. I already got mine. I'm happy. Just come find me when you're ready for another one."

"Thanks, ol' chap," Talon tipped his cap at Myrick, comically assuming a cavalier demeanor.

He then grabbed Victoria's hand in his and spun her into his arms. Before she had a chance to completely react, he was already leading her into a send out and the beginnings of a swing-style dance. At the same time, Myrick's eyes met Victoria's, but only briefly, as Talon deftly swung her around in a mesmerizing display of lively movement.

This, Myrick understood, *was what Lindy Hop was really supposed to look like.*

He was blown away by how effortlessly Talon went from pattern to pattern, and it was almost impossible to keep up with the fast-paced way it was carried out. There was no way that Myrick would *ever* be able to dance Lindy as well as the real pros like Talon and Victoria did.

Realizing it was time to go, Myrick made his way back through the other dancers, all of whom were swinging and bouncing around in wild fashion, eyes wide and grinning from ear to ear. He remarked to himself just how incredibly different the Lindy scene was from the more chill West Coast Swing environment. In fact, they really couldn't have been more contrasting in nature. And Myrick wasn't sure which one he liked better.

"This seat taken?" Myrick asked as he came to an open table, a young woman sitting at the far end, taking in all the dancing going on.

"Don't think so," she answered back.

Myrick sat down into the wooden chair, so that the woman was positioned behind him and out of his line of sight. In front of him was the entire hardwood floor, and despite his best efforts *not to*, he somehow spotted Victoria in the crowd. Sure enough, Talon was dancing with her beautifully, and although Myrick knew there was zero romantic interest between the two, it was still hard not to dwell on the understandable affinity being displayed.

Eventually the song came to an end. Myrick could see that Victoria's eyes were darting all around the darkened room, as if trying to track him down. He was about to stand up so that she could see him when another dancer came up to her, clearly hoping to steal her for the next song. Not wanting to be rude, Victoria smiled and obliged, but there was an undeniable hint of dismay on her face.

It then dawned on Myrick that she wasn't going to allow herself to have a good time if she was simultaneously worried about *his* wellbeing. The only solution was for Myrick to find someone else to dance with himself. He was going to have to be brave; he was going to have to venture *way* outside his comfort zone. Fortunately, he also remembered that he wasn't the only person in the room without a dance partner at the moment.

Turning in his chair to face the other person at the table, he could see the face of a woman in her late twenties with dark hair swept over her eyes so that they concealed her rather ordinary looking face. There was very little remarkable about her appearance, and it was easy to see why she could get lost in a crowd, no one yet having asked her to dance as far as Myrick could tell.

"Would you like to accompany me for the next song?" Myrick took a deep breath and posed the question before nervousness got the best of him.

"Yes, of course," the woman's response was pleasant, but her smile disappeared almost as quickly as she flashed it, as though she was simply going through the motions.

Standing, she made her way over to Myrick who led her out onto the floor. He then surveyed the crowded space until he spotted a small patch where he was relatively certain they'd have freedom to move.

Once they were there, Myrick quickly took the dark-haired woman's hand in his, not nearly as confident as he'd been when he danced with Victoria earlier. He then started to sway, hoping to develop a connection with the girl, while also getting a feel for the rhythm of the music.

His heart sank once he started to realize that the song they'd picked was a fast one. Lindy was already a lively dance, the rapid beat meant Myrick was definitely going to have to step up his game or else he was in for an embarrassing situation. Making matters worse, the girl still had an emotionless expression on her face and it was difficult for Myrick to get any sort of read on her. Rather than linger on that concern, he decided to do like Victoria always insisted - *just keep moving.*

Catching the first refrain in the music, Myrick seized on his opportunity and led the dispassionate girl into a swing out. He pulled it off, but the rhythm of the music was so fast that there was no time to savor the fleeting success. He reflexively led her in what might pass for a spin move. Then went back into a six-count basic: rock step… triple step… triple step; repeating the move, as if he was perpetually stuck in a looping pattern.

With Myrick on the verge of *complete* humiliation, the dance came to a merciful end almost as quickly as it had begun, the three minute song hitting a final verse. Myrick, meanwhile, couldn't have been more grateful that it was over. As the song faded out, he and the dark-haired girl stopped in the midst of a pattern. The two were caught standing there, awkwardness prevalent in the air, neither sure what to say or do next.

"So, um, thank you for the dance," the girl finally broke the silence.

"You were great. Really enjoyed it," Myrick was honest with the first part, but *not* the second part of his response.

The girl made no attempt to return the compliment, but did at least offer what could pass for a smile, then she turned and walked slowly off. That was it. She simply disappeared amidst the other dancers, like a fleeting apparition. Myrick was left defeated, knowing that he'd failed at the Lindy attempt.

He would've remained mired in that state, except a delicate hand grabbed his, then ducked around effortlessly, eventually coming face to face with him. Myrick realized instantly that Victoria had found a way to free herself and had come to find - *rescue* - him. She was just in time too, immediately aware of what needed to be done.

Before he had time to dwell on things further, she got him dancing again. Like falling off a bike, the best thing to do was to try again. The same rationale applied to dance. *Especially* for someone who couldn't help but dwell on things - which was an undeniable flaw of Evann Myrick.

CHAPTER THREE
Use Compression To Create A Spring-Like Energy

It was close to eleven o'clock when Myrick walked into the dueling piano bar - *The Phoenix & Dragon* - which was located with most of the ship's other entertainment on the 6th deck. Talon had mustered his way into their company yet again and Victoria even offered up that he could join them for drinks. The three were seated at a table tucked away in the back of the room. Myrick was *famished*. He'd been dancing for over five hours and had worked up quite an appetite during that time.

"What's everyone getting?" Victoria asked, sizing up the menu in front of her, which had mostly American-fare.

"Maybe an appetizer for me," said Talon. "I'm going back to get in a few more hours of dancing after this and I *hate* dancing on a full stomach.

"Same here," Victoria replied, understanding where Talon was coming from. "I could go for a chef salad, at most."

Myrick, on the other hand, couldn't have disagreed more. He'd spent the better part of the day just getting familiar with the ship's dining options, aware that he really only had five days to hit them all up. He'd also been coming to dance events for nearly a year, finding out that one of the best parts of them was sitting down for a good meal after all that exercise.

He'd worked up an appetite... and not just for finger foods. He wanted something equal to the workout he'd just gotten in. It didn't hurt that everything on the cruise ship was included. He could literally eat all the steak he wanted. It was like a dream come true.

"I think I'll get a salad also. A caesar," he said, glancing over the menu. "And I could also go for an appetizer. The cheese fries sound fantastic. And then maybe a porterhouse for the entree. 24 oz... rare... sounds delicious about now."

Myrick could see over the top of the menu that both Talon and Victoria were staring at him, Talon with a look of astonishment... Victoria with amusement, as she was well aware of Myrick's hefty appetite by this point.

"What, no dessert?" asked Victoria, lightheartedly.

"Oh, yeah," Myrick flipped the menu over to see a large array of dessert choices. Looking it over, he quipped, "I do love tiramisu. Should probably save room for that."

This time, Myrick got a chuckle at his own expense as well. He also didn't mind the good-natured ribbing. He'd learned long ago what a simple pleasure food could be, and he never passed up a chance to indulge in a four-course meal.

"You're going to put yourself into a food coma, man," said Talon.

"He's right," Victoria agreed. "I want you to stay up late dancing with me. Save some energy for that." She placed her hand on top of Myrick's as she spoke, as if to seal the fact that their evening together was only beginning.

"I'll do my best," replied Myrick.

"You better," Victoria leaned forward to make eye contact with Myrick, artfully emphasizing her point, and she could see in his puppy dog brown eyes that she had him roped in for whatever she had planned for the rest of the evening.

"I don't know if I have another *breakfast club* in me though. I still haven't recovered from the last one," Myrick laughed but it was evident he was also somewhat serious.

"Don't worry, I've been suckered into teaching an early morning class thanks to *someone*," replied Victoria, rolling her eyes humorously at Talon. "And then I'm signed up to do a couple of the comps afterward. I do need to get rest at some point."

"Yeah, you do," Talon chimed in.

"Can't believe I didn't think to ask you about that yet. You compete in Lindy also?" Myrick asked.

"Um, she sure does," Talon added, as if to prove that he knew things about Victoria that Myrick didn't. "She's an All-Star in Lindy."

"Wow, you're a pro at *both* West Coast and Lindy?" Myrick glanced over at Victoria, astonished.

"Lindy, West Coast," Talon continued to speak on Victoria's behalf, his voice effusive. "And about four other ballroom styles, I believe."

"Yes," said Victoria, her eyes turning away from Myrick briefly, apparently uncomfortable that her accomplishments were being aired. "But not *four* other dances," she glared at Talon. "Only Salsa, Cha Cha and 2-Step."

"You're considered a pro in five dances!" Myrick's eyes went wide in disbelief.

"I'm telling you, man," said Talon. "Victoria's a big deal."

"Sort of like how Evann is the best of the best when it comes to detective work," Victoria deftly changed the subject of the conversation, preferring to brag about Myrick rather than talk about herself.

"Oh, I've heard all about him," Talon revealed. "He was the talk of the dance community after what he did for Ellen and the other Westies... solving those murders. You know, I was pretty broken up when I heard the news. Jade was actually a good friend of mine. I still have a hard time believing she was capable of doing those horrible things. Near impossible to know who you can trust sometimes. She definitely had me fooled."

Instantly, Myrick's gaze turned downward, his left hand placed on top of his flat cap, as if trying to conceal a pained expression. Victoria caught sight of Myrick's reaction, aware of just how deep a bond he'd developed with Jade and the sadness of having had to be the one to put her behind bars.

"He saved a lot of lives," Victoria added. "Likely mine also." She smiled at him, grateful.

"Do you mean like saved in the *earthly*..." Talon began, "Or the *supernatural* sense?"

"Um, I don't know... maybe a little of both," Victoria mused proudly, her attention on Myrick so she didn't catch Talon's instant reaction.

Myrick did though. He watched as Talon rolled his eyes, evidently unimpressed with Victoria's response.

"To each his own," Talon replied, his voice dripping with sarcasm. He'd known Victoria longer than most. They'd even dated for over a year. And he knew the *real* Victoria, not this pretend version that was under Myrick's spell, apparently even willing to assume an angelic air for him. "Me, I don't need a crutch to get through the tough times. I can save myself."

This time, Victoria did pick up on Talon's demeanor. She also noticed that Myrick's body language had changed as well, leaning forward ever so slightly, enough so that Victoria had a sense of what was about to happen next.

"Well, this conversation just got interesting, didn't it," said Myrick, his gaze steadfast on Talon, as if he was particularly interested in sizing him up now.

"Whoa, no need to get so serious on me, boss," Talon immediately responded, a look of amusement on his face, clearly proud of himself for getting under the renowned detective's skin. "We've all heard the stories. You know there are more than a few around here who refer to you as the 'Pastor Detective'. So go ahead, preach at us. I mean, I'm not sure how we've gotten along all these years in dance without you."

Victoria decided it was time to step in. She didn't like Talon's tone, but she was even more worried about what Myrick's response would be.

"Okay, you two, let's change the conversation to something else. We came here to have a good time," Victoria spoke, nervousness brimming in her voice.

"This is fun," Talon continued, throwing fuel on the fire. "Stop being such a downer, Victoria. The *old* you would've totally been on my side."

For Myrick, it was one thing for him to bite his tongue when the comments were directed at him, but Talon's condescending tone toward Victoria was enough to send him past the point of reasoning. Suddenly, he was amped up to engage in this conversation, which seemed to be going downhill fast.

"Not fun *yet*," said Myrick. "But it will be."

Talon sat back in his chair, a look of satisfaction on his face. "Told you," he directed over to Victoria.

Unhappy with the direction of the conversation, Victoria shook her head in disappointment, arms crossed over her chest.

"You know there are some pastors who are prophetic," Myrick added.

"Oh good, you gonna foretell my future?" asked Talon, amused.

"Something like that," replied Myrick, his eyes narrowing, searching for a read on his adversary. "You're a good dancer. I imagine you make decent money traveling the country, teaching and competing."

"I'm pretty certain anyone could have figured that out, Reverend. You'll have to do better to impress me," said Talon.

"You seem to be holding onto something though, as if you know this can't last forever and dance is - unfortunately - all you have. I gather you're a lot older than you look... dress as well. I'd peg you at 38 or so."

Victoria's eyes instantly cut over to Myrick, astonished and aware that he'd pinpointed Talon's age exactly.

"The years are creeping up on you," Myrick continued.

"Age catches up with *all* of us," Talon winked, as if to emphasize that Myrick was clearly older than him.

"I noticed that when you went to dance with Victoria, you stretched out your left arm and shoulder," noted Myrick.

"First dance of the night, gotta get those bones loosened up a bit," answered Talon.

"Which then attracted my attention to the large scar you have running down your forearm," said Myrick. "Common of surgery post ulnar fracture."

"Motorcycle accident. Left side tightens up sometimes. It comes and goes. No big deal," said Talon.

"Which is likely a sign of synostosis, a loss in range of motion that's difficult to treat. That would also explain the second surgical incision along your forearm, clearly in an earlier stage of healing than the other, and which must've been performed to alleviate the complication. Given the still-evident discoloration of the additional scarring, I'd venture the follow-up procedure was conducted no more than a month ago, am I right?"

"Sure. But again, I'm good," Talon answered. "Thanks for the genuine display of concern though."

"Of course," Myrick smiled slightly. "But I'm sure the treating physician warned that you're risking permanent injury if you don't allow the arm sufficient time to heal. And it's clearly *still* bothering you. Which brings me to my second point, you wouldn't be out dancing if it wasn't absolutely necessary. My best guess... you're in the midst of a tough patch financially."

"Nope, that's where you're wrong."

"And *that's* also why you pushed so hard to get everything comped at the check-in desk, *even* the cocktails, isn't it?" Myrick continued, unfazed by Talon's denial, "Because you're strapped for cash right now."

"I was out of pocket for a while and put off doing private lessons... like you said... to *properly* rest the arm. I'm back now. Arm feels great. Money is the least of my concerns."

"Maybe."

Talon no longer had an amused expression on his face, immense frustration taking hold. He'd opened up a can of worms and was quickly starting to regret doing so.

"You know what, I think I'm done with this conversation," said Talon. "Victoria was right, I came on this cruise to have some fun... *not* engage in self-analysis with an over-the-hill detective who fancies himself the hall monitor of dance."

Pushing the chair back, Talon finished his drink in one swig and stood up from the table. He then glanced over at Victoria.

"Care to dance?" he asked her.

Victoria was caught off guard and in no mood to oblige at the moment.

"Maybe in a few songs," she politely declined.

"Figured as much," said Talon, already turning to go find a place to ease his spirits, and the lengthy bar seemed to be just the opportune place.

Myrick watched in fascination as Talon went up to order another drink. He also noticed that just as Talon went to sit down at a barstool, a stunning brunette with long legs walked over and struck up a conversation with him. After she'd spoken a few words into his ear, Talon followed her out onto the dance floor. The two then broke into a captivating dance that exhibited a certain amount of sensuality.

Talon, it seemed, was proving a point. He still had the world at his fingertips, regardless of what Myrick *believed.* Yet as intriguing as the dance was, a perfect character study in ego, Myrick's attention drifted away and over toward Victoria, whom he noticed was eyeing him - and not in an approving fashion.

"What?" he asked, feigning unawareness at why she'd be so upset at the moment.

"You didn't need to do that to him," she finally spoke. "Talon's not a bad guy."

"I never said he was."

"Then why stoop down to that level?"

"There's a fine line between taking the high road and letting someone think they can walk all over you. Applied wisely, and under the right circumstances, there are virtues to be found in *both* approaches."

"And what if I told you that Talon actually harbors some dark secrets... ones he's confided in me... and ones that have caused a deep pain you wouldn't wish on the worst of your enemies."

It suddenly dawned on Myrick that Victoria's relationship with Talon ran deeper than he'd originally understood. She was also keeping things from him. He began to wonder just how much Victoria trusted him.

"If you're telling me to cut him some slack... I'll do that... for *you*."

"I don't want you to do it for me," Victoria paused mid-sentence, pondering how much she should tell Myrick. She didn't want to betray Talon's confidence. She also believed deep down in her heart that Myrick was the best man she knew and that he deserved to have a complete picture of where she was coming from. "I want you to do it for Talon," she continued, her voice somber. "He deserves some compassion."

"Why? From what I can see so far, he's already a big enough fan of himself."

"No, he's not. It's an act, Myrick. He's… Myrick, he's covering up his pain. He's a victim… of abuse… and from a pastor of all people."

Victoria's eyes were on Myrick now, desperately searching for a read on him and his reaction to what she'd said. She'd expected him to immediately gasp in disbelief, perhaps even dismissing the possibility that such a dark allegation could be true. Instead, his eyes turned sorrowful, intensely pained.

Not what she'd expected.

"I should've picked up that there was more going on… I never even gave the kid the benefit of the doubt," Myrick paused, his words purposeful and resolute. "I'd hate the church too if I'd been put through a hell like that."

"I don't think it's so much the hate inside that he can't overcome. Yes, I'm sure that's part of it… but there's something else going on. I know he feels deeply betrayed by the people he trusted most too. He's got his guard up. I know most people don't even believe him. Which is probably because people don't want to believe that something like that can even happen."

"Oh, I believe it's possible," Myrick's reaction was anguished. "Evil exists everywhere… even infiltrating the church. I've witnessed things that you can't even fathom in the course of my police work. I've seen the worst in mankind."

"Then why do you even believe? Why do you still have faith in a loving God… if you know such evil exists?"

"Because I've seen a good in people that is even greater. I've seen people risk their lives for others. I've seen bravery, even in children, that couldn't exist if not first planted there by God Himself. It's like the world is in a constant battle with an enemy that is both real… and infinitely dangerous. But for God and the people that place their faith in Him, I also believe that evil doesn't win."

"Then, I need you to do something important for me," Victoria's eyes grew larger and more pleading. "I need you to be that example for Talon. Show him that there is still a measure of good left in the world. That people aren't just there to use him. Because up to this point, that's all he's known. Watch and you'll see. He believes his value exists in proving he's the best. He loses that and he's convinced he has nothing... that his world will crumble."

Myrick listened closely to Victoria's words. She was also asking a great deal of him, as Myrick had a fair amount of Irish blood in him and he clearly wasn't used to pulling punches. Still, looking at Victoria, he could also see that there was a pained expression on her fair-featured face. He wasn't entirely sure if her concerns lay mostly with Talon's wellbeing or if she felt bad about the sacrifice she was asking Myrick to make - or even if it wasn't a little of both to it. Regardless, it only took a few seconds of listening to Victoria for Myrick to resign himself to putting her needs ahead of his own.

"I'll try," Myrick finally said. "I can't promise entirely... your friend is a piece of work... but I'll do my best."

"You know, some say being the bigger person is a sign of intelligence."

"Well, I've never been mistaken for a rocket scientist, if that's what you're getting at," Myrick jested, although not entirely in humor.

"I know I ask a lot of you," Victoria replied, her hand reaching over to take his; her doe eyes turning soft and searching, so that Myrick quickly found himself wanting to alleviate her concerns.

Eventually, the two looked away and toward the dance floor, no other words needing to be spoken. It wasn't long before Myrick caught sight of Talon and the girl he was dancing with. She'd stayed with him through the entire first song and into a second one and they were dazzling. So much so that Myrick almost missed the fact that there was a second couple on the dance floor now as well. Turning his attention to them, Myrick suddenly recognized who the two were.

"So, looks like our new friend Paul is a pretty good dancer," Victoria noted, her eyes following Myrick's over to the second couple, ready now to change the conversation to something (seemingly) less consequential. "I wonder who the girl is with him?"

"I actually met her at the nightclub. She and I got a song in earlier."

"Oh really," Victoria's voice instantly went proud. "Look at you, already getting comfortable with Lindy Hop."

"I wouldn't go that far. She's dancing a lot better with Paul than she did with me."

"I doubt that," said Victoria, then her voice turned curious. "What's her name? First time I've seen her around."

"Dunno," it suddenly dawned on Myrick that he'd not introduced himself before - or even during - their lackluster dance. "Never asked."

"Well remember to ask her next time. I'm curious."

The two then watched Paul and the mysterious dark-haired girl. They weren't nearly as accomplished dancers as Talon and the woman he was dancing with, but they had evident chemistry and it was equally enjoyable watching them. That connection, though, was more complicated than anyone observing from the outside could possibly fathom.

CHAPTER FOUR
Floor Awareness Can Help Prevent Injury

As soon as she realized she was being followed, Tempest Greylock picked up her pace. The time was approximately 2:30 in the morning, and she'd only just recently finished her closing shift at *The Phoenix & Dragon*, but she was clearly not alone as she proceeded out into the night air.

One of the unique perks - *and there were many* - of this cruise line job was that she could walk out onto the promenade deck at the end of a hard night, break out a cigarette uninterrupted and take in the stars and open seas; eventually retreating to her Deck 0 crew quarters once she was ready to call it an evening. There was really nothing in life quite like that experience.

The downside, though? *Rare* moments like this. Working at a bar on a cruise ship with inebriated passengers on international waters sometimes meant you dealt with creeps looking for some unsolicited attention. One particular individual though had caught her entirely off guard, as it wasn't due to any sort of flirtatious encounter at the bar that night. Instead, the interaction between the two had been fleeting at most, as it lasted only so long as Tempest took what should have been a rather routine drink order.

Now as she was being followed, she began running through the strange conversation once more in her mind, reflecting on it and what might have led to her now being stalked:

"I'll have a Vodka Martini, blood orange," the passenger had ordered, walking over to the rather crowded bar.

"Sure, I'll be right back with that," Tempest had then went to work on the drink, only to have several other customers vie for her attention also, all wanting specific cocktails of their own. She got distracted trying to fulfill the multiple orders and by the time she returned with the martini in a v-shaped glass, the patron wasn't happy.

"That's not what I ordered," her blunt customer had replied.

At first Tempest thought perhaps it was in jest, as she was positive that she'd heard the drink order correctly. But as she'd chuckled back, the customer became even more adamant. "I said a whisky, neat."

Rather than argue, Tempest took back the cocktail and went to remake the order, this time returning with the pure spirit whisky. It was then that the conversation had gotten even stranger.

"Huh, I think you mixed up my drink with someone else's," the customer pointed out, although not in the same terse tone as before. "It's okay though. I'm fine with it."

And just like that, the strange customer had taken the lowball tumbler in hand, walking away from the counter in what appeared to be a pleasant mood. Meanwhile, Tempest had been completely thrown off by the encounter, shrugging her shoulders and then turning to help one of the more amiable customers, who *didn't* make her feel like she was entirely losing her mind.

Now, with the bar closed, and for there to be no good reason to see that same person again on the otherwise empty promenade, Tempest understood she was definitely being followed, causing her to grow increasingly concerned with the situation. Suddenly, she wished the mass of passengers - that normally roamed the external walkway - were out and about.

Instead, there wasn't another soul in sight, just the eerie sound of the night breeze cutting across the side of the mammoth ship. Fortunately, the heavy footsteps coming from behind her seemed to slowly drift off into the distance as she passed a row of lifeboats, creating an opportunity for escape.

The crew quarters were located on Level 0, which was the lowest deck and below sea level. To get there, she'd developed a routine of navigating the walkway toward a secluded back stairwell, knowing that most passengers weren't even aware that it was there, and which led down to a crew walkway, oftentimes referred to as *I-95* on the ship. After a long night of taking care of bar duties, the last thing she wanted to do was engage in conversation with passengers and this was the easiest route to avoid seeing people.

Reaching a section where two of the larger lifeboats were located, she decided to play it safe, ducking around the side of one, the edge of the boat giving her just enough cover so that she could look and listen for anyone who might be approaching. But from her concealed location, she spotted no one behind her and the only sounds evident were those of the waves crashing against the side of the cruise ship and the swirling ocean breeze.

All was going to be okay. Her overactive imagination had just gotten the best of her... yet again.

On her wrist, there was a minimalist tattoo, entirely black in color. The tattoo was simply of a heart inside parenthetical brackets, and intended as a reminder to guard her feelings. Tempest glanced down at it and instantly became emboldened, remembering all that she'd overcome up to this point, including a cheating boyfriend, who was actually the reason behind the spontaneous decision to apply for the job on the cruise ship, as she'd wanted to get as far away from him as possible.

As it turned out, the job wasn't an easy one though, and it was a struggle to adjust to life at sea, especially being housed in a 100 square foot cabin, which wasn't even fitted with a porthole view of the outside. The hours were arduous as well, and she was often expected to work seven days straight - sometimes even more depending on the length of the cruise.

Meanwhile, it took awhile to get used to the food options, which were served to the crew buffet style, and only offered during certain times of the day. Since Tempest worked an odd shift, breakfast fare was rarely an option. Instead, she subsisted on a steady diet of hot dogs, burgers and pizzas from the midnight crew buffet, none of which were her first choice.

As with most things, Tempest found a way to adapt over time. Six months into the job, and she'd gotten herself on a healthier routine, oftentimes hitting the crew gym late at night. Adjusting her schedule was a worthwhile sacrifice, her focus on how much of the world she was getting to see and how interesting her days had become. *I'm finally living life on my terms*, she often thought to herself.

Now, comforted by the reminder tattooed on her wrist, Tempest composed herself and maneuvered back out onto the platform. The light from one of the overhanging fixtures revealed her path, only to be instantly obstructed by a figure springing in front of her, a hazy aura present around her assailant's head and face.

Before Tempest could react, the deft attacker slipped a cloth bag over her head, pulling on one end of the drawstring so violently that no air could possibly get inside. Frightened and confused, she grasped with her hands at the object around her throat, which was already constricting her breathing, causing her to become disoriented as well.

Panicked, and close to blacking out, Tempest swiped at her attacker, who had slipped to the side of her and out of her grasp. While she wasn't able to get ahold of the perpetrator, her arm swinging at an awkward angle in the attempt to do so, she did feel her long fingernails glance across the edge of what felt like the surface of a person's face. In return, the assailant pulled tighter on the bag, clearly angered that Tempest was struggling to fight back.

Tempest gasped once more for air, instead gagging on the cloth bag which made it impossible to breathe, and her head felt like it was about to explode with an intense pressure building up around her brain from the obstruction to her arteries. She could also feel the sickening sensation of the assailant's heavy breathing, who had apparently leaned in closer, as if savoring her painful death. Tempest's fair skin went flush and her resistance began to weaken. Underneath the constricting bag, her eyes had gone wide, blood rushing to them so that the cells were bursting, turning them a ghastly red. Seconds later, and her body finally went completely limp.

Her attacker continued to pull the drawstring tight, even with the life already gone from Tempest's body, just to ensure she was indeed dead. Once certain, the killer removed the bag from her head, folding it neatly and then placing it inside a jacket pocket, ensuring that no incriminating evidence was left at the crime scene.

Next, Tempest's body was dragged toward one of the larger lifeboats. After breaking the flimsy lock open, the killer stepped inside the two-story covered mega lifeboat's catamaran hull, glancing around to get a better feel for its interior.

Concealed behind the rows of longitudinal benches were two stretchers. Tempest's body was gently placed in one. Her arms were carefully placed across her chest. Her eyes peacefully closed. Finally, the killer carved what had the appearance of an 'X' into the side of Tempest's neck, then stealthily crept out of the lifeboat, scurrying along the platform walkway and disappearing into the darkness.

*****

Myrick was sitting in a rocking chair on the main deck of the cruise ship, drinking a cup of warm coffee, watching the sunrise and enjoying the brisk morning open air of the sea. It felt inviting and peaceful; and Myrick, *for once*, didn't seem to have a care in the world.

Glancing down at his phone, he noticed an alert from the cruise ship's app, which indicated he had a text from Victoria. It read, "awake now & getting dressed to teach the workshop, but hoping for a few minutes with you before heading over to the club." A smile on his face, Myrick texted back that he was just relaxing in a lounge chair on the main deck, overlooking a stunning sunrise - and that Victoria needed to come have a cup of coffee with him.

Seeing her quick reply that she would be there soon, Myrick placed the phone back inside his herringbone jacket, the same one he'd worn for decades, and which was as comfortable as anything he owned. He then took a large sip of his coffee, its aroma doing as much to awaken him as the caffeine.

The wooden deckchair had a curved appearance with a lounger-style cushion fastened to it, aqua in color and reminiscent of Myrick's marine surroundings. All around the pool were cozy cabanas, available only to suite passengers, and which had already been stocked with artisan snacks, champagne, wine and caviar. A 42-inch railing ran along the circumference of the entire deck to provide safety while still allowing passengers to take in the cloudless sky and seemingly endless ocean all around.

This, Myrick thought to himself, *is my idea of heaven.*

The ocean liner's massive 20 foot propeller hummed along beneath a steady wake of sea water - the monotone nature of it incredibly calming - and. the smell of salt air awakening his senses to the beauty of his surroundings. Myrick loved the outdoors. He was an avid adventurer. The speculator design of God's creation was particularly beautiful to a mind as unparalleled - and as seeking for truth - as Myrick's, and he could spend hours contemplating the impossible brilliance it took to create such a world.

Myrick had once read that the oceans were so vast that, even with modern day technology, close to eighty percent of it had never been observed by human eyes. And in that moment, in his silent contemplation, he marveled that God had designed creatures that could not only exist but literally thrive in the dark ocean depths where man was incapable of venturing.

One day you'll have to explain some of these mysteries to me, Myrick thought to himself as he took in the edge of the sunrise, coming up along the ocean's horizon, like God was painting a many colored masterpiece. *But not quite yet. For now, I'm enjoying watching You show off out here.*

Lost in thought, Myrick almost missed the lone figure in the distance, practically staggering, head down and on a direct path for the glass doors that led to the 14th floor elevator. But as the man's approach grew closer, he ultimately caught Myrick's attention - especially given that Myrick enjoyed people watching - and then it became evident that it was Talon who was stumbling wearily along the deck.

There was a cigarette in Talon's hand, the smoke curling upward along his body as if carried by the wispy morning air. He took a quick final drag, then flicked the spent end of the cigarette to the ground, crushing it with the sole of his shoe.

After proceeding through the glass doors, he spotted the button that summoned the elevator up ahead, went over and pushed it. As he waited for its arrival, he took a moment to stretch his weary body, as if he'd gotten absolutely no sleep that night and was paying a heavy price for it. Eventually, the elevator doors opened and he quickly moved to step in.

"Talon!?" a confused voice spoke, almost colliding head on with him, emerging from the elevators at the exact same instant.

"Huh," Talon glanced up, still having a hard time holding his head up, his eyes tired and concealed behind round hipster-style sunglasses, tinted a dark gray.

Victoria was clearly unamused, well aware that the two of them were going to be teaching a workshop together in approximately an hour. Without warning, she reached out, her hand snatching the metal frame of Talon's sunglasses and pulling them off. Instantly, she caught sight of his red, glossy eyes and knew that her suspicion was correct, and that Talon had been out partying all night, only now returning to his interior cabin.

"Where have you been?"

"Just went out for an early morning walk, trying to get the juices flowing," he lied, unconvincingly.

"In the same exact outfit you were wearing at the piano bar?" Victoria glanced over Talon's attire, which had looked sharp the evening before, but now appeared as unkempt as his hair and overall appearance.

"Look, I'm not in the mood for this at the moment. You gonna let me by or not?" Talon glanced down at his watch as he spoke. "I'd like to get a good thirty minutes or so of shuteye in. I'll be good to go after that. You know me. I'll make it happen. I always do."

"I really hope so. *You* volunteered us to lead a workshop together at 8:00 this morning. I don't want to get stuck teaching alone."

"Relax, I've got my dance shoes," Talon held up a pair of stylish red suede shoes in his hand. "I'm good to go."

"You lose your dance bag?" Victoria asked, having never seen Talon walk around without the cloth bag that protected his prized shoes.

"It went missing last night. Someone stole it right off the chair where I'd left it."

"*No one* took your bag, Talon. You must've misplaced it. Or maybe someone picked it up by accident... they *all* look the same. Don't worry though, I've got an extra. You can have one of mine."

"Thanks, but shouldn't you be more worried about your boy Myrick. Where's he disappeared to?" Talon retorted, unaware of the wooden deckchair where Myrick sat only a few yards away, quietly observing the encounter.

Victoria hadn't spotted Myrick yet either, and was making no attempt to search for him, her attention completely on Talon and contemplating what to make of the unfortunate situation. She'd been in this place with him many times before. In fact, his immaturity had been the nail in the coffin for their relationship, Victoria ending it after the two had been together for less than a year.

Talon was a brilliant dancer, but in Victoria's estimation a complete train wreck otherwise. He clearly hadn't outgrown his partying ways yet either. She just had to trust that he'd pull himself together in time to teach, as he'd done many times in the past.

"Just go please make yourself look presentable," Victoria reached out her hand again, this time to return the sunglasses.

Talon didn't reply, instead shrugging his shoulders in resignation. He then took the glasses out of Victoria's hand, placed them back over his eyes and instantly the rest of his features appeared more relaxed as well.

In turn, Victoria finally stepped aside, as if to indicate that the conversation was now over, and Talon disappeared through the elevator doors, which closed behind him with a soft thud.

Immediately, Victoria lowered her head in exasperation, massaging her forehead, still trying to process the situation.

"He'll be alright," a familiar voice called out and it then dawned on Victoria that Myrick was nearby and that he'd likely overheard the whole exchange.

Victoria glanced over to see a handsome man, wearing dark jeans, brown cowboy boots, a thick overcoat and a tweed flat cap, sitting in the rocking chair. Her eyes instantly came to life, overcome by how distinguished Myrick appeared sitting in the chair, simply taking in his surroundings. Even his weathered features had an alluring aspect to them, as if Myrick was more of a rugged outdoorsman than she'd realized initially. Life at sea definitely suited him.

"I know he will be," said Victoria, although her reply lacked conviction. "More worried about if *I* can take much more of his antics on this cruise," her exasperation possessing a hint of amusement as well.

"You want to get a quick warmup dance in?" Myrick stood up from his chair, immediately aware that his body had stiffened in the early morning cold, but purposefully evidencing no sign of it for Victoria to see.

"I'm always up for one with you."

"Good." Myrick was already a few steps away from Victoria, indicating that they should head over to the club, only he caught sight of something on her hand and it instantly alarmed him. "You cut yourself?" he asked suddenly.

"No, why?"

"There's blood on your finger."

Victoria glanced down, turning the palm of her hand over so that she could see and inspect it, a look of confusion on her face. She then spotted a dab of blood smeared on the inside of her index finger.

"What the…" she began, trying to figure out where the cut was, but not observing one. "That's just weird. I don't see anything."

"I wonder if it came off Talon's glasses," Myrick surmised.

Immediately, Victoria's expression changed as she realized what she must have done. "Oh no, I snatched them off his face. I must've cut him somehow when I did that. I can't believe I didn't even notice."

"Possible," was all Myrick replied, not dismissing Victoria's assumption, but also curious as to whether there might be a different explanation for the appearance of the blood.

"Not a great start to my morning. I feel like I'm completely out of sorts," Victoria glanced up from her hands, looking at Myrick longingly. "Can we *please* get that warmup dance in now? I obviously need it."

"Come on," Myrick quickly responded, confidence brimming in his voice. "You've got this."

As he boarded the elevator and proceeded down to the sixth floor, where most of the entertainment venues were located, it was clear that the ship was slowly coming to life. Passengers were milling all about, including dancers, many of whom were making their way to the club to catch the first workshop of the day. Myrick didn't recognize many of the faces and there didn't seem to be too many dancers from the West Coast Swing scene that crossed over to the world of Lindy also. He guessed that Victoria was one of the few that did.

Eventually though, Myrick did recognize a familiar face, although he couldn't put a finger on who exactly the person was.

"You're the detective, right?" the man spoke, evidently doing a better job than Myrick of remembering how they might know each other.

"Yes, and I know we've met before… I'm better with faces than with names though." Myrick explained, studying the countenance of the man, noting that he had a low pompadour fade haircut and equally stylish 40s attire, complete with suspenders and a bowtie.

"Terrance. We met at the bar in Colorado Springs. I was teaching East Coast Swing. You mentioned you were a detective with the Police Department."

"That's right," replied Myrick, recalling the exchange. "And I *was* in law enforcement back then. But I've since retired and am trying my hand at private investigative work."

"Congrats, my friend. That's a cool gig."

"Not as impressive as teaching dance though. I remember your group. And I remember how great your lesson was that night and how welcoming everyone was. That's a real credit to you."

"Thanks, I appreciate it. We've worked hard to build our community. Several of us even compete now and are on this cruise. We tend to travel in a pack. That's just what we do."

"I recall getting to dance with a member of your group that night - Susie. She's a lawyer, I think. She here?"

"Oh yeah, Susie's here. Kind of surprised me that she showed up to be honest. I hadn't seen her since she moved."

"She doesn't live in Colorado Springs anymore?"

"No, she hit a rough patch and went looking for a fresh start. She'd taken on a legal case defending a guy who turned out to be *severely* twisted in the head. He started stalking her after the case was over. I remember Susie ended up getting an injunction against him after he showed up unexpected at one of our dance events and wouldn't leave her alone. The whole situation creeped her out... and I could tell it messed her up pretty badly. She just wasn't the same outgoing person after going through all that. She ended up moving to California... Oakland area. She's not even practicing law anymore. At least she stuck with dance."

"Well, maybe being back around her friends will do her some good. I can't believe she's here after all that. Small world."

"Dance is a tight-knit community. You'll run into the same people all around the country. By the way, I actually recall Susie telling me that night that she really enjoyed the dance with you... that she thought you were a natural."

Myrick was taken aback and flattered that Susie had mentioned their dance. From his perspective, he'd been a disaster. He'd assumed that Susie was way too skilled a dancer to have enjoyed it, but apparently Myrick had been wrong. The compliment instantly bolstered his confidence.

"That was nice of her to say," Myrick replied. "You think she'll be at the workshop this morning?"

"Not sure. Although she did ask if she could sign us up for the Intermediate ProAm comps, which are at noon," Terrance glanced down at his leather cuff mechanical watch as he spoke, checking the time.

"You compete as an Intermediate?" Myrick was confused again. "I would've thought for sure you were a pro given your expertise."

"Oh, well actually this is a Follower ProAm. Susie signed us up for it. They're a ton of fun. I'm the pro. Susie's the intermediate."

"Sounds intriguing. I'll definitely be there to watch." Myrick still wasn't sure what he was in for, but knew he'd be entertained regardless.

"Good. Looking forward to hearing your thoughts on how we do." Terrance reached out a hand to shake Myrick's. "Well, again, great to see you, Detective."

"It's just Evann now," Myrick laughed back.

"Oh, right. Well, great to see you, Evann. I'm off to go give a private lesson. I'll see you around later."

"See you around. And good luck with the ProAm."

Terrance thanked Myrick, then turned to walk off. Myrick, meanwhile, found himself fascinated that Susie was on the cruise also. *I'll have to track her down for a dance at some point,* he thought to himself, grateful to learn that there was someone else on the ship that he knew - even if only fleetingly.

Eventually he spotted Victoria, who was heading back in his direction, a glowing smile on her face. She was evidently eager to head inside to *Club Deception* and get their dance in, pre-workshop. So was Myrick. The cruise had already been full of unpredictable moments, and there were - unbeknownst to him - even more intriguing ones to come.

CHAPTER FIVE
When Things Speed Up, Take Small Steps

Batsheva Rotem was nearing the end of an eight month contract, her first that she'd signed with the cruise ship industry. In that time, she'd learned a great deal about the demands of security staff, particularly that it was a 24/7 job and that as soon as she let her guard down, *that's* when incidents cropped up.

She sipped her morning coffee, weary from the night before. The evening had started off uneventful enough and the seas were calm and tranquil as Batsheva - "Shev" as she was referred to by the other crew members - had been making her final walk through of the various decks, conducting routine checks to ensure there were no leaks, deficiencies in the fire equipment or passengers attempting to enter restricted areas.

Seeing no problems, Shev had been preparing to return to the security office on Deck 0 when she'd run straight into a panic-stricken passenger, who was completely convinced that she'd been witness to foul play. After calming her down, Shev had walked the passenger down to the security office, gotten the woman's statement and then requested a meeting with the chief of security so that she could debrief him on the situation.

"I'm sure she's just mistaken, Shev." An older gentleman wearing a dress white officer's uniform with three bars on the top of each shoulder, indicating he was the chief of security on the cruise ship, had spoken in a gravelly voice. "I know she's convinced she heard someone in distress... but at 2:30 in the morning... and out on rough seas... there's a great deal of sounds that can trick the mind. I'm betting she just got confused."

"Maybe, but good luck explaining that to her, Chief Moretti. She seems dead set that she heard a woman cry out in distress."

"I take it you did some follow up already... have you uncovered anything that bolsters her concerns?" Moretti asked, his hand placed along the base of his aged neck, which was flabby and lacked definition, giving him the appearance of a minke whale.

"Not really. Per protocols, I walked the entire promenade and searched the nearby stairwells to see if there was any indication of a disturbance," she explained. "I canvassed the entire port side of Deck 7, focusing on where the witness said she heard the situation unfold. Nothing."

"We aren't far from the Baja Peninsula. Could've easily been a brown pelican that ventured out to sea and was perched along the side of the ship. If startled, it would've made quite a commotion taking flight. Lots of things can fool the mind this late at night and in the pitch black. My guess is our good Samaritan probably had a few drinks in her also."

"She did."

"Thought that might be the case," Chief Moretti grinned. My instincts are *rarely* wrong. What else can you tell me about her?"

"She's with the group from the dance convention. Name's Harriett Cribbs. Traveling alone and staying in one of the interior staterooms. She says she'd been at *The Phoenix & Dragon* till about closing and ventured outside to do some star gazing afterward. She was heading back to her cabin when she swears she heard a loud commotion… and the muffled sound of a woman's cry."

"Hmmmm," Moretti tapped his bony fingers on the desk in front of him, deep in thought, his jaundiced fingernails evidence of his advanced age. "Well, I'm sure it's nothing. But then again there are a good 200 plus people that go missing on cruise ships every year, never to be found. Let's *hope* this isn't one of those cases. Regardless, better to play it safe and conduct a thorough investigation. I leave this in your capable hands, Shev," Moretti eyed his watch as he spoke, exhausted from having been up since they'd starting boarding passengers in port earlier that day. "I'm going to get some shuteye. You go ahead and see what you can find out. If anything serious materializes, you know where to find me."

Shev had watched as her superior officer turned to walk out of the security room, knowing that he was probably right. So far, there'd been no reports of anyone that'd gone missing or even that there were concerns about the welfare of a passenger. Harriett Cribbs, it seemed, had an overactive imagination.

Curious by nature, Shev relished the opportunity to solve a good mystery, having wanted to go into police work ever since she was a young child. Raised by a single mother, she was the oldest of three children. Her mother had worked multiple jobs and odd shifts to make ends meet and Shev had been forced to grow up fast, taking care of her siblings in their quaint apartment on the outskirts of New York City, where crime was a *constant* concern.

One night, when Shev was nearing her sixteenth birthday, her mom had received a last-minute call that she was needed to work a late shift at the local convenience store. Shev had made sure her two siblings had gotten bathed and in bed early enough so that they'd be good for school in the morning. After that, she'd turned on the television, eventually falling asleep while watching a reality show.

When she'd woken up, still sitting in the lounge chair, she'd immediately searched for her phone, wondering what time it was. At most, she'd figured she'd been asleep for an hour. So when she noticed the time was close to 1:00 in the morning, it had thrown her off entirely.

Shev had known that her mother typically got home no later than midnight, even on nights when she'd been roped into the night shift. Confused that she hadn't heard her mom enter the residence, Shev had dragged her tired body down the darkened hallway toward the master bedroom, expecting to see her mom passed out inside. But when she'd peeked in the doorway, she could see that the bed was empty, sheets still neatly made.

That's when Shev's heart had suddenly leapt, knowing that her mom would *never* leave the three of them alone overnight. Worry turned to fear as Shev called her mother's cellphone and it'd gone straight to voicemail. Sleep was no longer an option. She was alone and terribly concerned.

By 2:00, she'd become desperate enough to call the convenience store that her mom worked at. The crotchety old man on shift at the time explaining that he'd relieved Shev's mother long before and that she had headed home close to 11:30 that evening.

Shortly after police were called, they'd located the body. She'd had been robbed, stabbed and left for dead. Her assailant, meanwhile, was never found. Eventually, Shev and her siblings had gone to live with an aunt and uncle. Nothing was ever the same for them again after that.

Over time, Shev had found herself drawn to police work, desperately wanting justice for people who'd suffered like she had. She even volunteered at the police athletic league, helping as an assistant coach in sports. But her school work suffered and by her junior year, she'd made the fateful decision to drop out entirely. Unfortunately for Shev, a basic requirement to enroll in the Police Academy was a high school diploma or GED - at minimum. Shev had *neither*, and so that dream got put on indefinite hold also.

With limited options, she'd gone to work in a convenience store just like her mother had. She then found a second job working security at a budget motel, which was the closest thing to a law enforcement type gig she could find. Her sharp mind, keen instincts and street smarts all made her ideal for the job. Three years later, she was promoted to supervisor of security at the motel, which just meant more responsibility at essentially the same grade of pay as when she'd first started.

A friend suggested that she put her talents to better use forwarding her an online link to an opening for an entry level position working in the cruise line industry. Shev had never even been on a boat before, let alone a cruise ship. Giving her even more hesitation, she had an *intense* fear of the water, not knowing how to swim.

Still, her adventurous side got the best of her - that, and she was sold on the fantastic salary and perks. So she went for a job interview and next thing she knew, she had the position.

Chief Moretti was already nearing seventy years old at the time, and clearly in the twilight of his career when Shev came to work for him. His knowledge of the demands of working security on a cruise ship was invaluable though, as he'd worked in the industry for nearly two decades.

Despite the fact that he was an extremely private person, Shev had somehow managed to pry a few other details out of Chief Moretti to date, particularly that he'd had a prior career with the *Polizia di Stato* in Napoli, Italy. Since Shev had always wanted to work in law enforcement, she would press him repeatedly for stories of what it was like. With each captivating tale he told, she found it more and more fascinating. Eventually, they'd developed a close bond. Chief Moretti took her under his wing, essentially guaranteeing that the cruise line would be renewing her contract.

In fact, she'd garnered so much of Moretti's trust that he now considered her something of a right hand on the ship, especially since the Deputy Security Officer had given his two weeks' notice during their last stop in port. Shev seized on that opportunity, working tirelessly to prove her worth, which didn't go unnoticed.

So when Moretti turned the reins of an investigation over to Shev, as he was doing now, the passengers were in good hands. Indeed, Shev wasn't likely to sleep until she got down to the bottom of a situation. While Chief Moretti was probably right that there was nothing to be alarmed over, this was still a mystery that needed solving. And Shev had already formulated a few more questions to ask of her curious witness.

"I've had an opportunity to run this by the chief of security," Shev offered as she stepped back into the interview room where Harriett was anxiously waiting. "We're going to do a thorough followup of your concerns. I will say it *may* be possible that you the commotion you overheard was made by an animal... maybe a pelican... diving from the railing area. You certainly wouldn't be the first passenger to mistake a sound like that late at night."

"Oh, well um, I highly doubt that's the case," Harriett had protested, but in a raspy and tired voice.

"Why don't we run this back from the beginning one more time just so I know I have the facts straight."

"Sure. As I mentioned, I was at the bar till closing. I then came up to Deck 7 to get some air. I ended up walking over to the serenity pool area and then sat down in a chair for a few minutes, just taking in the stars before heading to bed."

"Anyone with you at the time?"

"Not at that point. But earlier that night I'd met and was hanging out with a nice guy named Paul. He seemed a bit odd, but I can be too so we actually hit it off. We stuck around until near closing time and then went our separate ways. I remember seeing another couple still inside the bar as I was leaving. The woman... I'd never seen before tonight... but I do know the guy she was dancing with, he's a pro in the dance community. I believe his name is Talon."

"Was that the last you saw of them?"

"Yes."

"Anyone else around that you can recall?"

"No, that's about it. I mean, it was so late. I was tired too and eventually decided to call it a night when... I, um, thought I heard someone... or like you said *something*... make a sound like a brief scuffle taking place... along the left of the platform area."

"So port side of the ship."

"Um, yes, I believe."

"And you mentioned earlier to me that was near where the lifeboats are."

"Yes."

"Did you actually see anything or anyone when you went over to that area?"

"No."

"Okay, well I plan on going through the security cams tonight to see if there's anything on them. Not sure we have any that would show that particular railing, but it would at least give us an idea if someone was walking along any of the common areas that time of night and turns up missing. Likely we'll have surveillance footage of you on there as well."

"Yes, I'm sure you will. Kind of creepy to think that there's always eyes on you these days," Harriett said. "We live in a tech-driven world, that's for sure. Seemingly nothing goes unseen."

"Well, I appreciate you letting me know to expect to see you on it and where you'd been this evening. It'll help me pinpoint if anyone else suspicious shows up on the footage without a good explanation for being out this time of night."

"Is it okay if I return to my cabin?" Harriett asked, yawning. "I'd like to get some rest in before heading over to more of the dance activities in the morning."

"Of course. And thank you again for coming forward with information on the possible disturbance."

"You're welcome. I hope I was wrong about what I thought I heard… but I don't think I was."

"I'm going to do a thorough investigation just to be sure. I can take it from here. Have a good night Ms. Cribbs."

"You too," said Harriett.

*****

"*Je m'appelle Noemie*," the lovely girl dancing with Myrick spoke in fluent French. She had hair as transfixing as her voice, a magical aqua color that flowed to a sea green and perfectly accentuated her eyes.

The morning workshop had started and Victoria was teaching the class, *alone*. Talon hadn't shown up yet and Victoria was visibly annoyed by his absence. To kick things off, she had all the leads stand on one side of the room and all the followers on the other side. It was a packed house. The Lindy crew were surprisingly early risers. Victoria then told each of the followers to go find a lead and a place on the dance floor, asking them to form a circle pattern, perfect for rotational dance.

Victoria was completely in her element and the participants in the workshop hung on her every word. Myrick was amazed, as he was certain he'd be overcome with fear if he had to teach a class and speak in front of hundreds of people.

Better Victoria than me, he considered to himself.

To get everyone awake and moving, Victoria did a few stretching and footwork exercises, which Myrick was grateful for *even if* he was clumsy executing them. Victoria then put on a warmup song, explaining that she'd begin teaching an intermediate level move - a push out from Tandem Charleston - once the song was finished.

Myrick hadn't intended to dance, but then the girl with the flowing blue and green hair walked over and in broken English asked, "You would like to dance?"

A smile of amusement on his face, Myrick replied, "*Oui,*" immediately detecting that her accent was French and that she was likely to understand and appreciate his response.

Hearing his reply in her native language, the girl returned a pleasant smile and then the two took to the dance floor. Fortunately, the song was a slower one - at least for Lindy Hop - and halfway through the dance the girl decided to introduce herself, now aware that Myrick understood some French.

It'd been close to five years since Myrick had visited Paris. He'd done so with his wife at the time, Riley, who'd since passed away. Riley had longed to travel to France and Myrick had decided to make that dream happen for her. He also didn't want to be one of those foreigners that couldn't converse with locals and so he'd dived straight into an online French course, absorbing as much of it as he could in the limited time he had before the cancer forced Riley into inpatient treatment.

It wasn't until they'd arrived in Paris that Myrick spoke French for the first time with one of the taxi drivers, surprising Riley that he'd learned the language in secret. She was completely enamored with him for it.

Speaking French had made the vacation even more enjoyable. But he hadn't returned to France since that trip and Myrick hadn't any occasion to speak it over the next five years, relegating what he'd once learned to the back of his mind, lost in dusty memories and difficult to recall detail. Still, when Noemie introduced herself, Myrick decided to at least try to reply back in French, not certain of the exact conjugation of each sentence.

"*Tu m'appelle Evann*," he replied, clumsily.

Noemie laughed, grateful for his effort. "*Tu t'appelles Evann*," she explained with a glowing smile. "*Je m'appelle Noemie.*"

"*Oui*," Myrick winked and repeated the one phrase he knew he couldn't mess up.

The two continued their dance, now sharing a laugh and creating a bond. Dance was amazing like that. There was actually no need to speak the same language to make a friend on the dance floor. The common love of music and dance was all that was needed.

Noemie was, no surprise, also a phenomenal dancer. The French *always* were. Myrick had noticed this time and time again. They tended to fly to the States for their favorite West Coast Swing events and each time they did, Myrick was dazzled by the fact that all of them were excellent.

They also typically traveled together in a close-knit circle of friends. The head of their organization was a couple, two of the top pros out of the *Île-de-France* region, and their group all wore matching jackets with the name of their dance community on it, *Danse Swing Parisienne*. Myrick could easily spot them in the crowd, often walking into the ballroom in packs of three and four and wearing their distinctive red and black jackets. They were an affable bunch and brought a welcome international flavor and competitive factor to events.

While his attention had remained on Noemie throughout most of the dance, his eyes drifted to the far end of the room near the end of the song, noticing something was amiss. A security guard, in a dress white uniform, had entered the room, wearing a badge along the top right of the form-fitted shirt. She appeared all business to Myrick, her eyes darting around, searching the room, sizing things up and then she made a direct path over to Victoria.

As the song faded out, Myrick's attention turned back to Noemie, although he could instantly see that her glow had faded a bit, most likely aware of the distracted state of her dance partner.

"*Merci pour la danse,*" Myrick was sincere in his thanks.

"*Avec plaisir,*" Noemie answered. "Another one maybe later?" she continued in broken English.

"Definitely," Myrick replied, but as soon as he did so his eyes turned back in search of the uniformed security personnel, seeing that she was still speaking to Victoria, which had Myrick concerned.

Noemie was a tad confused that she'd entirely lost Myrick's attention, but another dancer swooped in to steal her for the next song and she was instantly swept away in the excitement of it. Myrick, meanwhile, was now free to do some investigating of his own, his curiosity piqued.

Walking over, he could see that Victoria had a concerned expression on her face, which told Myrick that the security guard wasn't there on a routine visit. The two women didn't seem to notice his approach either, and so Myrick decided to interject himself into the conversation.

"Everything okay?" he inquired.

"Oh," Victoria was the first to respond once she heard Myrick's question, "I think so. I mean, this is Officer Rotem. She's with ship security."

"Shev," the security officer extended a warm hand in greeting to Myrick, attempting to keep things light. She certainly didn't want to scare the other passengers, especially as it seemed so far that this was nothing more than a false alarm. "And you are?"

"Evann Myrick."

"Nice to meet you, Mr. Myrick."

"He's actually a detective," Victoria chimed in. "He might be able to help you more than I can."

"Was," Myrick interjected. "*Was* a detective. I'm retired now."

Shev smiled as soon as she heard his response, aware that even a retired detective was better with details than a typical civilian witness. She decided instantly to take Victoria's advice and follow up with him more. "Were you at the dueling piano bar - *The Phoenix & Dragon* - last night also?" she asked.

"Yes, why?"

"Probably nothing." Shev once again didn't want to unnecessarily alarm any passengers "More of a routine follow up than anything. Just wondered if you saw or heard anything unusual."

"Well, that's a pretty vague question," replied Myrick with a slanted eye. "I saw a great deal of unusual things last night. You can't go to a dance event expecting the mundane."

"Fair enough," Shev realized there was no mincing words with a former detective, knowing he'd see right through it anyway. "Maybe you can tell me if you saw any altercations, verbal or physical, between anyone that night. Let's start with that."

"No, none that I can think of."

"Aside from between you and Talon," Victoria added.

"I wouldn't exactly categorize that as a verbal *altercation*," Myrick clarified, defensively.

"Depends on whose perspective you were seeing it from," said Victoria.

Despite being intrigued by the change in the tenor of the conversation, picking up the sudden tension, Shev remained focused on what she thought was a more important detail to pursue further. "Talon," she spoke, "that's the second time his name has come up. Who exactly is he?"

"Just a friend of ours," explained Victoria. "He's one of the dance pros."

"Is he here now?" Shev glanced over Victoria's shoulder, surveying the room. She could see that there were approximately thirty other passengers out on the hardwood floor. The song playing was a lively one that seemed to be fading out as it reached conclusion.

"No unfortunately," said Victoria. "He better be soon, though. He's teaching with me."

"Oh, okay," Shev's attention was back on Victoria as she spoke.

"He hasn't gone missing though," Myrick interjected, certainty in his voice. "That's why you're asking, right?"

Shev's attention was now turned to Myrick, fascinated by his response. "Sort of," she replied. "Maybe not him specifically. But I am trying to find out if anyone has gone unaccounted for. How did you know that?"

"Intuition about things I guess. That, and there just aren't too many possible emergencies on a cruise ship that would necessitate a conversation like this in the presence of other passengers."

"Good point," Shev conceded, impressed. "I guess there really aren't." She then turned the conversation back to her original concern. "But what makes you so certain that this *Talon* is okay. He obviously isn't here now," Shev glanced around the room again to emphasize her point.

"Because we saw him already this morning. He was walking by the pool deck around sun up."

"That's interesting."

"I don't mean to be rude," interjected Victoria. The song that had been playing had now ended and there was silence in the room, as the other passengers who'd been dancing waited for their instructor to return. "If it's okay, I'm going to get back to teaching my class."

"Of course," Shev replied. "I'm sorry for the interruption."

"It's okay. Again, Evann's probably more help than I am anyway. He's the detailed one," she laughed.

"I'll keep that in mind," said Shev.

Victoria walked back to the center of the room, indicating to the other dancers that the workshop was beginning, *with or without* Talon. Meanwhile, Myrick nodded toward the door and Shev caught the cue that he preferred to speak with her outside the presence of everyone else.

Once outside the room, Shev continued asking questions about Talon, learning that Talon had shown up unexpectedly that morning, surprising both Victoria and Myrick. Myrick was forthright with any details he thought might be relevant, explaining that Talon had clearly not slept that night, looking disheveled and tired.

"Anything about the encounter make you think he'd been in a fight with someone?" Shev asked, clearly fixated on that possibility.

"That's another interesting line of questioning," replied Myrick, acutely familiar with interview techniques. "I take it you have more concerns than just a passenger who might have gone missing."

"We received a tip... from a passenger... that around 2:30 AM she was sitting by the serenity, adults-only pool located on Deck 7... and heard a disturbance. She thinks it came from off in the distance of the port side of the ship... likely along the outdoor promenade. Odds are, she was probably imagining things... it *was* late at night... and there are all sorts of weird sounds on a ship at sea... the possibilities are endless. More importantly, so far, there've been no additional reports of concern from that particular time period."

"You mentioned earlier that this is the *second* time you've heard Talon's name mentioned. "That leads me to believe that someone from the dance community is the one who saw something go amiss."

"Yes, seems like there's no use keeping any details from you. And, you are correct... it was a dancer. Her name is Harriett Cribbs. Is that someone you know?"

"The name doesn't sound familiar. Maybe I'd recognize her by face though. I don't know many people here." Myrick paused briefly before voicing a sudden thought. "What was Ms. Cribbs doing by the serenity pool? I'm assuming they'd have it closed off by that point."

"Just told us she was doing some star gazing."

"Hmmmm. Maybe also winding down from a long night of dancing. Everyone decompresses differently, I suppose."

"She did volunteer that she was hanging out with a guy named Paul at the bar. You know him?"

"Actually, I do know a Paul. Or at least I just met one. He was dancing with a woman with short, dark hair. About 5'3. Green eyes. Small scar on her forehead."

"Wow, that's quite detailed. You just described Harriett Cribbs to a *T*."

"Well, Victoria did warn you that I'm a very observant person."

"I can see. Must have come in handy as a detective."

"It did."

Aware that she'd lucked out that Myrick was on the cruise, Shev was about to hit him with several more questions about the night's events when a man raced by them, clearly in a hurry.

"Excuse me," the man spoke, reaching for the handle of the door as he did. He then rushed into the nightclub, not waiting for a response from either Shev or Myrick as he pushed rudely past them.

"Um, would that gentleman be...?" Shev turned to ask of Myrick.

"Yes, that's Talon."

"Well, that's convenient timing. I think I may head back in there and speak to him. He seems quite elusive."

"Might be wise to do so while you have him cornered," said Myrick. "You know where to find me if I'm needed further."

"Oh you will be," Shev replied, gratefully. She thanked Myrick for his assistance so far.

Shev pulled open the door and disappeared back into the club. Myrick remained outside, taking advantage of the fact that he wouldn't be expected to participate in the workshop after all. Instead, he was going to head back up to the pool deck. He wanted to do some investigating of his own. Suddenly, the cruise was shaping up to be even more exciting than he'd expected.

CHAPTER SIX
Swivel At The Hips, Feet In the 11 & 1 Position

Paul found himself completely transfixed by the mysterious girl, thinking back on her even as he slowly woke up that morning and headed down to find something to eat for breakfast. He already had a love interest; he'd not come on the cruise to find someone else. Still, Harriett had an intoxicating effect on him the first time they spoke.

It had only intensified as they'd exhibited an instant connection on the dance floor. Harriett was a skilled dancer, better than really anyone he'd done Lindy with before. She'd insisted that she hadn't been dancing much recently and that she'd only come on the cruise to get back in the groove, but evidently it was a skill that came *quickly* back to her.

After staying up late the evening before, Paul was in no hurry and took his time having breakfast alone. It was nice that the cruise ship's restaurant was relatively empty, as all the dancers were gathered in the club already to start the workshops.

Maybe Harriett is down there now also, he mused.

If so, he was going to go try to find her eventually. But not now, as the prior night had been eventful enough and it was nice just to have a quiet opportunity to reflect. And Harriett was a particularly intriguing subject to think on.

She'd told him that she'd come on the cruise alone, not just for the dancing but also because she'd hit a rough patch recently and was looking for an escape. Paul smiled and admitted that he'd been having the same thoughts, and that he'd actually been considering a career change, himself.

A change of scenery was often a great respite from the stresses of life.

Paul recalled how, after a few dances at the social, they'd stayed at a table talking late into the night. In fact, they'd been two of the last people to leave, the bar making a final call for drinks and even turning the lights up to subtly indicate that they were on the verge of closing time.

Thinking back, Paul couldn't remember seeing too many other familiar faces from dance left in the establishment after 1:30. The only face he did recognize for sure was that of Talon Andilet, the pro that had been rude to him earlier at the check-in table. He also remembered that there was a girl dancing with Talon. A stunning girl with long legs, an hourglass figure and whose movements were hypnotizing.

Similar to all good things, the evening came to an eventual end, Harriett leaning in to give him a hug, thanking him for the dances. She then walked over to the bar, settled her tab and exited the establishment, leaving Paul to consider when he *might* get to see her again.

A few minutes later and Paul had decided to call it a night himself. When he went to close out his own bill, he noticed that Talon was already at the bar, talking with the waitress - a no-nonsense girl with a tattoo of a bracketed heart on her wrist, whom he later came to find out had a name as mysterious as the tattoo - Tempest.

Paul had sat down at a stool, waiting for Tempest to finish up with Talon, when he noticed that the conversation between the two had grown lively. He couldn't make out exactly what was said between them, but it was clear that Talon wasn't happy and he saw Talon fiddling with the gold band on his wrist, giving Paul the impression that Talon wanted to make sure he wasn't being charged for drinks.

It wasn't much longer when a clearly annoyed Tempest had made her way over to where Paul was sitting, mumbling under her breath simultaneously, "some people are the worst."

As soon as she grumbled those words, her attention turned toward Paul, surprised, as if she'd only just noticed him sitting there. Flustered, she offered to bring the check and he agreed, although not before ordering one final drink, wanting to polish off a perfect evening.

Now, hours later, Paul was finishing his breakfast in another mostly empty restaurant, when he spotted Talon yet again. This time, Talon was clearly sober, probably more so than he wanted to be at the moment. He watched as Talon ordered a drink from a waitress, explaining that he was in a hurry and not making any attempt to sit down.

"Bloody Mary, huh?" Paul remarked, loud enough so that Talon, who was only standing a few feet away, turned to look at him. There was no one else around and so Talon directed his response back at Paul.

"Long night," Talon uttered, grimacing, in a hushed breath, as his head was pounding, and he couldn't tolerate loud noises. That was going to be a problem too; he was scheduled to teach a Charleston workshop and he was already five minutes late.

"Oh, I know... I was there," Paul smirked, keeping his voice low, realizing what a favor he was doing for Talon by doing so. "It was a night I won't soon forget."

"Might be better if I could," Talon shrugged back in a monotone voice, clearly not actually interested in the conversation, but also stuck standing there waiting for his drink.

"You and your girlfriend had everyone watching," said Paul. "She's stunning."

"You mean Soriya?" replied Talon. "Just met her last night."

"Oh wow, I'd of never guessed that."

"Yeah, well, sometimes things aren't what they seem," Talon shook his head, half bewildered and half amused. "But you're right, she is pretty sexy to dance with. Interesting girl as well, that's for sure. Seems to have latched on to me." He rubbed the back of his scalp. "And I do also have this splitting headache to remind me that we stayed out way later than I'd expected."

"Did you see the girl I was dancing with? She was pretty hot too."

"Um, no I didn't," Talon grunted, entirely uninterested in the conversation, especially now that his eager friend was attempting to prolong a talk which Talon couldn't have cared *less* about.

Fortunately, just at that moment, Talon spotted the waitress walking back, highball glass in hand, which was filled with a concentrated red liquid, celery stock jutting out of the top. Talon had been saved, and just in the nick of time.

"Well, good talking to ya," Talon ended the conversation abruptly. "See you around, man."

"Oh okay."

"Cool," Talon replied, then turned to walk out of the restaurant, taking a large gulp of the soothing blood-red liquid as he did.

"Can I get you anything else?" the waitress asked, Paul's attention still curiously on Talon as he walked away, almost as though he was in awe of being in the presence of a celebrity.

"No, I'm good," Paul's countenance had changed and his voice was distant.

"Okay, here's your bill," the waitress fumbled inside her pocket and pulled out a brown billfold, placing it on the table in front of him. "There's no rush." She smiled and was about to walk away when she realized that the downcast look on Paul's face had become even more pronounced. "Sorry I know it's not my place," she began. "But, um, you okay?"

"I will be," Paul returned, although the tone of his voice gave away that he was struggling with his emotions. "I just sometimes feel like I don't matter. Like no one can see me."

"Same here," the waitress chucked a bit, knowingly. "Trust me, I understand.

Paul opened up the billfold, glanced over it to make sure it was calculated correctly, then scribbled a hefty tip - like a lavish spender - before signing his name on the bottom line. The weekend had been an expensive and extravagant one already. A night out drinking… dancing with beautiful women… large meals at breakfast, lunch and dinner. Paul was living it up, but he didn't mind. Life was short and Paul knew that sometimes you just had to savor the opportune moments, never really knowing when - or *if* - they'll happen again.

*****

The security officer hadn't given him much to work with; still it was just enough for Myrick to make some early deductions.

According to a map on the cruise ship, the adults-only, serenity pool was located on Deck 7, near the bow of the massive ship. Coming from the piano bar, Harriett Cribbs would've likely taken the companionway to get to it, allowing her a short walk upstairs to the promenade rather than trekking all the way to the middle of the ship to catch an elevator just to ascend one level.

Myrick decided to attempt to retrace her steps by way of the companionway, realizing that actually led him along the right, starboard side of the ship. Taking this direct route toward the adults-only area, he passed a row of lifeboats, including two large mega lifeboats, each likely capable of holding close to 190 or so passengers in an emergency.

Finally, he reached a sign along the promenade that read "Serenity Pool - 18 And Over Only." There was a metal gate and so he pushed it open, proceeding inside. The wind - which was traversing the bow of the ship unimpeded - whipped fiercely against his jacket, wild and uncontainable like the racing of his heart, Myrick's adrenaline flowing now that he was on a case for the first time in what felt like an eternity.

Unlike the fancy main pool, this pool was rather smallish in size - no more than 8x10 in dimension, yet its design and location were convenient nonetheless, providing a private view of the ocean. There were lounge chairs all around and even a heated circular jacuzzi nearby, and Myrick imagined that this was an ideal spot to watch the stars and listen to the sea, devoid of the usual distractions.

Myrick noted to himself that he needed to come check this place out himself at some point on the cruise, as it was right up his alley, especially if he wanted to read the historical novel he'd brought out on the trip - Dr. Jim Nealis' *One Man*. But for now, his entire focus was on solving a mystery and his eyes scanned the expansive deck for any sign of clues. None stood out.

The sea air was blowing stronger than it had been earlier that morning, and there were a few sparse clouds in the distance. The wind was chapping his face and he rubbed his dry hands together. Kneeling down, he decided to dip one hand in the pool, realizing as he did that the pool was a salt water one, which didn't surprise him as he knew that most cruise ships recycled sea water for all the ship's aquatic needs, although the stale, sulphur-like smell bit at his nostrils.

On the other side of the pool area was a second gate, which Myrick guessed led around the bow of the vessel so that a passenger could exit toward the port side of the promenade. No doubt the security officer - Shev - had searched the general area, where allegedly the supposed noise of a disturbance had come from, and evidently found nothing of concern, otherwise her tone earlier would've possessed more of a sense of urgency.

Satisfied that there was nothing else of import in the general vicinity of the pool area for him to investigate, he decided to now explore the port side promenade. Much like the right side of the ship, he noticed lifeboats on the port side as well. The most notable difference being that there were none of the impressive mega-size lifeboats that he'd seen on the starboard side.

As he continued his walk, Myrick noticed that the railing was about four feet high and had steel bars running the length of it, making it impossible for a person to fit through. That said, especially with the breeze blowing, if there had been any evidence lying around the wooden promenade, it would've likely blown overboard long ago.

A ten minute stroll further and Myrick had made it from the bow of the ship all the way to the stern of the vessel, nothing of particular significance catching his eye along the way. If Harriett had heard something alarming in the early morning hours, there didn't seem to be *any* indication that it had been caused by an altercation.

Myrick couldn't rule out entirely that someone had fallen overboard accidentally. But he could reach other deductions of importance. Based on the height that fall would've taken place from, seven stories above sea level, and the crashing sound of the waves and winds, Myrick could tell it was *highly* unlikely Harriett would have heard the sounds of a person falling downward, as it would be near impossible for those cries to carry all the way over to the bow of the ship where the serenity pool was located.

Standing at the stern of the ship now, Myrick glanced out toward the vast ocean. Above him was a blue sky, but off in the distance he could see dark clouds were brewing. Fortunately, they were well behind the cruise ship, which was traveling in the opposite direction, leaving the potentially stormy skies behind, much like the problems of daily life.

Hopefully we won't be sailing back through inclement weather on the return trip, Myrick muttered to himself.

Incredibly, even though they were relatively far from shore, Myrick noticed a couple of seagulls hovering above. The determined birds circled the ship as if not wanting to venture too far from a potential resting spot or source of food if passengers discarded any scraps overboard. It then dawned on Myrick how incredibly likely it was that Harriett had simply heard a bird's call and confused it for a person's. He could see how easily that could happen late at night, especially for someone unfamiliar with the nuances of life at sea.

Myrick had been so lost in his thoughts and the search for clues that he'd lost *all* track of time. Finally glancing down at his watch, he then realized that it was close to 10:00 and that he'd been playing detective longer than he'd known. He hadn't even given Victoria a heads up about what he was off to go do, he was so caught up in the excitement of the investigation.

Equally concerning, he knew that Victoria was set to compete in just a few minutes and he was on the verge of missing it. Instantly, he lost interest in the investigation, his sole consideration getting back down to *Club Deception* in time to catch her performance.

From his position on the stern of the ship, he could actually see the starboard promenade and so decided to hurry that way. Meanwhile, he kept his eyes peeled for signs of the stairwell that could take him back down to the 6th floor. Eventually, and with a sigh of relief, he spotted one - a relatively concealed stairwell, probably used primarily by crew, but Myrick didn't care. He simply needed to find the fastest route back down one level.

The interior of the stairwell was bland and clearly not as eye-catching as most of the other parts of the ship, which Myrick took to mean it wasn't designed with passenger use in mind. Descending a floor, he came upon the entry door to the 6th level. He also couldn't help but notice that the person who'd painted "DECK 6" on the wall of the stairwell had left a sliver of red paint on a nearby handrail as well, evidently from the brush swiping it lightly.

Reaching for the door, he hurried back through the entertainment sector of the ship, following the various signs that pointed the way to *Club Deception*. His chosen path proved to be the right one when he saw several passengers decked in 1940s attire milling about a doorway entrance. Pushing past them, Myrick entered the club and almost instantly heard a familiar song - Caro Emerald's *That Man* - which he'd also known was a favorite of Victoria's and one she'd mentioned wanting to compete to. His heart fell as he could tell the song was nearing its end and that it was entirely possible so was Victoria's dance.

He quickly found a spot in the darkened club along a back wall, immediately surveying the floor in front of him - which had approximately twelve couples on it - until he spotted Victoria, who he could see was dancing with Talon (*of course*). Myrick knew the competition was completely random and that both the song and the dance partner were decided on the spot. Still it was almost a given that she'd draw Talon's name.

Myrick could see that Victoria was also killing it. She had a dazzling smile pasted on her face and was spinning, kicking and sliding in an incredible display of talent and timing.

Wow, she really is amazing at Lindy, thought Myrick.

The song though was coming to an end and as it did, Talon and Victoria walked off the floor, hand in hand, as the crowd cheered on the performances of all the competitors. Myrick noticed that Victoria had changed outfits as well, putting on a stunning flapper dress, which Myrick guessed was the one she'd mentioned at the outset that he was going to love.

He did. It looked absolutely breathtaking on her.

"She's good," a voice next to Myrick spoke amidst the darkness.

Myrick glanced over to see that there was someone standing up against the wall next to him. He hadn't noticed the presence of anyone else, as he'd rushed inside the club. He was even more taken aback when he realized that person was the security guard from before - Shev.

"Oh, didn't see you there," Myrick noted, an expression of surprise on his face.

"I thought you were supposed to be observant," Shev smirked as she spoke.

"Well, um, I *typically* am," Myrick stumbled with his words, clearly caught off guard.

"That's okay. I'm sure she'll forgive you for being late."

"Hope so."

"Just tell her she did amazing. And that she nailed the back flip thing she did. Not that I know much about dance," Shev chuckled. "But I think anyone could tell from the reaction of the crowd that she clearly hit a homerun with the routine."

"That's great," said Myrick, simultaneously appreciating that Shev had used a baseball term to describe Victoria's performance, as that was the sport he'd grown up playing.

"So what exactly is a former detective doing in the dance world? *If* you don't mind me asking."

"It's a long story," Myrick laughed back.

"I'll bet it's an interesting one."

"It is."

"But maybe not nearly as interesting as the story behind your boy."

"You mean Talon?"

"Yes. I got to speak to him for a little bit."

"And?"

"Well, for starters, he seemed a bit full of himself."

"Yep, that sounds like him," Myrick noted, his eyes following Talon, watching intently as he made his way across the crowded room, noting that Talon had done an admirable job cleaning himself up despite limited rest. "Although, I have reason to believe that's something of a facade."

"I figured as much. Although it would be nice to know *what* he's hiding," replied Shev.

Myrick chuckled to himself, impressed with Shev's keen observation. But the information Victoria had provided to him about Talon had been given in confidence. Myrick wasn't about to break that trust. Shev was going to have to do her *own* digging if she wanted to learn more about Talon's past.

Shev, meanwhile, was proving to have a natural gift for reading people, almost as intuitive as Myrick's. And she immediately noted his guarded demeanor when it came to Talon.

She silently wondered if that might also affect Myrick's judgment to a degree.

"What do you know about him that you're not telling me? Are you holding back something?" she pressed, distrust in her voice for the first time.

"Um, not entirely," Myrick kept his response vague, not sure how to answer yet, especially given the way it was posed. "Would it make you feel better if I told you I know that my opinion of Talon is affected by my friendship with Victoria?" Myrick wisely offered, catching Shev off guard with his candor and self-awareness.

"It would," she conceded.

"Everything I tell you about Talon *should* be taken with a grain of salt... *even* the positive thing*s*, as I might be trying to overcompensate on a subconscious level. But I am relatively certain of this, he's not a particularly bad guy. My gut is that life has dealt him an unfair hand and he's figuring out how to adjust. Assuming something *did* go wrong last night... and that Cribbs *did* hear something of concern... I highly doubt Talon has anything to do with it. Now that girl he was with... well, she's an interesting wildcard. Seems to me she's using him."

"Yep, you're definitely overcompensating," Shev gave Myrick a flash of side-eye.

"You think so?"

"Oh, I *know* so."

"Well then it's good that you're working security on this cruise and not me. Besides I kind of agree with your supervisor's fledgling theory. My guess is Ms. Cribbs did just mistake the commotion caused by a pelican or flock of seagulls for something more nefarious in nature."

"*Maybe*," said Shev, not necessarily agreeing or disagreeing with him. "Let me guess, you couldn't help yourself and did some investigating of your own?"

"I did."

"I get it. It's in the blood. I'd do the same." Shev winked.

"I promise not to get in the way."

"Good," Shev replied. "Although if anything does ever happen, I probably would come track you down. I'm always grateful for the help of an actual detective, retired or not."

"And you're not one?"

"One day… perhaps."

"I know a fellow investigator when I see one," Myrick quickly replied. "Twenty years of law enforcement will do that to you. I get a feeling you're the real deal."

"We'll see, I guess," Shev replied, secretly grateful for Myrick's compliment, even if she wasn't showing it outwardly. "In the meantime, my spider-like intuition makes me think you should focus your attention in *that* direction." Shev smirked and then turned her eyes to the side slyly, indicating to Myrick where to look.

Myrick instantly caught sight of Victoria heading their way. Somehow she'd found him in the poorly lit club, an elated look in her vibrant eyes as they landed on Myrick. There was only one person in the room she *really* wanted to hear the opinion of regarding her performance in the comps and she was desperately seeking it out.

It'd been a stroke of good fortune that Myrick had hurried down to the club just in time to catch the end of her performance. And so as he told her how great she'd done (*especially the aerial flip over Talon*) she beamed with excitement. All, it certainly seemed, was well again.

CHAPTER SEVEN
Rejection Inevitably Happens In Life... & In Lindy

He didn't want to admit it, but even the brief time Myrick had spent playing detective had been a highlight of the trip so far; his adrenaline pumping as he did what always came naturally, solving potential crimes. Dance, while he found it thrilling, was quite the opposite and did *not* come easy to him at all.

I feel like a dog that's been romping around the park all his life, and then suddenly has the genius idea to try and actually swim with the ducks in the nearby pond. Only I'm drowning, Myrick had jested to Victoria at one point; meanwhile, the visual had been rather amusing to her, and she did think that there were aspects of Myrick similar to that of a noble hound dog.

She'd then done her best to assuage his worries, reminding him that he was never meant to be a duck, instead emphasizing that he was born with unique talents and that he should embrace the gifts God gave him and not be so hard on himself about the things that didn't come as easily. As long as he could keep that perspective, he could trust that the dance community would look out for him along the way, aware that he was tackling a whole new skill. Victoria had promised him as much.

With that reinforcement, Myrick decided to turn his attention completely back to learning Lindy. He had hopes that he could pick up enough so that the two of them could get some good dances in at the evening social, which promised to be amazing as it was to take place on the ship's top deck, under the nighttime stars. It was actually pretty fascinating how much and how quickly it was possible to advance as a dancer at workshops and conferences where the only thing to do was dance, few other distractions around.

Well, aside from the rare murder… or two.

Myrick couldn't believe how far he'd already come in West Coast Swing. It'd been a year since he'd been introduced to it, but in that time he was nothing like the awkward dancer that he was when he first entered the Westie scene. He suspected that the same might be possible with Lindy Hop, *if* he put some serious focus into it.

The two glanced over the schedule for the afternoon and found a few workshops that they thought would be perfect to attend. The first was a class on swing-outs, and which Myrick was excited to learn was being taught by his friend Terrance.

Already relatively familiar with the basic swing-out, Myrick was excited to find out what new twists Terrance would mix into the pattern, as Myrick liked the idea of adding a few more moves to his limited Lindy arsenal. He'd learned the traditional pattern, the lead rocking back on the *one, two…* and the follower being "swung" into the pattern along the right side for the *three-and-four…* sent back out on the *five, six…* and then finally anchoring in place on the *seven-and-eight,* oftentimes with some fancy swivel-steps added in for style. And now he was ready for something more advanced to try.

Sure enough, as soon as they arrived at the workshop, it became clear that Terrance was going to push the class a bit, and it was evident from the expression on his narrow-featured face that he relished getting to do so. Terrance was a compelling teacher, and the other dancers seemed to hang on his every word. Not only was his knowledge impressive, but he was quite entertaining, and he had the class laughing right off the bat; a zen master with a dry sense of humor.

He briefly explained that the swing-out was performed to an 8-count pattern and then demonstrated how it was done as a basic. Afterward, he winked and explained that he intended to add some flair to the pattern. He was going to teach them a more advanced step, often referred to as a "Rejection Swing-Out".

As normal, the lead rocked back on the *one, two. No change there*, Terrance explained as he demonstrated that footwork simply enough. The "rejection", however, took place on the *three-and-four* as the follower was redirected to the left then sent back out on the *five, six* until finally anchoring in place on the *seven-and-eight*.

Asking for a volunteer from the crowd, a spritely woman came forward. She was pretty with a slim figure and flowing light brown hair accentuated by alluring blonde highlights. The skirt she wore was floral patterned and neatly tied around her waist with a thick chocolate brown belt.

Immediately, Myrick recognized the woman. She was dressed differently at the piano bar - and her hair had been tied up in a ponytail that night whereas it was down now - but this was definitely the same mysterious girl that had danced with Talon at the bar.

Terrance asked her for her name as she walked up. She told him Soriya - Soriya Danes.

Curious, Myrick glanced around to see if Talon had come to the workshop with Soriya, noting that Talon wasn't there. Seconds later and Myrick's attention was back on Terrance, who was leading Soriya through a fluid and seamless swing-out, directing her clockwise to the left and away from her normal *three-and-four* pattern. From the expression on his face, it was clear immediately that Terrance was surprised at how perfectly she'd performed it.

"Just like that," Terrance noted, a subtle grin of pride on his face. "Soriya took my cue perfectly. That's what makes this dance so fun - the variations possible on even the more basic patterns. Anyone have any questions or should we go ahead and give it a shot?" Terrance asked.

Many of the dancers nodded that they were good to test out the pattern, emboldened by Terrance's teaching style. Myrick was looking forward to it also and so he quickly turned and took Victoria's hand, standing in front of her in the open position, his left hand holding her right.

Once all the dancers appeared to be in position, Terrance counted them in and then indicated for them to begin the pattern. Myrick felt confident, knowing he had an advantage on everyone else in the room, as it was effortless leading Victoria on the dance floor. He started with the rock-step, which she followed perfectly, smiling at him as she did so. Then he led her forward on the *three-and-four*, suddenly aware that Victoria was actually doing her best not to back-lead at all, forcing Myrick to do the heavy lifting, which she knew was the *only* way he was really going to learn correctly.

Fortunately, Myrick quickly figured out his assumption about having an advantage had been wrong and so he stepped up his game mid-pattern, making sure at just the right moment that he gave a clear signal for Victoria to swing-out to the left, just as Terrance had instructed to do the "rejection" footwork. Effortlessly, Victoria completed the maneuver and then came face to face again with Myrick, finally tripling in place on the *seven-and-eight*, ready for the next pattern to begin.

"Are you going to talk to her?" Victoria whispered into Myrick's ear, leaning into him ever so slightly.

"Who?"

"The girl who was with Talon last night," Victoria continued to explain, her voice low. "I know you. I know what you were up to while I was teaching the workshop," Victoria smiled seductively as she leaned back to peer into his pointed, discerning eyes. "I'm sure you want to ask her a few questions as part of your investigation also."

"There's nothing to investigate," said Myrick.

"Oh okay," replied Victoria with a half-smile, not believing him. "Well, that's your forte... not mine. But, um," Victoria indicated with her gaze turned toward the woman on her left. "Here comes your next follower. You can fill me in later on what you found out."

As Victoria spoke, Terrance called out, "switch." On cue, the followers moved one lead to the right, so that an entirely different woman was now standing in front of Myrick.

Myrick stood in front of his follow, an older woman, maybe late-60s. She had a wide, welcoming smile on her face as she took Myrick's extended hand.

"Please tell me you've done this before," Myrick jested.

"Nope, just here to dance with handsome men," the woman replied, a smirk on her face.

"Oh, um, I'm Evann," Myrick introduced himself, a bit caught off guard by the woman's forward - *but endearing* - nature.

"Mildred," she replied.

Myrick reached out and took Mildred's right hand, which the older woman seemed particularly enamored about. Once all the leads and follows had done as instructed, Terrance gave the countdown to proceed.

Instantly, Myrick took a step back with his left foot. As he rocked forward again with the other foot, his mind suddenly went blank, as if he'd forgotten everything he'd just done with Victoria. He then led Mildred on a completely different pattern, somehow resulting in the two of them being back face to face by the end of it.

Mildred had a glowing smile plastered on her face, as if the pattern was less important to her than the man she was getting to dance with, which more than covered for the internal embarrassment Myrick was feeling.

"Good job." Mildred squeezed Myrick's hand.

Myrick's ego might have been wounded, but his gratitude outweighed it. "Thank you," he chuckled back, aware that he couldn't have butchered the move *any* worse.

Almost as soon as he did, Myrick heard Terrance call out yet again, "switch!"

Myrick knew what this meant, and he high-fived his partner, who then moved clockwise one dancer so that another follower took her place - the woman who'd danced with Talon at *The Phoenix & Dragon*. This was Myrick's chance, only he'd been so flummoxed by his dance with Mildred that he wasn't himself.

Fortunately, the stunning woman in front of him pleasantly introduced herself, breaking the ice.

"Soriya," she spoke.

"Evann," Myrick fumbled back.

"Oh, I know who you are," Soriya smiled seductively. "You're the detective."

"How do you know that?" asked Myrick, confused.

"Talon told me all about you. It was all he could talk about between breaks from our dances. Not exactly what I had in mind, of course." Soriya rolled her eyes. "But boys will be boys. And I could tell there's *quite* a rivalry brewing between the two of you it seems."

Myrick instantly started to wonder if Soriya wasn't trying to stir up a little trouble with her comments. No doubt, Talon *did* tell her about their dust up, but Myrick also was pretty certain Talon wouldn't have dwelled on it to that degree. He could see on Soriya's face that she was enjoying retelling Talon's secret and Myrick was wise enough to know that she was hoping he'd take the bait and give her even more ammunition to work with.

"No," Myrick finally replied, evenly. "No rivalry between us. Talon seems like an upstanding guy."

"I'm sure he is," said Soriya, an even more devious look in her slanted blue-green eyes, which along with her outfit had her looking reminiscent of Gene Tierney in her heyday.

Terrance had already given the cue to repeat the pattern, killing any chance Myrick had to ask questions of Soriya. He wanted to know how the two had met, or if perhaps their dance at the bar was their first encounter together. More importantly, he wanted to find out if Talon had been with her before returning to his room that morning.

Instead, he had to focus his attention entirely on the pattern, although he found out quickly that Soriya was quite the skilled dancer, smoothly performing the swing-out before triple stepping and extending her arm to create stretch at the end.

Myrick was about to ask a follow up question when Soriya purposefully beat him to it, cutting him off right as Myrick was about to speak.

"Well so nice to meet you," she reached out to high-five him, the normal etiquette among dancers in a workshop. She then turned to walk away, although Myrick noticed the mischievous grin return to her face as she did, clearly enamored with herself.

All the while, Victoria was watching as well. She'd seen how the encounter had gone, and she could tell by the look on Myrick's face that it was not as he'd hoped. Soriya was toying with him, Victoria had seen that game played before.

It was time now for Victoria to do some detective work of her own. *She'd* be the one to skillfully pry answers out of the vixen. She just needed to wait until the opportunity presented itself to do so.

*****

Harriett was sitting in her quaint cabin #347, alone, contemplating her conversation with the security officer, who'd introduced herself as Shev. Shev was young, but she seemed bright, perceptive, and quite frankly Harriett saw a lot of herself in Shev.

They were both the same age - 23. In talking to Shev, Harriett picked up on a New York accent, eventually learning that Shev had grown up in Tremont, which wasn't much safer than Bushwick where Harriett had spent her childhood. The only difference, the two had clearly chosen different paths in life - Shev pursuing a path in security work; whereas Harriett found herself trapped in a life of crime.

In fact, Harriett had garnered herself quite a lengthy rap sheet over the years. Nothing too heinous, mostly misdemeanors and civil driving infractions. The NYPD's 83rd Precinct had been on a first-name basis with her by the age of fifteen.

Harriett, though, had a fierce spirit and wanted to find a way out. She knew she'd never make it on the traditional path, education just wasn't for her. But she did have another gift, she was incredibly artistic. She could paint... she could draw... and she could dance. The latter eventually opening up doors that would've otherwise been unavailable to her.

The cruise was actually an unexpected gift from a wealthy customer. She made quite a living offering private lessons. She could teach really *any* type of dance. Lindy wasn't her favorite, she preferred Latin dances, as they were more sultry in nature. Still, she needed the break and she certainly wasn't going to turn down an all-expenses paid cruise.

The people onboard the ship weren't the type she typically spent time with either, especially the awkward guy with the herringbone coat and flat cap who'd asked to dance with her the night earlier. At the time, she'd actually been enjoying doing people watching in the back of the room, sizing up the crowd of strangers. Later, once she'd gotten more of a comfort level with her surroundings, was when Harriett had planned to get some dances in.

But then the man in the flat cap had sat down next to her, and she believed it would be rude to turn down a request to dance; so she'd painfully obliged, hoping that'd be their *only* one of the trip. Fortunately, later that evening, a much more skilled dancer did ask her to dance. He said his name was Paul. She found him to be an odd bird, but of course that was actually her *type* and it'd soon become clear that she could relate well to his quirky personality.

Among other similarities, *both* weren't really in the mood for socializing; they'd just come to dance and escape life for awhile. Paul did a wonderful job not only leading her, but did a fun thing where he could switch roles mid-dance; Paul becoming the follow and Harriett becoming the lead. They seemed to do it almost effortlessly, despite the fact that it hadn't been a planned thing at all.

The two continued dancing at the dueling piano bar late into the evening, with very little actual conversation taking place. In fact, Harriett hadn't learned much about Paul throughout the evening and she'd told him even less about herself, *which was a good thing*. Harriett had long since learned that the more people learned about the adverse circumstances of her upbringing - especially her troubles with the law - the more they tended to distance themselves.

By the end of the evening, Paul had grown increasingly distracted, most likely exhausted from being out so late. Their conversation growing awkward, Harriett had thanked him for the fun dances, gone up to the bar to pay for her drinks and then left the establishment. Still, the abrupt end to their encounter strangely affected Harriett and she'd found herself wide awake, not yet ready to head back to her cabin.

She'd decided to take a walk on the ship's deck, hoping that might tire her out. And when it didn't, she'd decided to go sit by the more private adults-only pool at the bow of the ship, her mind still racing with thoughts.

While Shev did seem to give credence to the recantation Harriett told her about hearing the sudden disturbance, she'd added the caveat that the commotion *could* potentially have been caused by a larger type bird. Of course, Harriett knew the truth… she'd not been mistaken that the cry that went out that night had been a *human* one.

Regardless, Harriett didn't actually care what the security team did with the information she'd given them; she didn't necessarily like or trust law enforcement types anyway. So after she provided the particulars of the situation, it made no difference to her how they proceeded from there.

She'd also *simultaneously* covered her tracks in case something was suspected to have gone awry and her presence was spotted on footage captured in that general vicinity. Harriett knew there were security cams everywhere on board the high-tech ship. And it certainly wouldn't be the first time she'd been caught in the wrong place at the wrong time.

Thwap. There was a knock on the door, startling Harriett. Then another. And another. Each one heavy-handed in nature.

The knocks now had Harriett's complete attention. Quickly, she pushed pause on her phone, stopping the music in the midst of a particularly foreboding verse. She then stood up from her twin-sized bed and made her way over to the cabin door.

"Who's there?" she asked, confused why anyone would be knocking.

"Ship's host, ma'am," a boyish voice responded. "Just coming by to remind you of the event you signed up for this evening."

Harriett opened the door to see a young man in sharp attire, black vest and bowtie, standing outside her room. He had a youthful face that matched his voice so that his appearance conformed to what she'd expected to see. The young host had a tablet in his hand, and seemed to be typing on it as she spoke.

"What event?" Harriett asked.

"The poker game. I see here that you'd checked it off during registration as one of the events you were interested in. It's a dancer-only event. Takes place in the casino, room *Lucky Seven,* in about fifteen minutes. There was a sign-in, but a few passengers didn't stop by and so I was requested to come check and see if you and those others still wanted to join the tournament. If so, you'll likely want to head that way soon."

"Oh, yes actually," Harriett straightened herself out as she replied. "I did want to do the poker tournament. It's just been a long day. I lost track of time. But I'll head that way in just a second. Only need to get a few things together first."

"Of course." The young man tapped the tablet to insert a black checkmark beside Harriett's name on the screen. "I'll let them know you're coming."

As the young man disappeared down the corridor, Harriett nodded her head while slowly starting to close the door, indicating the conversation was over. She glanced down at her attire, suddenly acutely aware that she was still wearing the same clothes she'd worn to the club the night before, so distracted that she'd not even taken the time to change yet. Harriett was prone to doing that, she could get fixated on a subject, losing all track of time. It was a trait that got her into trouble on occasion, *like now.*

Hurrying over to the small cabin bed, she reached underneath it and pulled out the only suitcase she'd brought on the trip, which was covered in stickers, souvenirs from all the places she'd been. Harriett was a wanderer.

She tossed the suitcase on the bed haphazardly and unzipped it. Inside were clothes, neatly rolled up, as if everything was packed military style, which she'd learned during a short stint in the Army. Her choice of wardrobe would fit that motif as well, mostly earth tones: greens, browns and tans. She pulled out a taupe single-breasted flare skirt and a black skinny fit sweater, and then quickly changed into both.

There was a round mirror in the solo-cabin. Unlike the night before, Harriett decided she wanted to make herself as appealing as possible, using all the wares at her disposal to her advantage. She'd not applied any makeup at all the night before, hoping to call as little attention to herself as possible, wanting to remain in the shadows. An introverted-extrovert by nature, she could also turn on the charm when she wanted to, and now that was suddenly *exactly* what she wanted to do.

Poker was her game. She loved everything about it, and it suited her personality well. Harriett liked to study people, get to know their peculiar idiosyncrasies. She enjoyed competition too, poker was indeed a game of skill, especially when you'd figured out the other players tells. But, most importantly, Harriett liked to win, even more so when *money* was involved.

Naturally unassuming, Harriett went to work enhancing her appearance with shades of makeup. Her mysterious green eyes, she accentuated with smoky eyeliner. Her thin lips were lined with a dark rouge lipstick, making them appear fuller. And her fair skin was powdered lightly along her cheeks. Suddenly, the ordinary seeming girl from earlier had transformed herself into an apparent femme fatale.

The weaker minded men at the table were going to be like putty in her hands. Those that didn't succumb to her looks, she'd outsmart and outplay. The shocking transition had turned her into a deadly combination of looks and intelligence; the odds were stacked in her favor even before the games had begun.

The last thing Harriett put on was a bracelet. It was a metallic gunmetal one, and it wrapped around her wrist, rope-like. Harriett's arms were thin and so she had to twist the bracelet around it four times, which made it look thick, covering up most of her wrist. The bracelet was also layered intermittently with dangling charms: among them a bullet, a dog paw print, a skull, an hourglass and a compass. Each of the charms had a deeper meaning to Harriett, even if she rarely shared those intimate details with others.

Glancing in the mirror one last time, Harriett liked how she was put together. The last thing she did was place a thick white belt around her waist, the center of which was shaped like a coiled viper wrapped around a small (but deadly sharp) dagger. After attaching the belt around her narrow waist, it had an alluring quality to it, showing off Harriett's stunning figure.

That, however, wasn't the *only* reason why she wore the unique belt. It was an essential accessory, the dagger capable of being detached from the belt, and she found ways to wear it whenever she went out. In fact, she'd worn it the night before at *The Phoenix & Dragon* as well.

And, indeed, while she'd been walking on the promenade of the ship - and in the dead of the night - she'd even pulled out the weapon that was concealed within the coils of the steel viper buckle. A detail she'd not divulged to the security guards when filling them in about the late night sounds that she claimed to have heard.

CHAPTER EIGHT
Practice Body Awareness & Isolation

Shev made her way into the back office of the dueling piano bar, which had only been open for a few hours. She'd gotten a call from the manager on duty that one of the shift workers hadn't shown up, the bartender - Tempest Greylock.

In speaking to the manager over the phone, Shev learned that Tempest was *always* punctual, having never missed a day of work before. The manager had called down to the crew quarters to check on Tempest, only to learn that no one had seen her in quite a while. They also checked her cabin quarters, but she wasn't there either.

Tempest, it seemed, had gone missing.

Ordinarily, a situation like this might not entirely alarm Shev. She'd been down this road many times before, aware that hookups were a common theme on cruise lines and that Tempest had most likely spent the night in someone else's cabin. She'd probably even overslept which was easy to do without an alarm, most of the crew working long arduous hours.

Tempest would most likely show up eventually. The only thing making this situation feel different was Harriett's account from the previous night. Shev wanted to personally make sure the two situations weren't connected in some way.

The manager of the dueling piano bar was Gunther Macklin and he ran a tight ship at *The Phoenix & Dragon*. Gunther insisted they meet in his office, as he was *incredibly* busy and also now running short staff thanks to Tempest being a no show. Shev, meanwhile, had never been in Gunther's office before. As she knocked on the door, she heard a voice on the other end bark out, "Come in!" Entering slowly into the dimly lit room, she spotted a man sitting down at a desk, paperwork scattered all over.

The room itself had a heavy smell of tobacco in the air, almost overwhelming. Shev's attention was trained on Gunther, who hadn't yet lifted his eyes to look up to see who his guest was, as he was deep in thought, rifling through some of the papers on his desk.

Gunther had a rough face, cratered like the moon. His hair was thinning, and he ran his nubby fingers through it, evidently troubled by what he was reading. In front of him was a Cuban cigar perched on a stand, thin waves of smoke lifting up toward the vent on the ceiling. Aside from designated regions on the exterior aft of the cruise liner, the ship was non-smoking, especially in the interior areas. No one *dared* enforce that rule on Gunther though.

He'd been in the cruise ship business for decades, addicted to the sense of pleasure that came from smoking. A man as stubborn as Gunther wasn't going to change his ways all these years later, and he was far too valuable to the cruise line industry to chance letting go. If the man wanted to indulge in a cigar or two - *or even twenty* - in his private office, then so be it.

Realizing he had a visitor, Gunther finally glanced up at Shev, an annoyed look in his wrinkled eyes that were barely visible underneath heavy lids.

"Well, have you tracked her down yet?" Gunther asked.

"No, I haven't. Might have just met someone last night and lost track of time," Shev threw out the possibility, as it was as good a guess as any.

"Or fell overboard," Gunther added, devoid of emotion. "Wouldn't be the first poor soul to do that. Then you're just shark bait at that point."

"I *highly* doubt that's the case. My understanding from asking around is that Tempest was constantly getting hit on at the bar. It's possible she just hooked up with someone. I'm not ready to assume the worst yet."

"You might if you know the girl like I do. Sure, guys constantly test their luck with Tempest. Can't say I blame them either. But that girl can handle herself just fine. She isn't the type to fall for that nonsense."

"Well, maybe this time was the exception. Even the strongest personalities are capable of a weak moment every now and then."

"*Sure,*" Gunther replied, clearly not convinced. He then took a long puff from the cigar, his eyes opening wider as he did so, giving Shev a better look at their bloodshot, tired appearance.

"You know something, don't you?"

"No, just a hunch is all," Gunther placed the cigar down on the tray and leaned back in his chair, arms crossed about his thick chest.

"You think she could've been the victim of foul play?"

"Could be. She was upset last night. Not often I've seen her get rattled. But someone or something had gotten under her skin. She cut out of work a few minutes ahead of quitting time. That's not like her."

"Was she upset to the point that she might have done something drastic? Jumped from the ship?"

Gunther didn't answer. Instead, he unfolded his arms and let out a belly laugh, revealing a stomach that looked as plump as an overstuffed turkey. "No, I highly doubt that," he replied through his chuckle, his cheeks and round face now a rosy red. He then ran his hand along his thick, unkempt beard, wondering at the impossibility of what Shev had said. "Tempest is tough as nails. That's one of the things that I like best about her. I'm not exactly the *easiest* person to work for-"

It took everything in Shev not to nod back her agreement, clearly perplexed by Gunther's bluntness. Instead, she simply feigned surprise at his self-assessment.

"I like to give Tempest a little *good-natured* ribbing. I treat her like one of the guys. But only because she can take it as well as she dishes it out. I enjoy our back-and-forth banter. She's feisty. She has no quit in her. She wouldn't do a thing like you suggest. If Tempest went overboard, it would only be by accident... unless of course someone purposefully shoved her. She's known to go up to the promenade and take a smoke break after work to unwind. I see her sitting on that bench by Lifeboat Station 9 all the time after work, sometimes a good hour after closing time."

"Let's hope that's not the case then. Right now, I'm still inclined to believe she'll show up. I'll keep asking around. *Someone* will have seen her."

"Send her my way if you do find her," said Gunther.

His businesslike demeanor threw Shev off, as she'd expected more concern from him regarding his valued employee. He seemed to know Tempest quite well, but before she could speak again, Gunther added a comment that made her realize that the gruff man did indeed have some humanity in him after all.

"And don't stop looking until you do find her," Gunther added after a pause, his voice suddenly serious. "*Even if* the powers that be act like her disappearance is no big concern."

"I won't stop searching," Shev replied.

There was an awkward silence between the two, as if Gunther didn't know what else to say. He was a man of few words, and the ones he did speak were rarely affable. He didn't like showing emotion and now that he had, he wasn't sure what to do next.

Gunther's eyes drifted down to the paperwork still in front of him, rifling through it again, trying to find the page he'd left off on at when first interrupted. Meanwhile, Shev turned to leave, more determined than ever to figure out where Tempest might have disappeared to.

Making her way out of the bar, Shev's attention turned to a curious tip that Gunther had unwittingly provided - Tempest had a habit of smoking cigarettes up on the promenade after work. His information was also something of a relief to Shev, as she knew that Lifeboat Station 9 was on the starboard side of the ship, whereas Cribbs had insisted the commotion she'd heard had come from the port side. It was nice to know the two circumstances weren't linked after all.

It was late afternoon and the sun was just setting in the distance. Shev had almost entirely lost track of time and her security shift was coming to an end soon. She'd report everything she'd found out to Moretti, although frustrated a bit by the fact that she'd accomplished so little in her search for Tempest.

As Shev made her way along the wooden platform, she passed a few passengers, all of whom seemed enamored by the view of the sun as it set in the sky, creating a stunning multicolored (red, purple and blue) hue in the distance. There was a couple walking toward her, both appearing to be in their mid-70s. The two were holding hands and Shev smiled at how endearing the two of them looked together, almost as if plucked from a Norman Rockwell painting. Cruise ships were *incredibly* romantic. It made Shev wonder if she'd ever find the right one to spend a lifetime with as well.

Just as the couple was passing by along the promenade, Shev noticed the glint of a gold circular object on the ground. Curious, Shev leaned over to pick it up, examining it in her hand briefly as she did. She then immediately turned to the couple.

"Excuse me, did one of you drop this?"

"Um, no, I don't believe so," the woman replied, a confused look on her face. She then glanced over at her husband to see that he didn't recognize the object either. "Must've been someone else. Thank you though, dear."

"You're welcome," Shev replied as the couple turned to leave. She then peered down at the object in her hand again, which was no bigger than a dime in size.

There was a solitary marking on it - "ᴛ.ᵹ." and it had a hook on the top, as if it had once been attached to a necklace. The latch was bent, indicating it must've been forcefully broken open at some point.

Shev glanced around, trying to sense if perhaps someone else nearby had lost it or was looking for the valuable trinket. Realizing that no one was, Shev tucked it into her pocket, deciding to take it down to the lost and found.

Eventually its owner would show up to claim it. Shev was just glad she'd spotted it before the wind or someone's shoe kicked it overboard, to be lost *forever* in the depths of the sea.

*****

Positioned against a wall, his back up against it and cap pulled down low as if he was trying to remain inconspicuous, Myrick peered out at the sea of people wandering around the casino. The room was alive with excitement. And Myrick relished the chance to take it all in from a concealed place in the shadows.

In many ways, not having to deal with people was an opportunity to recharge his batteries. He could turn on the charm if need be; but that tended to take something out of him as well. This was different, he could spend hours quietly observing things from a distance, awed by people's quirks, which was oftentimes entertainment enough.

It helped too that he was dressed in dark attire - a wool-inspired, charcoal gray outfit, complete with a pinstripe vest and two-toned Oxfords - that had him looking like Frank Costello overseeing an early 1900s gambling operation.

Adjusting the black tie around his neck, Myrick loosened it to provide some extra breathing room. He didn't like neckwear and rarely wore it, but Victoria said it completed the ensemble. She'd actually picked it out for him herself. And when she saw it on him, she gushed about how handsome he looked, which was more than enough encouragement for Myrick to keep it on. After satisfying herself that his entire outfit looked the part, Victoria placed a black handkerchief inside Myrick's vest pocket, then sent him away so that she could get ready as well.

Myrick, meanwhile, was fine with his marching orders, heading down to the casino to wait for her. She'd entered the two of them in a poker tournament, knowing that Myrick would really enjoy it. Although she didn't provide *too* many other details, she did mention that it was a Texas Hold'Em tournament and that she'd been in one at a prior dance event, explaining to Myrick that it was a great way to socialize with other dancers in a different setting.

The organizer of the entire Lindy event had secured them a private room inside the casino. So with some time to kill waiting for Victoria, Myrick found a tucked-away corner of the casino, simply waiting and watching as people passed by.

It was then that he noticed a familiar face scurrying through the entry hallway of the casino. She was in a hurry, passing quickly along a set of slot machines, which were alive with a dizzying array of colors and sounds, and then walked right past where Myrick was standing, not even noticing him, her attention clearly elsewhere.

"Any updates in your case?" Myrick called out from the shadows, just loud enough to get the attention of the security officer hurrying past him.

"Huh," Shev replied, a befuddled expression on her face, as if not certain who'd made the comment *or* if it was even directed at her. "Oh, hey," she continued, only then stopping in her tracks as she realized that the man behind the gangster costume was Myrick. "Didn't see you there." She then sized up his attire before continuing, the right side of her mouth rising into a smirk. "I thought you were one of the good guys?"

"Not tonight," Myrick's broad shoulders rose in a comical shrug.

"Hmmm, then not sure how I feel about sharing information with you."

"I wouldn't trust me."

Shev then noticed for the first time an object in Myrick's hand - a shiny quarter, and he was flipping it effortlessly from finger to finger.

"That's a neat little trick," Shev noted, changing the subject, eyes directed at the quarter in Myrick's hand, which was shifting from the knuckle of one finger to the next.

"Oh yeah, picked this up from a criminal, believe it or not. He was doing it in the middle of an interview. Not gonna lie, I was impressed. Halfway through the interview I asked him how he did it so he showed me. We bonded over the trick so much that he eventually confessed to his crime."

"Sounds like a win-win."

"I saw it that way. Not sure he did though."

"Interesting," Shev replied slyly, then chuckled. "Well, that kind of reinforces my original point. Not sure I should be sharing details with a guy who blends in with the criminal element so well."

"Your loss." Myrick winked, knowingly. "But I can tell by the tenor of things that you *did* find something… even if you aren't sure what to make of it yet."

"Dang, you're good."

"After twenty plus years of detective work, you get decent at sizing people up."

"Hope I can have that sort of sixth sense one day," Shev replied, impressed and envious.

"I'm sure you will."

Hearing Myrick's reply, Shev reached inside her pocket and pulled out the gold charm she'd picked up. Holding it in the palm of her hand, she showed him the cryptic markings "ᴛ.ᶢ.".

"What am I looking at?"

"Well, it appears to be a charm that broke off from a necklace. Seems like it might be valuable. Wondered if it might belong to our missing crew member - Tempest Greylock."

"It does," Myrick replied, confidently.

"How can you be so sure?"

"Those are initials on the charm… written in Gaelic Insular. The first is 'T'… and the second is 'G'… for Tempest Greylock, I'd assume."

"Oh, wow. But then why wouldn't she come looking for it?"

"Well, judging by the damage to the charm, Ms. Greylock's disappearance may be connected to the commotion that Ms. Cribbs insists she heard late last night."

"Possibly… although there's an obvious flaw to that theory. I found this on the *starboard* side of the ship, nowhere near where Cribbs says the commotion took place on the port side of it."

"You know I once had a case where my original theory was entirely disproven by the discovery of one piece of evidence. Changed everything so I had to start back at square one to solve the crime. Maybe that's what you're dealing with as well… some sort of clue to where Ms. Greylock has disappeared to, perhaps?"

"Maybe. I'm thinking I should show this to Cribbs and see if her story has changed at all since last night. Can't hurt to make sure she's got her facts right."

"Or to ensure she's not hiding something."

"*Exactly*. I really do love the way you think."

"Likewise. It certainly appears there'd be wisdom in a second interview of your key witness."

"Well, that's *if* my supervisor permits me to conduct a follow up."

"You know, luck might be on our side. There's a chance Ms. Cribbs will be at the poker tournament I'm headed to. If so, I'll try to do a little digging, get a better feel for what kind of person she is."

"That'd be great. Please let me know what you find out."

"Find out about what?" a voice spoke from behind Myrick.

Turning around, Myrick caught sight of Victoria. She looked *stunning,* an alluring sight in her flapper dress and elbow-length white satin gloves.

"Well, handsome, you gonna tell me what's up or do I have to pry that information out of you?" Victoria took a seductive step toward Myrick, placing a gloved hand on his chest, acutely aware by the look in his eye that she'd garnered his complete attention, *just as she'd intended.*

"So I, um, think I'll let the two of you get to your poker game," Shev interjected, amused that the man who seemed levelheaded mere seconds ago was so easily put under Victoria's spell. "We can catch up more later," she nodded over at Myrick, who was only *partly* paying attention to her, the touch of Victoria's hand on his chest a more compelling distraction.

"Right," Myrick replied, his voice cracking.

"Well, good luck," Shev simply replied, a wry smile on her face. She then turned to walk off, leaving Myrick and Victoria to themselves, which was what Myrick clearly preferred at the moment.

"Come on," said Victoria, knowing she needed to get Myrick to refocus. "The poker game is about to begin. I figured that'd be your favorite part of this cruise."

"You've got me looking forward to it actually. I'm a pretty decent poker player, you know."

"I'd believe it. You're a tough read *most* of the time."

Myrick's thick eyebrows rose as he replied, "Not always though."

Victoria suddenly blushed, which she rarely did, having spent a life in the spotlight and used to being hit with compliments, but none had *quite* the same effect on her as the current one from Myrick did.

"You don't look too bad yourself," she winked. "We'll be the perfect Bonnie and Clyde."

"I couldn't wish for a better partner in crime."

"Me neither."

"We need a plan if we both make it to the final table."

"Agreed."

"What's the signal if you have a good hand and I need to get out?"

"I'll tell you to fold."

"Got it," Myrick impressively kept a straight face and serious voice. He *loved* Victoria's humor. "And if I have a good hand and you have a bad one?"

"Same. You should fold."

This time Myrick did chuckle out loud. "What's the prize for first place?" he finally asked.

"It's winner take all, which I imagine will be a hefty sum with a twenty dollar buy-in and a room full of players."

"No second place prize?" Myrick was surprised.

"No money, but I believe Duncan will come up with something for the first loser," Victoria explained, wryly. "He's always keeping things interesting."

"Who's Duncan? That the guy running this event?"

"It is."

"Don't think I've met him yet."

"Oh, he's quite a character. Comes from a small town overseas... Islay, I believe."

"Ah, a Scot!" Myrick's voice had some levity to it suddenly. "Always a pleasure to spend time with a fellow from the British Isles. I'm sure he'll have some captivating stories to tell if he's from Islay. Now I'm looking forward to this even more."

"I had a feeling you two might hit it off. Anyway, he'll obviously be there and I'm sure he'll make it entertaining for everyone. If nothing else, this'll be a good way for dancers to get to know each other and talk away from the dance floor. Duncan's the glue for this event."

"Well that *is* good to know. Anyone else I should be aware of at the tournament?"

"Most of the pros will be there. Several are actually big time gamblers. Don't just assume they'll be pushovers."

"I won't."

"I'm hoping Talon will be there too. I saw him briefly after his interview with your security guard friend."

"How's he doing?"

"He's hanging in there. Seemed a little down. I still don't know where he went after the bar or why he stayed out all night. He hasn't said a word to me. I hope he didn't get mixed up with the wrong person. He can be gullible sometimes."

"I know you'd mentioned that you'd never seen that girl before that he was dancing with."

"Nope, but she sure seemed to click with him fast. Weird how that all went down."

"Well, that's a guy for you. Easily seduced. Although, it's probably not the worst thing in the world that he found someone to spend time with on the cruise," said Myrick, an air of hopefulness in his voice, betraying that he'd prefer Talon have his sights on someone *other* than Victoria.

"And if he does come to the poker tournament-"

"I'll be on my best behavior," Myrick finished Victoria's sentence, still sorry for his juvenile response at the bar and deeply affected to have learned about Talon's painful past.

"Thank you."

"You're welcome."

"Let's just go be *us* and make tonight memorable. I only get a few days with you."

Victoria's words hit Myrick a little harder than he'd expected, suddenly aware of how fast the time was flying by. Before he knew it, the cruise would be over and Victoria would be back on a plane to New York. He'd gotten far too caught up in Shev's investigation, which was a problem for security to solve and not one of the paying customers.

"We will. Especially if I win tonight," Myrick finally added.

"That's a *huge* if," Victoria laughed. "But then again, nothing you do really surprises me anymore. I'm curious to see what kind of poker player you prove to be."

With that, Myrick and Victoria made their way over to the *Lucky Seven* ballroom, Myrick no longer consumed with the investigation. Tempest Greylock's disappearance didn't likely have anything to do with attendees of the Lindy Hop group anyway. She'd eventually show up with a good explanation for where she'd been. In the meantime, Myrick was going to make the best of every minute he had with Victoria.

Or at least that was his hope.

CHAPTER NINE
Use Non-Verbal Cues to Telegraph Your Next Move

There was an ivory card on the table with Myrick's name printed on it in sophisticated *Roundhand* lettering. He picked it up to see that'd they'd badly misspelled his name, inscribing it as, "*Evan Miric*", which he found amusing.

Locating Victoria's card, he picked that one up as well and walked over to where she was standing, chatting away with several friends. He then slipped the card into her hand, which she glanced down at to inspect.

"I'm at Table Four. What about you?"

"Table Seven."

"Seriously, you even got a number that's lucky," she laughed. "I wonder how many people are getting in on the poker game."

"Well, usually you sit 8 to 10 at a table so we're talking at least 60 or so players."

"*Victims* you mean," Victoria winked.

"Exactly," Myrick replied, channeling his best gangster impression. "Them chumps won't know wut hit 'em, sugar."

"Oh dear, I've created a monster, haven't I?" Victoria laughed, rolling her eyes in amusement.

Feigning concern, Victoria placed her hand to her neck, which was accented by a slinky boat-neck flapper dress. The swirling sequined pattern of her attire matched the elegant sheer mesh capelet around her shoulders, with an embroidered cloche hat placed atop her soft strawberry-blonde hair. The white gloves adorning her hands were ruched through the elbow, and Victoria could see that they'd done a nice job drawing Myrick's attention to her sultry neckline.

"Perhaps."

"Yes, perhaps," Victoria replied, giving Myrick a hint of side-eye.

"Well, I'll see you inside." Myrick decided it was best to let Victoria catch up with her friends, who *all* wanted her attention while she was with them.

Just as importantly, Myrick wanted to scout out the competition, many of whom were already scattered throughout the poker room.

Proceeding through the ornate double doors and into the ballroom, he could instantly see that the room was decked out in Art Deco decor. Much like Myrick and Victoria, the people milling about wore vintage-era attire that fit with that particular theme as well.

This was indeed going to be an intriguing evening, Myrick thought to himself.

"Please tell me you're sitting at my table," a familiar voice caught Myrick's attention and he turned to see a beautiful blonde walking toward him with a twinkle in her deep set eyes, wearing a polka dot print belted dress; her hair combed in Dutch Cat style, her lips pouty.

"Susie," replied Myrick, a smile coming over his face, immediately recognizing the girl who'd coincidentally introduced him to East Coast Swing nearly a year earlier. "Terrance told me you were on this cruise. Nice to see you again."

"Nice to see *you* also," replied Susie, the rouge of her lipstick accentuating her grin, impressed that Myrick remembered her. They'd only danced together that one particular evening at the bar, but apparently it had been enough to leave a lasting impression on *both* of them. "I take it you must have gotten more into dance after that night, huh? Is Lindy your thing now?"

"Wish I could say that, but actually I'm only here because a friend invited me. That's her coming in right now." Myrick pointed toward the double-door entryway, just as Victoria was entering the ballroom. His eyes followed her as she made her way over to what was marked as *Table Four*.

"Just a friend, huh?" Susie smirked, picking up on both Myrick's effusive tone and Victoria's undeniably captivating nature.

"Yes," Myrick laughed. "*Just* friends."

"Okay, then... so back to my original question - what table are you?"

"Table Seven. And you?" Myrick asked, glancing down at the ivory-colored place card in his hand one more time as if to make sure he remembered correctly.

"Seven also."

"Oh good, at least I'll know someone else there."

"Well, we'll see how you feel about that *after* we're done playing," Susie grinned.

"Fair enough." Myrick smiled back, accepting the challenge.

Almost as soon as he did, a voice with a thick-Scottish accent belted out from the front of the room, announcing that it was nearing time to kick off the event. Myrick glanced over to see an older gentlemen with long wavy gray hair and thin wire-rimmed spectacles addressing the crowd, a black microphone gripped in his hand and held up close to his interesting face. As the man surveyed the room, his thick bushy salt and pepper eyebrows angled up in a discerning fashion.

"Good evening, you'll see that your names are all positioned in front of the chairs at assigned tables," the gentleman began. "Aye, we've selected these spots completely in random fashion." He winked as he spoke, as if to indicate that he *might* be fudging a little. "If you *happen* to be sitting next to a dance rival or foe… well, that's just a wee bit of coincidence, I'd venture to say." He smiled widely, which only accentuated the droopiness of his reddish cheeks and his aged face.

Placing the microphone back down on a podium stand. The older man then made his way toward the far end of the room, as if he too was in search of his table. Taking the cue, Myrick decided to do the same.

"Let's go find our seats," he motioned to Susie.

"Let's." She smiled back.

Myrick spotted Table Seven, which had a bold numeral "**7**" visible on a stand in the center of it. His seat was on the far side of the table, marked by a card with his (still misspelled) name placed in front of it. Susie, meanwhile, was directly across from him.

There were ten seats in total at the round table and slowly all ten seats were filled. The last, interestingly, was occupied by the same old man who had earlier opened up the event over the microphone. The old man's seat happened to be just to Myrick's right and so after the gentlemen sat down, Myrick did the cordial thing and introduced himself.

"Evann Myrick." He extended out a friendly hand to the elder gentleman.

"Aye, glad to meet ya," the man replied, his eyes blinking furiously, as if he suffered from a nervous tick. "Name's Duncan Campbell."

As the two men shook hands, Myrick noted that Duncan's hands were aged and coarse, but his grip was firm. He then watched curiously as Duncan placed one hand on his wire-framed glasses, adjusting them slightly as he spoke.

"I've heard of ya. They say you're quite the detective."

"I've heard about you also. My understanding is you're a true Scot... from Islay. My family line traces back to Dublin."

"Well isn't that tidy. Tis a bonnie day when I run into an Irish cousin. And seems you've done your homework on me, detective. Quite impressive, indeed."

"Well, actually, it was Victoria Monroe that mentioned your hometown to me."

"Victoria. Aye right, she's one of my favorites, ken. I always look forward to her coming to my events. The people absolutely adore her. That lassie's one fantastic dancer."

Myrick noted that as Duncan spoke, his hands moved wildly, as if he was almost talking *through* them. It was equal parts mesmerizing and distracting, almost like watching mismatched wind turbines churning in front of him.

"Well, I'll be curious to see if your detective skills translate to this here game of poker," Duncan continued, his hands still moving back and forth for emphasis. "That'll be interesting to see."

"Is that why you put me to your direct left?" Myrick noted, astutely.

"Aye, well that would be the idea now, wouldn't it? I know these other players. I've seen 'em a time or two. You're *wee* bit of a wild card at this event, ken. Hopefully I'll have developed a good read on you by the end of the game. Or," Duncan paused for emphasis, "Perhaps it'll be *you* that has developed a might good read on me."

"Guess we'll just have to wait and see."

"I do believe we will," Duncan turned back to the rest of the table, addressing the others who were now ready to get things started. "As you know," he began, breaking open a new package of cards as he spoke, the plastic wrapping still covering it, "we'll be playin' Texas Hold'em." The cards were now out of the box and neatly cupped in his hand. He then began dealing one card to each of the players. Once dealt, Myrick flipped his over to reveal it was an Ace.

"Not bad," Duncan began, his eyes glancing around at the cards in front of the other players. "It looks like Detective Myrick will be our first dealer." Duncan referred to Myrick by a title he no longer had, but Myrick made no effort to correct the amiable Scot. "We'll start the big blind at four chips, small blind at two."

The two players to Myrick's immediate left, the small and the big blinds, placed their respective chips in front of where they were sitting. After shuffling the new deck of cards, Myrick then began dealing them out to each of the players at the table.

The first few games played out rather uneventfully, everyone taking a conservative approach, as if no one wanted to be the first to get knocked out of the tournament. Myrick's play was the most curious at the table, at least to Duncan, as Myrick lost on a hand that he played to the end only to reveal his best cards were a pair of eights, and easily beaten by Susie's full house.

As play continued, there were other times when Duncan noticed Myrick bowing out quicker or staying in longer than he might have expected. The uncertain manner of his play made it hard to discern Myrick's tells. And Duncan couldn't decide if Myrick was a very skilled or particularly *green* poker player. Either way, it was confounding not to develop a good read on him.

Slowly though, the aggressiveness of play picked up. Finally, a player went "all-in" with what remained of his chips, only to lose on the *River* card.

One player out, nine remaining.

Then, as if the flood gates had been broken wide open, another lost his last chip, this time after Susie brilliantly outplayed him. Within thirty minutes five more players were knocked out, leaving only only Myrick, Susie and Duncan to do battle.

Duncan glanced down at his watch, aware that exactly an hour had passed. He then made a brief announcement to the rest of the room. "Blinds will now be increased to twenty chips," he explained. "With a wee bit o' luck, we'll have a final table soon."

Sure enough, and just a few minutes later, the last remaining player was announced at Table Four. Curious who it was, Myrick glanced over to see it was a familiar face... Talon.

Of course, he'd make it to the final table, Myrick mused, trying hard to remind himself that he'd *promised* Victoria that he'd be on his best behavior. It then occurred to him that it might be judicious to purposefully sacrifice the next few hands, as that was probably the safest way to alleviate the potential for repeated antics between him and Talon.

Then again, Myrick was entirely too competitive to go through with such a notion. Dismissing the idea almost as quickly as it got into his head, he instead trained his sights on the two remaining players in front of him, both of whom seemed to be worthy opponents, if in *distinctly* different ways.

Susie, he'd learned, was a very aggressive player. She'd gone toe-to-toe with several players at the table, even effectively bluffing them into folding, as if she savored the chance to take each one of them down. Myrick surmised that her fearlessness likely translated well to the courtroom as well. *The best attorneys always had a measure of pit bull in them.*

And of course, anyone who was willing to give up a stable career in law and relocate halfway across the country to take on an entirely new challenge was probably something of a risk taker. That unpredictable nature, in combination with her spirited disposition, was making Susie a *dangerous* opponent at the poker table indeed.

In contrast, Duncan slow played just about every hand. He spent more time talking than it seemed he did deciding whether to raise, fold or call. Several times, Duncan would go to make a decision, only to hesitate and re-examine his own cards, as if he'd forgotten what he'd had. At first, Myrick considered that might even be part of a ruse, but with time he came to believe that Duncan really *was* that distracted, more interested in the camaraderie of the event than actually winning the final pot.

Fortunately, Duncan had a very discernible tell, and Myrick almost laughed out loud when he eventually spotted it. Duncan's hands, always in unbridled motion during conversation, ceased moving entirely when he'd been dealt cards that he wasn't sure exactly how to play. It was as if Duncan didn't want to be distracted by his own gestures, focusing all his energy on the difficult decision to be made.

So, when Myrick was dealt a pair of pocket kings, he furtively glanced over at Duncan, noticing that Duncan's hands had stopped moving, pausing for a length of time before eventually deciding to match the big blind.

This might be my chance to knock the Scot out finally, Myrick thought to himself. When the Turn card came up as a jack of spades, giving Myrick a second pair, it only confirmed his suspicion and he decided to push the envelope, raising the pot considerably.

Hands completely still, Duncan ultimately called the raise, concern evident in his eyes, aware that his luck might have finally run out.

The last card dealt - and revealed face-up on the table - was a three of hearts. Based on the cards now visible, Myrick surmised that the odds of him winning were heavily in his favor and decided to go "all-in". Almost instantly, it was clear by Duncan's reaction that he didn't want to do the same, but was already so committed with the chips he'd previously thrown in the pot that there was no point folding.

And, just like that, Myrick's pair of kings and jacks had knocked out the host of the event, leaving only two players remaining at the table.

Duncan was gracious in defeat, wishing both Myrick and Susie well. There was a brief pause as he pushed his chair back and stood up, slow and deliberate like an aged sloth. Meanwhile, this was the first break in action that Myrick had had in a good while and so he used it to survey the rest of the room, now understanding that his table was actually the *only* one without a final competitor determined. There were six other table winners, and they were all waiting, with bated breath, for the seventh player to be announced for the final table.

The room was abuzz watching Susie go head-to-head with Myrick, as their contrasting styles made for good entertainment.

"You ready?" Susie finally asked.

"Ready as I'll ever be," replied Myrick, as he watched Susie deal out his cards, her stack significantly smaller than his now that he'd racked up all of Duncan's chips.

Susie's strength was in her aggressive play, but she quickly found out that it was near impossible to bluff Myrick. Still, she managed to steal a few hands from him, prolonging the game longer than most could've hoped, Myrick exhibiting a masterful understanding of what cards to play and what cards to fold. By the time Susie had tossed her last chip into the pot, even she recognized that the end was inevitable.

Poker was indeed Myrick's game, his unique ability to read people honed during his time as a detective. He'd sized all of his competitors up just like he'd done with thousands of suspects over the years. Susie was just his latest victim.

A more daunting challenge, however, still lay ahead at the final table, and not just because of the card game that they were all playing.

*****

Soriya Danes hadn't been particularly interested in the poker tournament, but she *was* interested in Talon; and so when he'd asked her to join him, she'd quickly agreed. It was fascinating to her how drastically her fortunes had changed. She'd come on the cruise alone, not knowing anyone in advance. Talon, however, seemed to have ins with everyone on board.

She'd set her sights on him early on in fact, having overheard a conversation between Talon and his friends by the poolside at the dance check-in desk. Soriya wasn't part of the Lindy Hop group, but she had heard about it prior to them setting sail, and she'd secretly hoped she could ingratiate herself into their company, getting to be a part of some of their activities.

Listening in on their conversation, she'd also learned enough to figure out that Talon possessed a high opinion of himself, which was a character flaw that she could easily twist to her advantage. Soriya, after all, was mesmerizing in her beauty, and perfectly willing to play those enticing attributes to get what she wanted; and *this* happened to be one of those occasions.

Fortunately, later that night, as she'd slipped into the private party at *The Phoenix & Dragon* - acting if she belonged there - no one questioned the long-sleeved jacket that she wore to fend off the cool night air - *or* that it was used to cover up the absence of a purple colored Lindy wristband on her wrist.

With her eyes trained on Talon the entire time, she waited for her opportunity to strike up a conversation with him. It wasn't much longer until she spotted an argument between Talon and one of his friends. She then watched intently as Talon got up from his table and walked over to the bar, creating the perfect chance for Soriya to ensnare her hapless victim.

"You care to dance?" Soriya had said, batting her angelic-seeming eyes at him as she spoke, which were anything but indicative of her not-so-virtuous intent.

"Of course," Talon had replied, glancing over at the curvaceous woman standing mere inches away from him, making no attempt to hide the fact that he was sizing her up.

After Talon confidently took her hand and led her onto the floor, the two had danced several songs together. Then, aware of the sparks between them, they'd sat down at a table and talked for a good hour more. It wasn't too long into the conversation when Soriya knew that she had him, her flirtatious manner impossible to resist, especially as she leaned slowly and subtly closer to him, hanging on his every word.

Soriya may have come on the cruise alone, but she'd met someone already, and it was a someone that she *definitely* intended to spend the entire cruise getting to know on a more intimate basis, even if only to suit her own egocentric purposes. So, at the moment, as she stood in the private poker room, watching the last remaining players taking a seat at the final table, she had a vested interest in the player she was rooting for most - Talon Andilet.

She whispered into his ear to *go get them*, to which Talon confidently winked back to her that he would. He also told her to find a spot *close by* so that she could watch how masterfully he took out his opponents. Obligingly, Soriya stood only a few feet away, able to even glance over Talon's shoulder, allowing her to catch a glimpse of the cards that he was dealt each hand.

Over time, and as the game dragged on, Soriya predictably lost interest. Her mind drifted to the prior night's events - how they'd left *The Phoenix & Dragon* only a few minutes before closing time and then walked out onto the 7th Deck promenade together. It was there, under the light of the stars and moon, when they'd kissed for the first time; a kiss that Talon would likely later come to regret once he fully understood the purpose behind it.

Talon had then forwardly mentioned that she should come to his cabin for a nightcap. Seizing on the chance to brag, he revealed that they'd even upgraded his room to a suite. Soriya was impressed, but she hadn't been persuaded enough to join him *just yet*; she needed to keep him baited long enough to make it through the entire seven-day cruise.

Instead, she'd asked Talon to walk her down to her own room, 365. It was there that Talon had attempted to follow her inside, only to once again experience rejection. Toying with his emotions, Soriya had slipped in one more seductive kiss, reminding him of why he wanted to keep her around and then disappeared into her room to call it a night. It was a kiss that Talon had dwelled on for hours afterward, his emotions a conflicted mess, the romantic atmosphere out on the open ocean only exacerbating his confused thinking.

Fortunately for Soriya, and as she'd planned, Talon was even easier to manipulate the next day, especially after a night of no sleep, unable to get her out of his mind. He'd taught a workshop and been dancing in competitions all morning. When she finally did get his attention, he mentioned the poker tournament and that he'd already entered it. With a wide smile on his face, he added that she could come to it also. Although it *was* an invitation-only event, he had a great deal of sway and could pull some strings to get her in. Sure enough, after a brief conversation between Talon and Duncan, Soriya was a last minute entry into the poker game as well.

At first, Soriya was fine with the idea. She knew it was nothing more than a chance to ingratiate herself with Talon, while killing some time before she coaxed him into drinks and dancing later on that evening. It wasn't long though until Soriya began to dislike some of the company that Talon kept, especially a woman named Victoria.

That nosy girl, Soriya came to the quick conclusion, *needed to quit with the questions and stay in her lane.*

Talon had secured Soriya a seat at his table, right next to him, but he was also all business as soon as the card game started, and he barely said much to her, more fixated on his opponents. It was at that same Table Four that she'd met Victoria Monroe for the first time. Almost immediately, Victoria was full of questions for Soriya, and Soriya sensed that the woman was protective of Talon.

"What happened to your wristband?" Victoria asked, already knowing the answer, but wanting to push the conversation in that direction.

"Oh, um," Soriya fumbled back. "I don't have one. Talon had to get me into the event. He's great. He even got me into some of the workshops."

"He *is* great," Victoria had purposefully looked past Soriya and over at Talon, who'd been oblivious to the stare being directed at him. Soriya though watched it all, aware of the sardonic nature of it. "So do you dance much?" Victoria had finally continued, her attention back on Soriya.

"Sort of. I used to. Long ago. It's coming back to me though. Maybe more so because of Talon than me."

"I know. I saw the two of you out on the dance floor last night. You danced well together."

"Thank you," Soriya had responded, intending to keep her responses short, as she'd hoped not to have to reveal much about herself. It was easier said than done though, and Victoria had kept finding ways to pry into more details about Soriya and how she'd met Talon.

Eventually, Soriya came up with a new plan. She'd decided that she was going to throw the poker game, purposefully trying to lose as many chips to Talon as she could along the way. None the wiser to what was happening, Talon seemed genuinely apologetic as she'd stayed in on a hand where he was the only other player remaining, generously tossing chips into the pot, then folding before the *Turn* card had even been dealt, so that Talon won most of her chips by default.

With just a handful of chips left, Soriya had drawn pocket queens. One by one the other players folded, until just Victoria was left, who raised the pot considerably. To match the aggressive bet, Soriya pushed almost all that remained of her dwindling stack toward the center of the table, leaving her with just a single chip left if she lost. Then, as luck would have it, another queen showed up on the *River*.

The first move had been up to Soriya. No raise had been made and Soriya could have easily checked. Instead, after a few minutes pondering her cards, she'd folded, sliding her cards, not yet revealed into the stack of those already discarded during the game.

"Whoa, don't do that," Talon had quickly spoken, trying to stop Soriya.

"Did I do something wrong?" she'd replied, coyly.

"You could've checked," Talon had frowned, feeling bad at how the hand had ended for Soriya. He also knew that it was already too late for Soriya to take her cards back. The rules of poker were clear, once a player folded or played a hand or even raised, it was set in stone. There was no going back.

"I'm sorry, I don't really understand this game. This is my first time playing."

The damage already done, Soriya predictably wasn't able to mount a comeback and soon lost her final remaining chip, feigning disappointment in the process. Now out of the game entirely, she turned to Talon and wished him luck, secretly squeezing his hand under the table as she did.

"You did good," Talon offered, believing that Soriya needed to hear the words of encouragement. "You mind at least sticking around to root me on?"

"Of course. I'd *love* that. I enjoy playing the role of cheerleader."

Soriya had gotten her wish and Talon was none the wiser. Victoria *was* though. She'd seen right through Soriya's ruse, shooting Soriya a distrusting glance as she'd gotten up from the table and turned to walk away.

Although Soriya had created a brief reprieve from Victoria's prying questions, it didn't last long. She'd made a mistake agreeing to Talon's request that she stick around until the end of the tournament. She realized the extent of her mistake as soon as Victoria lost her last chips as well, and in circumstances *suspiciously* similar to how Soriya had conceded defeat, freeing Victoria to continue her conversation with the only other player knocked out of the game at Table Four at that point.

By the time the final table was announced, Victoria somehow had found a spot right next to Soriya yet again. Soriya was suddenly in a bind, unable to avoid Victoria's prying ways. Talon had asked her to stay close by and watch, a request Soriya had originally savored, aware she could use it as an opportunity to observe more of Talon's personality, which she could see was as precipitate as she'd guessed based on the hasty way he played his poker hands.

There were seven final players at the table, Talon being one of them. Only a few hands into it and Talon impressively knocked one out with his aggressive play, leaving only six fighting to win the cash prize. Next it was Myrick's turn, slow playing a hand until the end when he matched an all-in, displaying that he'd drawn a full house.

All the while, Victoria just kept peppering Soriya with questions, so that Soriya found herself wishing Talon would *just lose already*. That, though, didn't seem to be an option; Talon proving to be as determined and competitive in poker as he was in dance, unaware of Soriya's prolonged agony.

CHAPTER TEN
Switch Things Up Between 6 & 8 Count Moves

While Myrick was sizing up the other competitors remaining at the final table, Shev was equally busy trying to solve the truly bizarre mystery of Tempest's disappearance. *None* of Tempest's coworkers had seen or heard from her in nearly 24 hours. Multiple announcements had even been made over the ship's intercom system for Tempest to report to *The Phoenix & Dragon*, but to no avail. The situation was becoming increasingly worrisome with each passing minute.

Currently, Shev was down on Deck 0, which was relatively empty at the moment, as most of the ship's crew were already hard at work on the upper decks. Reaching inside her pocket, Shev pulled out a universal keycard, which security had to get into all of the cabins on the ship. She then placed it against a digital reader located outside cabin #019, and the lock went from red to green. Shev then proceeded inside the darkened room.

The particular cabin was no more than 100 square feet in size. It had no port window, as all the rooms on Deck 0 were below sea level. Shev didn't talk about it much, but she actually possessed a healthy fear of the ocean - or really *any* large body of water for that matter.

The job, itself, she loved, but there were aspects of working security on a cruise ship that forced her to face her *darkest* fears. Oftentimes, Shev would wake up in a cold sweat, woken by a nightmare that the cruise ship had gotten caught in a storm, throwing her overboard into the icy waters, leaving her gasping for air above the violent waves. And, no matter how hard she tried, she couldn't completely overcome that foreboding sensation, almost as if it was doomed to eventually come true.

Still, Shev found a way to force those - seemingly ever-present - trepidations to the back of her mind. She'd become dead-set on uncovering where Tempest might have disappeared to. Searching Tempest's cabin seemed the most logical next step.

There wasn't much to the room: a TV, nightstand, closet, mini fridge and a few other nooks and crannies meant for storing things. At the end of the room were curtains, which provided privacy to a set of bunkbeds. Tempest had originally been assigned a roommate, but her bunkmate had quit at the end of the last cruise and there hadn't been enough time to hire a replacement before the next voyage disembarked, leaving Tempest as one of the few crew members lucky enough to have a room to her own.

Fumbling around in the dim light, Shev reached for where she knew the light switch was situated and turned the overhead bulb on, instantly revealing that the curtains had been drawn closed by the bunkbeds. Despite being relatively certain Tempest wasn't actually sleeping in the room, Shev couldn't help but feel a tinge of apprehension as she made her way over toward it, pulling the curtain back to investigate what lay on the other side.

Sliding the cloth divider away, Shev could see that both the top and bottom bunk were still neatly made. Indeed, the rest of the room was tidy as well, everything in its place. The TV was off and Shev placed her hand on the top of it to feel that it was cool to the touch, evidently unused for some time. Opening the drawers, Tempest's clothes were all folded neatly inside, including a clean crew uniform to wear to work at the bar.

Most telling, Shev opened the mini fridge to find that there was a container of fresh fruit in it, apparently placed there by Tempest the previous day. A crew member had explained that she gave it to Tempest who'd been saving it as a late night snack, intending to eat it as soon as she got off work. Clearly though, it hadn't been touched at all, the seal still intact.

Done scouring the cabin for clues, her search revealing nothing helpful to Tempest's whereabouts, Shev left the room, closing the door back behind her. While the hallways were usually filled with the sounds of crew talking, it was quiet other than for the sound of the engine room, which was accessible from this level. There were well-traveled tales that the crew deck was actually frequented by a ghost and Shev's heartbeat ramped up as she walked alone down the narrow hall, closer to where the sounds of the clanking engine room echoed.

The stories of the hauntings arose because a crew member had passed away at sea years ago after claiming to have been poisoned. No official investigation was ever conducted, the cruise line sweeping the incident under the rug to avoid bad publicity and the potential of scaring customers away. Meanwhile, after the death of the crew member, he'd been taken to the ship's morgue, which happened to be on the same floor as the crew quarters, and which was bound to stir up some speculation.

For four days the ship had continued to sail, until its eventual return to port. During that time, strange sightings started to take place with crew members convinced a ghostly specter was roaming the ship. The captain insisted it was nothing more than paranoia, but the stories stuck, and years later crew members still bemoaned hearing inexplicable and frightening sounds at odd hours of the night.

A telescoping baton was fastened to a belt along Shev's waist and she tapped her hand alongside of it, as if to make certain it was still there in the *highly unlikely* event it was needed. Fortunately, she reached her destination at the end of the hallway without incident or need for the weapon. She placed her hand up against a door, knocking on it lightly, speaking as she did.

"Agnes, you awake in there?" she asked. "If so, I *really* need to speak to you."

Coming from inside the room, Shev heard the distinct sound of feet shuffling. She then waited patiently until Agnes finally opened the door, a heavy dose of makeup half applied to her face - the beginnings of a marvelous makeover evident.

Agnes was a show performer. But not just *any* artist. She'd been a staple on the ship for over a decade and repeat customers routinely proclaimed that Agnes' performances were one of the cruise's main attractions. In that time, she'd garnered a sort of legendary status, and it was understood that she didn't like to be interrupted during her time getting ready, which routinely took place an hour or two before dusk, since Agnes' shows ran from 8:00 PM to midnight.

Given that, it wasn't a surprise to Shev that Agnes seemed annoyed at first by the unannounced visit.

"I'm sorry to interrupt, Ms. Fischer. There's been a bit of an emergency and so I just need to ask you a few questions. My understanding is that you're good friends with one of the workers over at *The Phoenix & Dragon* - Tempest Greylock."

"I am," Agnes replied, an expression of sudden interest in her aged, beguiling face. "Tempest is like a daughter to me. She comes to me for advice all the time. She and I talk about everything. Life on a cruise ship can be surprisingly lonely at times. Why do you ask?"

Agnes had the door opened completely now and Shev could see that she was dressed only in a thick plush robe, dazzling white and fluffy like her hair. The stark white attire only made the brightly chosen colors of her makeup stand out even more, her eyes lined in a beautiful shade of emerald green and her cheeks a dazzling rouge with hints of glitter. Even with her makeup only partially applied, she was a sight to behold, and her appearance was almost as striking as her singing voice. Agnes was a fascinating creature.

"She didn't show up for work tonight," Shev explained, not wanting to alarm Agnes, but also needing to fish for information from the person who could probably help the most.

"That's not like her."

"So I've heard. That's really why I felt the need to follow up. I'm sure she's fine. But I'd feel a lot better if I knew where she's disappeared to."

"Nice to see that the well-being of the crew does matter after all," Agnes replied, her response biting in tone. It was *no* secret that Agnes didn't hold the captain of the ship in high regard; she also wasn't one to pull punches, often referring to the man who helmed the mighty cruise ship as - *Cephissus of the Seas.* "Did anyone check the crew mess?" asked Agnes, focusing on the important. "She always goes there for coffee and a meal before her shift."

"We did. No one had seen her there today."

"Well, now that *is* strange also. *Please,*" Agnes stepped aside, waving Shev in to her cabin. "Let's talk more in the room."

Agnes had a very direct way about her and so Shev didn't argue as she stepped inside, instantly seeing that Agnes had one of the largest rooms in the crew quarters, comparable to an upper deck suite. The interior was furnished and decorated in a very inviting manner, and it was evident that Agnes had put her own personal touches into it, as this was where she'd resided for such a long period of her life.

Shev, in turn, was instantly impressed with the decor, appreciating the artistic flare it possessed. A nice touch compared to the other barren crew cabins.

"Again, I apologize for intruding like this," said Shev, as she hesitantly proceeded inside, not sure yet if she wasn't overstepping her bounds.

"Of course, dear. Anything for Tempest. Please, take a seat." Agnes pointed to a chair that extended out from under a vanity table. On the desk were a myriad of makeup items scattered in an impressive array of colorful options, and which Agnes had clearly been using prior to the interruption.

Before Shev could get any questions of her own out, Agnes was already starting in with her own theories. "I'll bet you she's with Bernard. She really fancies him," Agnes winked as she spoke, revealing even more of the mesmerizing green eyeliner. "You should talk to him."

"Already did," Shev replied and Agnes seemed instantly taken aback by that answer. "He says he hasn't seen her either."

Agnes went silent, clearly at a loss for words now. Shev decided it would be a good time to ask a pressing question, fishing in her pocket for the charm she had concealed inside it.

"You ever seen Tempest wearing this before?" Shev opened her hand to show Agnes the gold circular charm with the distinctive initials "Ⴀ.Ⴆ."

"Yes, of course," Agnes replied, leaning in closer to make a better inspection of it, as if she'd grown concerned at the sight of the object. She then glanced back up at Shev, wondering aloud if she could hold the item, "May I?"

Shev nodded that it was okay and so Agnes took it in her own hand, flipping the charm over as if to size up its condition. "The latch is broken," she noted with alarm.

"I know."

"Tempest *never* takes this off," Agnes emphasized, gravity in her voice. "Her father gave this to her. It's her favorite keepsake. I've never seen her without it. Where did you find this?"

"Outside platform. Picked it up off the deck not long ago."

"And no word about Tempest coming to look for it?"

"None."

"This is bad," Agnes wasn't mincing words. "You *need* to find her."

"That's what I'm trying to do. Chief Moretti has been apprised of everything as well and is on top of the search."

"That bumbling old fool," Agnes' eyes flashed. "You and I both know he doesn't know what he's doing. He's simply become part of the ship's decor at this point in his career. It's going to be up to you and me to find her."

"Us?"

"Yes."

Shev appreciated the offer, but wasn't sure that Agnes' idea was the best one. She did, however, agree that Moretti wasn't going to be of much help either. For the first time since she'd taken the job, she suddenly understood how *entirely* alone she really was in an emergency situation.

A person had gone missing. Details of her disappearance were scarce. And then it dawned on Shev just how lucky she was to have a certain passenger on the cruise with her. It was time to seize on that stroke of good fortune and turn to him for help.

*****

"And just like that we're down to our final four players," Duncan announced, no longer in the game but relishing his role as MC even more. Who'll be our grand champion?" Duncan waved his hands, wildly and unimpeded for effect. "Aye, who'll walk out with the grand prize… fifteen hundred dollars… and *two* all expenses paid tickets to our partner event - *Wild West(ern) Weekend?*"

Myrick rolled his eyes, learning for the first time what the prize actually was. He'd assumed it was just a money pot, focusing on the $20 buy-in each participant had kicked in. The last thing he'd wanted was to win a prize to a dance event also, knowing *full well* that would mean Victoria would want him to learn an entirely new dance - Country 2-Step.

"The final four, three suckers and me," Talon said under his breath, although purposefully loud enough to be heard, clearly hoping to get into his opponents' heads.

"You gonna talk or deal?" Paul asked, bluntly.

"Whoa, what happened to the pleasant fellow who struck up a conversation with me at the restaurant this morning?"

"Different place. *Different* circumstances," Paul retorted.

"Fair enough," Talon shrugged his shoulders, amused. *That was at least one player he had already gotten under the skin of.* He then broke open a brand new deck of cards, fanning them out in his hand then shuffling them, expertly.

Talon wasn't the only one intrigued by Paul's remark, Myrick was also. It appeared that there was increasingly bad blood between Paul and Talon. Interestingly though, Paul was now handling that situation much differently than he had the day prior, when Talon had rudely bumped into him. Paul had been contrite about the incident at the time. *Clearly* the gloves were off now, and Myrick was intrigued by this unexpected new development.

The only thing more interesting to Myrick than the interaction between Talon and Paul was Harriett's relatively reserved demeanor. The fourth player at the table, she was incredibly unassuming, skillfully waiting in the wings while other players did battle and knocked each other out.

Myrick liked the way Harriett played the game. She was both calculating and observant, wisely getting a feel for the style of play of the others as the game moved along. In fact, Myrick was doing the exact same. He thought it would be quite a battle if the two of them were the last remaining, considering the possibility that Harriett *might* have a better read on him than he did of her.

Cards went sliding across the table as Talon finally dealt a hand. All around, spectators gathered, almost as intrigued by this game as they'd been watching the dance competitions take place earlier in the day. Duncan had done a phenomenal job hyping the event and creating suspense. Anything, it seemed, could happen now.

Out of the corner of his eye, Myrick noticed that there were even a few side bets taking place as well, people wagering on who would be crowned the eventual *LSS* Poker Champion. A title coveted by Lindy Hoppers the world over - or at least that was the rumor Duncan had started.

After the second card was dealt to each of the players, Myrick glanced down at his, briefly taking note of what he had, yet careful not to react visibly, an emotionless expression on his face. Immediately he could see that he was in trouble, having been dealt an off-suited two and seven.

No longer peering down at his cards, Myrick decided to assess the other players at the table, trying to get a read for what they might have. Talon, he could tell, had garnered himself a bad hand as well, his eyes blinking repeatedly, which Myrick had figured out Talon did when he had particularly useless cards.

Talon will fold, Myrick thought to himself.

Paul was a harder read, not really giving any indication of what he might have, simply glancing down at his cards then back up again, not making eye contact with anyone, as if in his own world. In fact, it seemed like Paul spent more time debating with himself what cards to play and what not to, which - *purposefully or not* - worked to his advantage, making his decisions difficult to predict.

Don't know what to make of that, Myrick wondered silently.

Finally, there was Harriett. Myrick was pretty certain that Harriett had directed a sly smile at him just as his eyes turned to her. He was going to get nothing of use from the girl, especially now that she was on to him. She had quite a poker face.

Toughest read at the table, Myrick admitted to himself.

The one clear advantage Myrick had at the moment was that he was the small blind and wouldn't have to make a decision until *after* both Paul and Harriett had already gone. First Paul was up. He hesitated momentarily to consider his move, as if second-guessing his decision, but then decided to call, matching the big blind.

Harriett was up next. Evidently possessing a losing hand, she wasted no time folding.

With eyes now on him, Myrick threw in an extra couple of chips to match the big blind. Finally, Talon tapped his finger on the table to indicate he wasn't going to raise. Given that quick response, Myrick felt even more confident that Talon didn't possess particularly good cards and was going to have to get lucky on the flop or - to use a common poker term - he'd be *drawing dead.*

Since he was the dealer, Talon burned the deck's top card, then placed three more across the table, all facing upward - consisting of a two of clubs, a four of spades and a seven of hearts. Terrible flop for most, although surprisingly perfect for Myrick; his hand going from useless to intriguing in an instant.

Unlike before, Paul didn't hesitate, immediately raising the pot significantly, catching Myrick totally off guard by the aggressive move.

Since Harriett had folded already, Myrick was next up and didn't have time to process things as much. He glanced at Paul and then down at the three cards face up on the table, trying to understand what Paul could *possibly* see in them. Still, it was too hard for Myrick to give up his suddenly valuable pair, and so he pushed a hefty stack of chips into the pile, matching Paul's raise.

Seconds later, and Talon tossed his cards toward the middle of the table, indicating he was out, wisely cutting his losses.

Only two players were left.

Talon kept the pace of play moving, turning over the *River* card to reveal it was an ace of hearts. Not great for Myrick, but potentially very helpful to Paul *if* he'd been playing a pocket pair, which seemed entirely possible given his high bet earlier. Surprisingly though, Paul called this time.

Myrick remarked to himself that Paul was the most unpredictable player he'd ever gone against. It was hard to get any sort of definitive read on what the guy would do, but it sure seemed like Paul hadn't gotten the card he needed on the *River*. Myrick decided to raise, figuring this was the right time for him to go on the offensive, maybe convince his opponent to fold.

Immediately, he looked over at Paul, who matched the bet without any sign of hesitation.

Again, *not* what Myrick had expected. *I'm apparently losing my touch,* he thought to himself.

The room had come alive, and the murmuring reached a fevered pitch, as the final card was revealed by Talon - a king of hearts. Now Myrick was in serious trouble. His pair had tricked him into staying longer than he should've. It seemed he was in danger of losing most of his (once formidable) stack.

And then, as Paul indicated he was all-in, an air of confidence in his eyes, Myrick came to understand just how dire his situation was. All eyes were on him now, wondering what he would do - fold or call.

Myrick glanced over at Victoria, who had an amused smile on her face, aware of his predicament. She then shrugged her shoulders as if to say that he might want to take the same tactic as Talon, preserving what chips he still had and hoping for a better hand next time around. Myrick chuckled to himself, then winked back at her. Seconds later, he turned his attention back to the table, pushing the rest of his stack in, which practically matched Paul's.

"Hold your horses… I understand there's been an all-in call!" Duncan announced in excited fashion.

Suddenly, the room came alive. Duncan asked for a count to be made, and when it was done the stacks were almost entirely the same, save for the fact that Myrick would have exactly two blue *$5 dollar* chips left if he lost, not even enough to match a big blind.

Finally, it was time to flip the cards and reveal what each player had. Myrick showed his, the off-suited pair of twos and sevens. He then glanced up at Victoria, who seemed to laugh almost immediately. It was a foregone conclusion that Myrick had pushed his luck too far this time.

Turning his attention to Paul, Myrick watched curiously as his unpredictable foe flipped his cards over, exhibiting no real emotion either way as he did. Paul's cards were an unmatched nine and jack. He had been completely bluffing. Myrick *couldn't* believe it.

Cordially, Paul reached across the table to shake Myrick's hand, respectfully conceding defeat. Unlike his altercation with Talon earlier, Paul couldn't have been more gracious in defeat. Myrick was both impressed and confounded by Paul at the same time, wishing he could ask what the man could've possibly thought was going to happen going all-in. Instead, and without any explanation forthcoming, Myrick came to the conclusion that Paul was evidently an extreme risk-taker.

The next few hands were played rather anticlimactically, the fireworks settling down some. Eventually though, Talon drew a good hand; Myrick could see it in his wide eyes almost instantly. He assumed Harriett would also, but she hadn't, surprisingly taking Talon to the end and pushing all her chips into the pot, only to lose in shocking fashion. Harriett had three Kings. A solid hand. Talon's was better - a straight flush.

The final two would be Talon versus Myrick. Once again, Myrick glanced over at Victoria, although it was clear that she didn't find this development nearly as amusing as the earlier situation, mouthing to Myrick a reminder to *stick to his earlier promise*.

"She can't help you, buddy," Talon asserted, proving as predictable as ever.

Well, at least I have a read on one person, Myrick noted, instantly amused.

Thanks to knocking out Harriett, Talon had a significantly larger stack of chips and a clear advantage. It didn't last long though, Myrick playing hand after hand expertly, almost as if he was able to look at Talon's cards and know what to do each time. Talon, conversely, seemed visibly frustrated as his chip stack dwindled away. Soon, it was Myrick with the clear upper hand, and now that he had it, the time had come to go for the jugular.

As it turned out, Myrick did have a discernible tell and someone else in the room had already picked up on it. Fortunately for Myrick, that person *wasn't* Talon.

"I'm all-in," Myrick declared, after being dealt two cards, but before the flop had even been turned over.

As he spoke, he tapped a solitary chip three times on the table for effect. Meanwhile, Victoria instantly caught sight of Myrick's one tell and laughed. She'd figured out that anytime Myrick did things in a sequence of three, it was a sign he was on to something good.

A dead giveaway that had somehow gone unnoticed by anyone other than Victoria.

"You don't want to wait and see what comes up on the board?" Talon replied immediately, not even attempting to conceal his disbelief.

Myrick knew what that meant, Talon had a solid - *but not spectacular* - hand. He wanted to play it, but not with the stakes this high. That said, losing hand after hand had grown frustrating enough and so as he tapped his cards on the table for emphasis, Talon stared down Myrick.

"I'm all-in also," Talon finally announced, flatly and without emotion.

A hush went over the crowd as the rest of the cards were dealt - first the *Flop*, then the *Turn* and finally the *River*, so that both players had five cards visible and at their disposal to use: a three of diamonds, a three of spades, a five of clubs, an eight of spades and an ace of hearts.

"Alright lads, let's see 'em," Duncan announced.

A crowd had gathered around the table and they were on pins and needles as Talon finally flipped over his cards to reveal that he was holding an eight of hearts and an ace of diamonds.

"Aces and eights," Duncan announced. "The dreaded *Dead Man's Hand*," he added cryptically, for effect. "Aye, and you, Mr. Myrick? What do you have there?"

Myrick flipped over his cards, allowing everyone to finally see.

"Pocket threes," Duncan announced, incredulous. "What a hand. Mr. Myrick's four of a kind takes the pot. Can you believe it, we have us a winner!"

Myrick stood up from the table, reaching over to shake Talon's hand. Talon had played marvelously and had definitely earned the respect of everyone present, only Talon clearly didn't feel the same, pushing his chair back in disappointment. It was one thing to lose the game. *That* Talon could live with. But not to Myrick.

Not wanting to cause a scene, Myrick made no attempt to stop Talon. But he *did* notice with interest Soriya's reaction. She dutifully followed behind Talon as he left, making no attempt to console him, but also not wanting to lose sight of her free ride on the cruise.

For Myrick, it was an auspicious ending to an otherwise entertaining poker game. A precursor of more excitement to come as the night progressed. Victoria was impressed with Myrick's victory, but was quick to inform him that now he needed to turn his attention to the main event - the dance under the stars on the ship's main deck.

CHAPTER ELEVEN
Maintain Stretch & Tension In The Dance

For a man like Myrick, anonymity was a cherished thing. Not knowing anyone else on the cruise other than Victoria had been a huge plus. He wanted to spend time with her, get some dancing in and then spend the rest of the vacation enjoying (much needed) rest and relaxation. Thanks to his poker game victory, that was no longer going to happen. From the moment he was announced the winner, he was bombarded with impressed well-wishers, offering him congratulations and trying to get to know the curious new member of their Lindy family better.

"This is your fault," Victoria whispered in his ear. "You just can't stand to lose, can you?" she chuckled.

"Oh no, I've *definitely* lost," Myrick replied, clearly vexed by the newfound attention.

As soon as he answered, another dancer came up to speak to him, congratulating him on his victory and starting polite conversation. And Myrick was in no mood to engage in small talk, although he did his best, especially as Victoria nudged his side repeatedly and insisted he be *accommodating*.

Eventually, Duncan reminded everyone that the main dance on the outdoor deck was starting soon, and then surprised them all with news that there was also going to be a dazzling fireworks show to watch from the bow.

Amazing the lengths Duncan had gone to make the night memorable.

Myrick knew that Victoria wouldn't want to be late for it either and that he needed to prepare for a *long* evening of dancing ahead. He was just going to have to embrace his sudden celebrity status.

But an unexpected reprieve was on the way. As they were walking up to the 17th deck, Shev came hurrying over. She apologized to both Myrick and Victoria for interrupting them, aware that they were on the way to the social, but she did want to know if she could briefly procure Myrick's assistance.

"I really can't take you anywhere," Victoria tilted her head, impishly. "Go ahead." She smiled. "Go play detective. You know you want to."

"You sure?" Myrick asked, although there was already a hint of hopefulness in his voice.

"Yes, just come find me when you're done."

"I promise I will," Myrick replied. "This won't take long."

"It better not," Victoria laughed. She then slipped a kiss onto Myrick's cheek, partly to remind him what he'd be missing if he was delayed too long. She could see by the look on his face that he instantly got the message. She then immediately turned to walk away, her alluring silhouette disappearing into the night air as she crossed along the boat deck, practically being enveloped by the darkness.

"I'm sorry, I don't mean to be such a pest," said Shev, regret in her voice.

"No, it's okay. She understands. I'm guessing that you haven't heard from that missing crew member yet... and have reached a standstill in your search efforts."

"How did you know?"

"Mysteries that take longer than 24 hours to solve often go unresolved. The trail just tends to go cold," added Myrick, matter-of-factly.

"I really don't know what to make of it... But there's no sign of Tempest Greylock *anywhere* on this ship. She's just vanished into thin air. At this point, I'm convinced something bad's happened to her. I also don't have a whole lot of actual experience in investigating things like this... missing persons and such... and I don't have anyone to bounce ideas off either. Except," Shev paused, "*Maybe* you."

"Well, that is a predicament indeed," Myrick kept Shev in suspense, still sort of in character, given the poker game he'd just played and the gangster costume he wore. *He was enjoying this entirely too much.* Finally, he spoke again, "Lucky coincidence then that I came on this cruise."

"Almost seems preordained, wouldn't you say?"

"A person of faith might consider that a strong possibility."

"I'm hoping then that's who you are."

"I am."

"Good, because I'm starting to think that Ms. Cribbs may have lied to me and I need to bounce some thoughts off you. Maybe she might even want me searching on the wrong side of the vessel. I could use your thoughts on it. You think that's possible?"

"Could be."

"Because I just don't see how Tempest could get off work at 2:30... be seen leaving in the direction she was... the gold charm with her initials show up on a route that would lead to the crew stairwell... and somehow a commotion takes place on the complete other side of the ship at the exact same time, indicating someone's in danger. The two must necessarily be linked. But if Ms. Cribbs is to be believed, they can't be."

"Sounds about right."

"Okay, are you going to actually *help* me or simply agree with me?"

"I'm not going to disagree just for the sake of doing so. I'm actually quite interested in how you're processing the evidence. Of course, sometimes a detective has to step back and look for the thing that's *not* there. By your own estimation, there's a hole - *a missing fact* - in the evidence. We can't be sure whose fault that is. Assumptions alone can easily sidetrack a case."

"So then what's your solution?"

"Why don't we start with a search around the area where you located the medallion. You mentioned that was on the starboard side of the ship?"

"Yes, by one of the two larger lifeboats."

"If I remember correctly, I know exactly where you're talking about," Myrick, replied, proud of himself for already having gotten his bearings on the ship. He then turned to walk off, figuring that'd be a cue for Shev to do the same. He did want to help her. He also didn't want to spend *too* long away from Victoria.

"Where are you going?" Shev suddenly asked. "I thought you said you were going right?"

"I am," Myrick turned, confused.

"That's the left side of the ship. Starboard side is *this* way," Shev pointed in the complete other direction, amused to now be the one correcting the trained detective.

"Oh, I was sure that…"

"It's okay, happens all the time. People get confused where they are on the ocean. Easy to lose their sense of direction."

"Must be." Myrick shrugged his shoulders, now following Shev in the correct direction.

As they walked, Myrick caught the sounds of music and laughter off in the distance, coming from the bow of the ship. The party had begun and was already kicking into full gear. Reaching the elevators and taking them down to the 7th Level, Myrick and Shev then proceeding along the promenade, which was mostly empty, haunting in some aspects.

The night sky above was breathtaking, endless stars and a full moon shown amidst thin lines of gray clouds. As Myrick continued on, he peered over the railing to see that the lights of the ship reflected off the dark waters far down below. The drop was higher than he realized, and it even made him a bit queasy just thinking about it.

If Tempest had tumbled overboard - even if she'd somehow survived such a fall - it was easy to see how she'd be lost to the seas, impossible to hear or locate in the vast ocean.

"Have you ever heard of anyone falling over the railing during your time as a security officer?" Myrick finally broke the silence.

"*Two* people actually. Both were suicides, I think - or at least that's what we eventually concluded - but there isn't often much evidence to go on when something like that happens. There are an average of 200 deaths on cruise lines per year... although that number is probably a little low. Cruise lines don't always accurately report deaths for fear that it'll scare passengers away. We travel all around the world and many international ports aren't as strict about reporting those things."

"So just the two deaths on your ship though?"

"Oh no, there's been others. Just during the short time I've been working in the cruise industry, I've seen people die of sickness... heart attack... even food poisoning. There's a reason we have a morgue onboard... and it *does* get put to good use."

"Kind of disturbing to know that."

"You get used to it."

"Ever had a suspected homicide onboard the ship?"

"No, I can confidently say that's never happened. But it's actually an interesting place for one to occur, we sail under a Panamanian flag for tax purposes. It also means that while on international waters, we're subject to Panama's specific jurisdiction if a crime were to occur. Or at least that's what I understood when Chief Moretti hired me for security. It's never been an issue of course. If there's a theft or fight or whatever, it tends to be easily handled in-house. Worst case, we just turn the investigation over to a police agency at the first port we stop in. *But* if a murder occurred while at sea, that would definitely complicate matters. Truthfully, no one on the security team is trained to deal with something of that magnitude. Moretti is our most experienced person. But his law enforcement days were long ago and he's been in the cruise ship industry for decades since and honestly I think all he wants to do is ride things out till his retirement in a couple of years."

"Funny how life works and the unexpected nature of things. Seems like the cruise line would've planned for a contingency like this. Guess not though."

"You ever investigated a homicide case before?"

"Several actually. More than I can - *or wish* - to remember."

"Wow, I wanted to be a police officer."

"Tough career. You might be better off staying where you're at. Being a cop isn't all it's cracked up to be. Long hours. Dangerous situations. And yes, paperwork... *Lots and lots of paperwork,*" Myrick laughed, although it was the laugh of someone who clearly suffered from PTSD simply recalling those arduous days.

"Maybe I'll dazzle you with my investigative skills and you can put in a good word for me with an agency?" Shev replied, clearly unfazed by Myrick's warning.

"Hmmm, we'll see. A search for a missing person isn't *quite* the same thing as a full blown homicide investigation."

"Well, what makes you so sure this wasn't a murder?" Shev threw out the possibility.

It dawned on Myrick that she did actually have a point. Tempest Greylock had now been missing for over a day and there were only so many places she could've gone on a cruise ship. In Myrick's estimation - s*omeone should've long since located her.*

He'd also been pondering the broken medallion, which Shev had explained had special significance to Tempest and that she *always* wore. The theory that Tempest could've accidentally fallen into the sea didn't jive with the discovery of the cherished keepsake. It simply wasn't feasible to Myrick that the charm would break off... land where it did... and then, Tempest would somehow accidentally tumble overboard.

There had to be a better explanation for the events that had taken place. Unfortunately, however, Myrick hadn't come to any definite conclusions yet.

"Here," Shev finally came to a stop along the platform. "This is where I found the charm." She pointed to the ground just in front of her feet.

Myrick glanced down, then his eyes turned to his surroundings, trying to get a better sense of what might've happened, as if capable of reimagining a possible sequence of events in his mind.

It was quiet. The music and laughter from the social dance was so far off in the distance but he could still hear it, as they were within earshot of the bow of the vessel. He did also pick up on the sound of splashing water, guessing that some of the guests had even jumped into the infinity pool.

"Didn't Ms. Cribbs say she was by the adults-only pool when she heard the cries?" Myrick asked of Shev.

"Yes, that was her story."

"And are we about the same location distance-wise that she said she heard the disturbance?"

"Technically yes. But again, she insisted other side of the ship... port side. This is starboard. But yes, if we were on the port side of the ship, we'd be standing right about the spot that Ms. Cribbs insisted she heard the commotion take place."

"Interesting," Myrick observed, glancing toward the railing. He could see that there were two mega-size lifeboats - both impressive in appearance - secured in place along this side of the ship. Their combined girth actually blocked access to the railing, although there was a small gap in between the two boats, and a thin person would likely be capable of slipping in-between them.

"I guess it's possible Tempest could've ripped the pendant off her necklace in a fit of final despair... tossed it aside... and then jumped to her death," Myrick offered a potential explanation, although from the tenor of his voice it was obvious to Shev that he wasn't convinced by that explanation.

"Why would she do something like that?"

"Don't know. Maybe she couldn't bear to think that the one memory she still held onto of her father would be going overboard with her. People do bizarre things when contemplating the end of life. Suicide, itself, is an irrational act."

"Manager at the restaurant says that she'd never take her own life. He said Tempest was strong willed. Her friend Agnes insisted the same. There were no red flags she was on the verge of something so drastic."

"People dealing with severe depression oftentimes are good at concealing the pain. Possible that was the case with Ms. Greylock as well."

"You don't buy that," said Shev, impressing Myrick once more with her intuition. "I can tell."

"Oh, you can, huh?" Myrick replied, becoming increasingly convinced that Shev was a natural at detective work with each deduction she made.

Taking off his flat cap, Myrick scratched his head in consternation. He wasn't saying it aloud, but Shev appeared to be onto something, and his gut was telling him that this wasn't a case of someone accidentally falling overboard, no matter how hard he tried to convince himself otherwise. All signs pointed to a more troubling explanation.

It increasingly seemed to Myrick that there'd been foul play aboard the ship. And that poor Tempest had been the unfortunate victim of it.

*****

Victoria had finally pried herself away from the social long enough to step aside and see if she couldn't figure out what was delaying Myrick's return. It'd been close to an hour, longer than she'd expected it to take for his "brief" investigation. She understood he was needed elsewhere, but she also wished he was back with her now that the festivities had reached a midpoint.

All evening, she'd been pulled out onto the dance floor, one lead after another excited for the opportunity. Victoria did her best to enjoy the dances, but her heart just wasn't completely in it. She was incredibly distracted. This was supposed to be her time with Myrick, and he was missing maybe the best part of it.

For the first time, she started to wonder if perhaps she'd misread things. Maybe he *didn't* feel quite the same about her as she did him. That thought alone immediately caused an ache in the pit of her stomach.

Standing in the darkness, the music of the twelve-piece big band's nostalgic songs playing in the background, Victoria felt surprisingly wistful. She was surrounded by people that loved and adored her. There were men lined up that would practically kill to be with her. But the man *she* wanted at the moment was nowhere to be found, even as her eyes desperately searched the platform in the distance, hoping she might spot his impending return.

Distracted by her thoughts, Victoria failed to notice a figure come up from behind her, steps so light on the deck that they barely made a sound.

"Are you looking for *him*?" a voice spoke out of the quiet, startling her.

A chill went up Victoria's spine, as if spooked by a ghostly apparition. She turned quickly, jumping a little, her hands curled over and across her body, an effort to fend off the cold night air - *and* the feeling of sudden fright.

"Oh my, you scared me!" Victoria exclaimed, her voice trembling, but with a mixture of relief in it, recognizing the face of the woman in front of her.

"I'm sorry. I didn't mean to startle you. I should've given some sort of warning before coming up on you so unexpectedly."

"No, no," Victoria stammered, almost apologetically, "It's my fault. And yes, I was looking for him. I was looking for Evann."

"Is that Myrick's first name?"

"Yes."

"Funny, you're the first person I've actually heard use it with him. Everyone kept calling him Myrick at the poker table."

"Oh right, I've noticed that also. Not even sure why," Victoria paused, eventually extending out her hand in greeting. "It's Harriett, right? I don't think we've formally met yet."

"Yes, Harriett Cribbs."

"Nice to meet you, Harriett."

"Nice to meet you too. And if it makes you feel better, I think it's really sexy that you're the only one he seems to go by Evann with," Harriett slyly winked as she replied.

"Thanks, I probably needed to hear that right now."

"No problem. We all have our moments."

"So true."

"So where is he now... Evann?"

"Don't know actually. Security asked if he could assist with an issue. He's a former detective so *of course* they'd steal him away from me," Victoria replied, consternation in her voice. "I just figured it wouldn't take this long."

Victoria glanced behind herself as she explained, her attention back to searching for Myrick, leaving her so distracted that she didn't notice Harriett placing a hand in her pocket as if to pull something out of it. Slowly, Harriett removed her hand back out of the pocket, an object now clutched in her fist.

"Myrick!" Victoria suddenly belted out, excitement in her voice. "That you?"

Harriett was startled, jerking backwards. Her eyes quickly following the direction of Victoria's so that she could see a tall man coming into view, appearing suddenly out of the foggy night air.

"Well, that took longer than I'd hoped," Myrick announced, his face now clearly in view and his distinctive Irish accent impossible to mistake. "You save some dances for me?"

"I saved *all* the best dances for you," Victoria smiled, making no attempt to hide her elated state.

"Good," Myrick replied. He barely showed any emotion in life, but it was clear from Harriett's vantage point that his eyes lit up the moment he was next to Victoria.

Harriett didn't say anything, still she couldn't help but feel a tinge of jealousy. She'd never experienced anything like that before. Her relationships had always been short lived, not really forging anything resembling a lasting feeling. She *did,* though, believe in fate. She imagined that Myrick and Victoria were likely soulmates, even if they weren't entirely aware of it themselves yet.

"Oh, good. I see the two of you have now met," said Myrick, suddenly aware of Harriett's presence and turning his attention to her. "Harriett was at the final table with me."

"I know. I was there watching," Victoria laughed, finding it amazing that someone as smart and as observant as Myrick could forget an obvious detail like that.

"You're just fortunate Talon knocked me out," Harriett added. "He got lucky."

"Sometimes luck is more important than skill," Myrick noted.

"Apparently," replied Harriett, shrugging her shoulders. "I do regret that we didn't get to go toe-to-toe at the end. Might have been an intriguing battle."

"Agreed. I would've liked to have seen how that would've panned out also. You impressed me with your poker play."

"Maybe we'll get another chance to see who's the better player at another game. Maybe one that is less about luck and more about skill."

"Let's hope."

"Can we please dance now?" Victoria interjected, no longer willing to waste anymore time. "Come on, handsome," she slid her arm into Myrick's. "Let's go cause some trouble."

"Some good trouble."

"I'm pretty sure that's the only kind."

"Especially when it's with you," Myrick added, slickly.

"Oh, and don't worry, I promise not to monopolize *all* his time," Victoria winked over at Harriett, then turned her eyes back to Myrick. "I'm sure Harriett will want to get a dance in with you at some point also."

"Um, that's *if* she'll dance with me again. You didn't see the first one. I felt pretty bad about it."

"You did fine," Harriett offered up, pleasantly. "I'll come steal you away for a dance or two when the opportunity presents itself." Harriett then turned her attention to Victoria. "Thanks for looking out for me."

"Of course," Victoria replied, turning to walk back toward the social event with Myrick. "You coming also?" she asked Harriett.

"No, you two go on ahead. I'll be there eventually."

Harriett's willowy shoulders visibly sank as the two walked away, leaving her alone. She had on a black v-neck wraparound sweater to fend off the cool breeze and she clutched it tightly around her chest for warmth… but also to guard herself against a strange feeling - of *what,* she couldn't quite explain.

In fact, Harriett had possessed a heightened awareness of things and people ever since she was a child, oftentimes causing her to retreat from the world around her. Growing up, she rarely spoke and her mother had even taken her to a psychiatrist when she was only ten, thinking that perhaps she had some sort of mental disability. The psychiatrist, thankfully, was good at his job, figuring out that not only was there nothing wrong with Harriett, but that she was actually *incredibly* gifted, just not in ways that her mother or even her peers could completely understand.

As it turned out, Harriett saw the world through an entirely different lens than most, sensing things in others - almost empathic in nature - and it was a struggle to dismiss those powerful emotions. The present circumstances were no exception, and Harriett was acutely aware that some of the Lindy dancers had been acting increasingly peculiar ever since the social at the dueling piano bar, even keeping secrets among themselves. Harriett was beginning to wonder if perhaps some of those hushed conversations didn't have to do with observations about her in particular.

If so, it was ruining an otherwise promising voyage. Up until that point, the dance cruise had actually been a nice escape from reality, as Harriett was tired of people constantly judging her. And she'd been glad she'd decided to go on it, even if she wasn't a fan of everyone on the ship, particularly Evann Myrick. Harriett trusted her instincts and she didn't like the vibe she got when the former detective was around. He always seemed to be studying her every move, whether it was on the dance floor or at the poker game.

She finally came to the conclusion that she needed to keep him at a distance. Although it seemed that no matter how hard she tried, their paths were still destined to cross, even at the most inopportune of times.

CHAPTER TWELVE
Keep Your Knees Slightly Bent

Shev had stayed behind even after Myrick left to return to the dance, determined to piece together the limited clues at her disposal. Based on their analysis of the facts, she was also now *certain* that she (and Moretti) should've taken the matter more seriously on the front end. Worse, given the discovery of the broken charm, it seemed entirely possible that Tempest could've been pushed overboard during some sort of violent altercation. If so, the disposal of her body at sea - and in the dead of night - was the perfect crime. They'd never find it in the vast ocean.

No body... no corpus delicti... no proof of murder.

At a complete loss, Shev walked along the railings, casing the area, searching for signs of blood or other subtle clues of a struggle that she might have somehow originally missed. At first, nothing of particular significance stuck out. That was until she happened to peer over at the entry to one of the mega-size lifeboats, noticing that its door was damaged, as if it had been pried open, still slightly ajar.

Shev was surprised, as the ship's maintenance took painstaking measures to ensure that the lifeboats weren't tampered with by passengers. Nobody was allowed inside the lifeboats, and Shev had always known the doors to be closed and locked securely when not in use. This one clearly wasn't though, which instantly piqued her interest.

Without even having to turn the handle, Shev was able to pull the door open, allowing her to peer cautiously inside. The interior opened up to rows upon rows of passenger seating, as the lifeboat was built for a large capacity. It was massive in size, and a technological advance.

Squinting her eyes to get a better view inside the hull, Shev had no idea where the light switch might be - *or even if the boat had one*; it was dark inside so it was difficult for her eyes to adjust as she proceeded through the doorway. Fortunately, Shev had a flashlight on her, security issued. She fetched it from her utility belt, then switched it on, a thin beam of light cutting through the otherwise thick darkness.

Each forced step she took felt weird, surreal - almost as if she'd stepped off the cruise liner and into a separate reality, one in which she was suddenly completely alone. That sensation felt particularly creepy to Shev. Meanwhile, there was a strange smell, thick and cloying, worse than anything Shev had ever experienced. The putrid air was almost impossible to navigate, forcing Shev to pull the top of her shirt up to cover her nose. Still she pressed on, aware now that something was amiss inside the boat and that it likely had to do with Tempest.

Reaching the back of the enclosed vessel, Shev angled the flashlight in front of her, illuminating the walls and rows of empty benches. The light then came to a rest on what appeared to be the handles of a stretcher. As she inched closer, Shev spotted the ghostly pale features of a woman's face as well, which appeared almost inhuman and mannequin-like.

Instantly panicked, Shev could now see that the woman was lying upright on the stretcher, her arms crossed about her chest. With her eyes closed, the woman appeared in a state of rest, although Shev knew immediately that *wasn't* the case. The color was completely drained from the woman's body and there were red marks and dark bruising all around her neck, as if something constricting had been placed around it.

Shev had seen enough pictures to recognize the woman's face and know that she'd finally found Tempest Greylock. Her next reaction was to check for a pulse, reaching and picking up Tempest's wrist, which was cold and rigid to the touch. There were no signs of life left in her, and judging by the state of her body - *rigor mortis* already setting in, she'd been deceased for some time. A sense of dread came over Shev, aware that this was the worst possible outcome, the gut feelings of both her and Myrick proving true.

Tempest had indeed been the victim of foul play.

Snatching a radio from her side, Shev twisted a knob on the top and it squealed to life, white noise transmitting loudly over the preset channel.

"Chief, you there?" Shev's voice was troubled. "I've found Greylock. Chief... she, um... she's dead. I need you to answer me-"

"She's what?" a startled voice came back over the radio.

"Dead... I, um, think she's been murdered," Shev stumbled over her words, trying to hold it together as she described the situation to Chief Moretti.

"Hold on, where are you? I'm coming to you now."

"Starboard side, Deck 7. Lifeboat #2A. I found Greylock's body inside here, lying on a stretcher."

"I'll be there in just a minute. *Don't* move her. I'm going to inform the captain as well."

"Okay," Shev whispered, the conversation already over.

It felt like an eternity as Shev stood inside the lifeboat, the lifeless body of Tempest next to her, waiting for Moretti to show up. When he finally did, Captain Salazar was with him as well, both of whom were deeply disturbed by the sight of a deceased member of the crew.

But Shev hadn't completely prepared herself for the fallout from her discovery. Captain Salazar, who was responsible for the well-being of *all* of the inhabitants on the ship, immediately turned his sights to damage control, his overriding concern to stave off the potential for panic. And - much to Shev's dismay - that mindset would be a compelling factor in the decisions made aboard *The Savoy of the Seas* from that point on.

*****

It'd been an incredible and memorable evening, as the Lindy Hop group frolicked and danced on the bow of the ship, oblivious to darker events unfolding elsewhere. The front of the ship was completely decked out in Rockabilly style props. The entertainment team - at Duncan's insistence - had gone all out, determined to create a magical experience, transporting the dancers back to the 1950s.

At the entry point, there was a pastel-colored arch with faux columns on each side and a sign that read, "SoCK HoP". In addition, there were seamless black velvet tablecloths draped over all the tables, with gold foil spray serving as the centerpieces on each. Even the silverware was wrapped in customized napkins, featuring the silhouettes of Lindy dancers. And all around were multicolored lights and streamers, 45-size plastic records dangling down from them.

The most impressive sight though was the live band that played and which had everyone out of their seats at the moment. Well, everyone *except* Evann Myrick. He'd danced song after song with Victoria. Then, when someone would finally steal her away - making it seem as though Myrick would be able to take a break, another dancer would come snag him as well. It was an absolute whirlwind; and Myrick was having a wonderful time. He just wanted a chance to rest his tired feet for a brief spell.

The minute he sat down and caught his breath though, his thoughts returned to the mystery of Tempest's disappearance. Interestingly too, the exercise from dancing had him thinking clearer and he almost instantly began to piece together a theory of what likely happened to her, eyeing some *potential* suspects who just happened to be in the immediate vicinity as well at that exact moment.

Victoria had also filled Myrick in regarding her conversation with Soriya. By her description of her and how she'd so quickly latched onto Talon, Myrick got the impression that Soriya was an opportunist. The question though at the moment was why target Talon among all the other potential eligible bachelors on the ship. Surely, given his financial circumstances, he seemed like an unlikely initial choice for someone in search of a free ride.

Several tables away, tucked into a far corner, Talon and Soriya sat alone. They'd been that way for most of the social.

Soriya was in a chair inched close to Talon's, and Myrick noticed how she'd whisper into his ear from time to time, pointing at various people on the dance floor. She'd not only ingratiated herself to him, but she seemed to be the only one he wanted to be with at the moment, which Myrick guessed was exactly how Soriya wanted it.

Myrick's attention stayed on Talon and Soriya's secluded manner for quite some time, rousing his interest. But after a while, his eyes strayed back to the dance floor - just in time to see that Victoria was now dancing with Paul; this time to a lively Count Basie song. It was a curious display too. At times, it was clear that Paul was leading Victoria in patterns. Others though, it appeared he was the one doing the following, as if mid-dance the two had switched roles.

Completely in awe of their smooth transitions back-and-forth, Myrick was truly intrigued by the dance. It was quite impressive, like nothing he'd seen before. And so he carefully studied their movements, curious as to how it could be pulled off so effortlessly.

The band was nearing the end of its session, playing one final song, encouraging everyone to come back out onto the dance floor one last time. Myrick had been dancing almost nonstop all night. With so much practice over two days straight, he was already getting comfortable with Lindy.

Throughout the evening, he'd danced several songs with Victoria, but there were at least 4 or 5 other follows he'd danced with as well, including one with Harriett near the end of the night. By her reaction to it, he sensed that he'd somewhat redeemed himself in her eyes as well, and she even offered up a half-smile as the Ella Fitzgerald song faded out, which he considered something of a miracle. *But then the evening went south again… and fast.*

Victoria had walked over to him and so he reached for her hand, expecting to take her in a closed position. Instead, she chuckled and shook her head *no*. She then pointed around her, emphasizing how everyone was basically closing in together, practically shoulder to shoulder and faced in the same direction.

The Lindy Hoppers were gathering for a group-style dance; and apparently Myrick was the only one who didn't realize this was how the night would end. Had he, he wouldn't have allowed Victoria to lead him out there. Now though, he was trapped, immediately noticing that everyone else was moving to the music - displaying clever footwork, air kicks and all other sorts of acrobatics. This was Lindy at its finest, full of spontaneity, smiles and laughter all around as if somehow they were all in on a choreographed musical number - everyone *except* Myrick.

Suddenly nauseous, Myrick knew he needed to formulate an escape. Unfortunately, just as he was about to make his getaway, he made the mistake of glancing over at Victoria, whose eyes were already on him, as if she'd never been happier with him than at that exact moment. Now he was *really* stuck.

To her, the dance that broke out seemed whimsical and simple enough. She had both hands on the edges of her dress, pulling it up just slightly so that it was up to her knees, then kicking her legs up in reveling fashion. She then glanced down at Myrick's feet, urging him to do the same. Immediately, he shook his head no, but she wasn't going to give up that easily.

Seconds later and Victoria, along with everyone else, jumped to a complete stop, hitting the beat of the music just perfectly, as if it had dictated it. Victoria then flashed her hands out in front of her, wiggling them wildly like jazz hands.

Myrick rolled his eyes. He'd seen enough. But he was also a good sport. And so he raised his hands, jumped about a half-inch off the floor (which was not in unison with the music *at all*) and then landed with jazz hands waving comically in the air. In turn, Victoria broke out in the widest smile he'd ever seen, getting a great laugh at Myrick's expense. *She was also completely enamored with him for at least trying to keep up with the other dancers.*

An incredible thing then happened, a booming sound echoed from out of the darkness. And then another one. Myrick turned to see bright fireworks lighting up the night sky, bursting in dazzling fashion all around the ship, while the lively music continued playing in the background. It was like nothing Myrick had ever seen or experienced, and it was happening all because he was with Victoria. This was entirely her idea, he'd have known nothing about this beautiful side of life without her.

Suddenly, out of nowhere, she stopped in place, grabbed his hand and then began to pull him away from the dance floor. Confused, he allowed her to lead him away, willing to follow along wherever she took him.

The bow of the ship was just up ahead, and the tip of it provided the perfect location to watch the fireworks show. Many of the other dancers were still caught up in the last song, leaving Myrick and Victoria alone to stake out an idyllic spot to watch it, which Victoria wisely did.

The two then gazed out at the endless ocean, the moon shining off the sill waters, fireworks exploding in a thrilling display of bright colors up above. It was a picturesque moment that *seemingly* couldn't get better. Although Myrick realized there was one thing that he could do that might make the moment even more special.

Tugging lightly on Victoria's hand, which he still held in his own, he turned to her. She did the same, so that the two were now eye to eye. Victoria's silhouette lit up with the array of fireworks going off all around her. She was already irresistibly beautiful, but this was like nothing Myrick had ever seen or imagined.

Myrick wasn't the type to take risks. He was a deliberate person who carefully considered all the possible outcomes before ever proceeding into the unknown. But allowing himself to get lost in the magic of their surroundings - and aware that moments like this only come around once in a lifetime, he slowly leaned in toward Victoria, gently releasing her hand at the same time. He then reached along her back, placing one hand just above her slim waistline and the other along the base of her neck. As his lips touched Victoria's, her eyes softened to a close. His heart, meanwhile, leapt as she returned his embrace, the two quickly lost in an unforgettable, passionate kiss; one which Myrick found himself wishing would never end.

CHAPTER THIRTEEN
"Cup & Hook" Your Partner's Hand

Captain Alejandro Salazar was a confident man, and at just 36 years old, one of the youngest in the industry to be promoted to cruise ship captain. He rose up the ranks quickly, impressing others in the industry with his savvy and credentials, receiving his master's in marine engineering from the University of South Hampton. Fortune was also on his side, being taken under the wings of a mentor that had incredible connections in the cruising world.

That same mentor pulled enough strings so that Salazar went from third officer to staff captain in record time. It wasn't long thereafter that management recruiters came calling and he was hired to a position as captain of the newest commissioned ship in their fleet - *The Savoy of the Seas.*

Blessed with strong genetics, Salazar had dark black hair, bronzed skin and piercing eyes. He was tall, 6'1, with an imposing stature and a temper of equal measure when angered. Those under his supervision rarely questioned his decisions, even those who'd been in the cruise industry longer than him. Pride also tended to get the best of him and oftentimes his ego was a hindrance to his development. At sea, there was very little substitute for actual experience. Much of captaining was the ability to read circumstances - recognizing subtle changes in weather patterns, motivating crew and navigating unforeseen situations, all skills which he'd not yet mastered.

Despite his shortcomings, Salazar hadn't really faced much adversity in his young career. The potential murder of a staff member on his ship was certainly a first. His resolve was about to be severely tested, and his *only* hope of succeeding was to rely on the collective wisdom of the crew under his authority.

"I'm not going to rush to any conclusions," Salazar quickly informed them. "We don't even know if this was a murder or a suicide."

"Captain, what about the marks on her neck... the blood vessels that have burst in her eyes? It looks like she's been attacked, suffocated to death," Shev protested, but as soon as she did, she could see that she'd misread her place in the conversation, a mere peon in the ship's pecking order.

Salazar had a scathing look in his dark eyes, disapproving of Shev's decision to second-guess him. After giving her a soul-crushing death stare, he turned his attention to Chief Moretti. The old man simply stood there, a blank expression on his ashen face, not making any attempt to defend Shev. Salazar relished the opportunity to wield his power and authority in such a setting.

"Well, speak up. This crew member is under your direct supervision. Do I need to step in to correct her behavior? Because I will if you can't-"

"He didn't..." Shev foolishly attempted to defend her boss, only to watch Salazar snap his neck in her direction, the look in his eyes making clear he didn't want to hear another defiant word from the young crew member.

"Moretti?" Salazar pressed again, his attention back on his chief of security. "*You* want to explain this?"

"Well, it's just that," Moretti fumbled for words. "I think what Ms. Rotem is trying to say is that there do seem to be some peculiar aspects to Ms. Greylock's death."

While Moretti's words did seem to offer up a semblance of defense on Shev's behalf, his actions did not. Moretti stood meekly in front of Salazar, like a scolded dog showing deference to an overbearing master.

At his age, Moretti wasn't likely to find another job that paid or offered the benefits that this cruise ship position did. Acutely aware of that fact, the last thing he wanted to do was get on the captain's bad side. Moretti liked Shev, but not enough to risk his *career*. So, a feeble defense was as far as he was willing to go on her behalf.

"I've been all around the world," Salazar decided it was time to boast about himself, as weaker men often do when trying to prove their self-worth. "And so I've seen strange things. In Barcelona, there's a case pending in the courts where a woman was found stabbed multiple times in the back. Everyone cried homicide. But, do you know what... it was *nothing* of the sort. Police investigated and ruled her death a suicide. Bizarre yes. But also a great example of why the people should let those in authority do their job. It's been decades since you were *Polizia*, correct?" Salazar pressed his chief of security.

"Yes, that was a lifetime ago," Moretti conceded.

"My point exactly. And I know you certainly don't have any law enforcement experience," Salazar turned to Shev, speaking dismissively.

Shev didn't dare utter a reply this time, knowing that Salazar was entirely unreceptive to what she had to say.

"And of course, I don't either," Salazar continued. "Which means none of us should be injecting our own preconceived notions into this. We need to work only within the cold hard facts available to us at the moment. We have a dead body. We don't know *how* she died or what demons she might have been secretly struggling with. That sort of in-depth investigation is a job for the police. Let's get her to the morgue. Do so in a manner that doesn't alarm any passengers. We don't want anyone to become spooked by this tragic - but *isolated* - development."

"We may have lucked out though, Captain," Shev tried to remain respectful in her tone, knowing that her opinion wasn't wanted, even if it might be *needed.* "There is a detective on board. His name is Evann Myrick. He was actually helping us in the search for Ms. Greylock." As soon as she added this last detail, Shev knew she'd made a second crucial mistake, the look on Salazar's face nearing disbelief.

"You consulted with a passenger about the situation?" Salazar bellowed, as if the last of his restraint was being tested.

"I mean, we're fortunate…" Shev glanced over at Moretti for help, instantly aware by his timid body language that none was coming.

Shev was on her own with this one. It was a difficult realization - *shocking to witness this side of her boss* - as she'd looked up to the man for so long. Fortunately, Shev had an inner strength about her. Years of having had to fend for herself under impossible conditions had been a strange sort of blessing, so that her spirits were *not* easily broken.

Her eyes turned back to Salazar. "If I was wrong, Captain... I'm sorry... but the most important thing on my mind was finding a missing crew member. We did. Although mostly because of his help."

Salazar hadn't spoken a word, appearing expressionless as Shev explained her reasoning. *None* of what she said justified that level of subordination. And with every word she uttered in her defense, he grew increasingly angrier. Finally, unable to stomach any more, he spoke again, his voice surprisingly flat, but in a way that made his potential fury seem even scarier.

"From this moment on, any security decisions are to be run by me. That understood?" He glared at both Shev and Moretti. Moretti nodded emphatically, his eyes on Shev as if to emphasize the gravity of the situation. Fortunately, he could see that she did (mercifully) nod her agreement as well.

"Good," Salazar spoke directly to Moretti. "Something like this will not happen again on *my* ship. Make arrangements immediately to get Ms. Greylock's body out of here. I assume I can trust you to handle that without incident?"

"Of course," replied Moretti, contritely.

Done with his orders, the captain turned to leave the lifeboat, confident that he'd sent the necessary message to his security team. Meanwhile, he now had other concerns. They were only a few hours away from Cabo San Lucas. If he docked there, they'd be under the jurisdiction of Mexican authorities and would have to turn the body over to them. Salazar wasn't entirely sure what would happen from that point.

His greatest concern - that the *Policia Federal* would insist upon a full investigation while docked in their port, potentially delaying their trip for hours, maybe even days. While Salazar had feigned his belief that Greylock *might* have committed suicide, he could clearly see from her injuries that wasn't the case and a full homicide investigation was inevitable. He just couldn't risk that taking place in Mexico. It was better to deal with this situation back in their home port, California.

The company would be grateful if he handled this well, rewarding him accordingly.

Convinced he'd have to turn the ship around, this was at least the most opportune time to do so. Most of the passengers were likely either asleep or heading back to their cabins below deck. Very few would be aware of the ship's gradual change of course. By the time they woke up the next morning, they'd be well on their way back to San Diego, and Salazar would have formulated a reasoned explanation for them by that point.

In fact, he was already thinking that the wisest course was to admit that there had indeed been a medical emergency to a crew member on the ship, offering up a hint of truth. Then he'd inject a little more creative wording to it, adding that there was no cause for alarm, even if there *clearly* was.

Thoroughly enamored with himself for already coming up with a plan of action, Salazar returned to the navigation deck. There, he barked out orders to his crew to reset their course, beginning the lengthy turnaround of the approximately 220,000 ton ship, which was a monumental undertaking. To head off any concerns from his team, he briefly explained that there'd been a medical emergency, although he'd kept details of the incident purposefully sparse.

Once he was sure that his crew was on top of things, the captain beckoned for his first officer to follow him to a private room. There, he picked up a handheld radio, accessing a secure line, which allowed him to communicate with the mainland. Using *seasspeak*, and commencing with one of the eight understood message markers of open seas communication, Captain Salazar finally spoke into the receiver, his first officer hanging on every word, "Request, corporate assistance with the removal of a corpse at the San Diego port. Murder... suspected."

*****

Paul was in his cabin when he felt the ship begin to turn, gradually changing course. At first, he'd assumed that it was simply the captain maneuvering around rougher waters, no surprise that they'd make a small change in direction to do so.

And he would've been satisfied with that rationale except he was already unable to sleep for other reasons, his mind racing a mile a minute. Something just didn't seem right, and he had an unnerving feeling about one of his foes from the poker table - Evann Myrick, especially after he'd spotted Myrick speaking to a member of the security crew earlier that evening inside the casino.

Although he hadn't overheard any of the conversation, Paul was an incredibly observant *and* inquisitive person. He also noted a curious change in Myrick's demeanor after the talk had taken place, which manifested itself pretty obviously in the poker room.

In Paul's estimation, Myrick was an affable fellow, seemingly easy going. But at the poker table, something was different. Myrick's disposition had changed. Paul watched with intrigue as Myrick seemed to be carefully analyzing a select group of individuals, almost as if Myrick was playing detective.

Paul knew cops. He'd spent plenty of time around them. He understood what made them tick and he knew how to play their games. He could see it in Myrick's eyes, the man was creating a mental profile of everyone around him, including Paul. If that was the case - and he was *certain* it was - Paul was more than willing to oblige.

Meanwhile, sitting at the final table with the detective had been particularly telling for other reasons, affording Paul an opportunity to observe things up close, especially the awkward dynamic developing between Myrick and Talon. Talon was clearly no actual threat to Myrick, but the rivalry did afford Paul the knowledge of one important character flaw in Myrick - *the man was vulnerable to jealousy.*

After getting knocked out of the final four, Paul had been incredibly disappointed. He'd wanted the winner's pot as much as anyone. The loss did, though, at least force him to step back and take in the bigger picture, including the developing tension between Myrick and Talon... Victoria's protectiveness for *both* of them... and *just as importantly*, Soriya's predatory behavior in regards to Talon.

Soriya had evidently mastered what Paul would best describe as the Marilyn Monroe effect - raising her eyebrows and lowering her eyelids, as if giddy with excitement every time Talon glanced over at her. Men were suckers for subtle flirtations like that, and Soriya was exploiting that to her advantage masterfully, even if Victoria's presence was making things harder than they needed to be.

But, of course, Paul understood women like Soriya *all* too well. Soriya was a parasite, searching for a host that she could bleed dry and then move on from. Paul didn't need to talk to her to know that Soriya was using Talon, as Paul had done the same to plenty of people himself over the years as well. It was just part of the game. And interestingly Myrick apparently had picked up on it as well, suddenly showing sympathy for the same man that was the cause of his jealousy. *Things were getting interesting, indeed.*

Chuckling to himself, Paul thought back on how brilliantly Harriett was playing the room as well. Unlike Talon, Harriett posed a far bigger threat to Myrick. Even Paul, despite spending so much time with her dancing, didn't really know much about the mysterious girl. She remained incredibly guarded, but was clearly capable of more trouble than she was letting on.

Still fascinated, Paul had watched as the same security guard approached Myrick - *yet again* - after the poker game was over, this time saying something that even convinced Myrick to leave Victoria and go assist. Now, Paul was certain something was up. Something quite serious.

Not privy to the secret obviously being kept from the other passengers onboard the vessel, Paul resigned himself to heading over to the dance social at the ship's bow. He then spent the rest of the evening getting dances in, all the while frustrated at being kept in the dark. Yet, as the hours passed and the captain made no announcements, he also knew that answers wouldn't be forthcoming anytime soon.

Dwelling on that fact for a good hour, Paul noticed the ship was still turning. By this point, he guessed they must actually be going in the entire opposite direction, away from their port in Cabo San Lucas. Suddenly, Paul started to truly worry. The captain wouldn't turn the ship around mid-cruise with no warning to the passengers unless it was the result of a particularly *dire* occurrence.

Completely awake, Paul sat up in the small bed. Glancing down at his watch, he could see that it was nearing 4:00 AM.

No sense trying to sleep at this point, Paul bemoaned to himself.

Deciding it would be best to venture out and find a place on the ship that was open 24/7, Paul threw on some slippers, resolved that it might do him some good to get a glass of wine, maybe calm his nerves some. After proceeding out of the room, he noticed how eerily quiet it now was in the usually-busy hallways. Throughout the entire cruise, there'd always been something going on, even late into the night. So for it to be so still - practically devoid of sound other than the din of the ship's massive engine - was a stark and jarring contrast.

As he proceeded down the corridor, unexpected movement far up ahead suddenly caught his eye. It *appeared* to be a woman, dressed in all black, and she was walking toward the door of a nearby cabin. Quickly the woman slipped a key out of her pocket and - just as swiftly - disappeared through the doorway. The entire scene happened in a flash, but even from that distance Paul was certain who the person was. It was Harriett.

What could she possibly be doing up this late? he wondered, silently.

Beset with yet another chance development, Paul walked quietly over to the door he'd seen her enter in through. The room number was 347. After listening for movement inside the room, Paul heard nothing.

Starting to lift his hand toward the door, he considered knocking on it, *just* to ask if she was okay. It then dawned on him how creepy that might seem, as she clearly hadn't noticed him in the hallway and it would make for an incredibly awkward situation for him to interrupt her at such an odd hour of the morning, regardless of his motives.

His hand a mere inch away from the door, he ultimately pulled it back. Standing in the silent hallway, Paul scratched the back of his head in consternation, aware that he needed to stop letting his overactive imagination get the best of him.

None of this is even your business, Paul chastised himself under his breath.

The elevators were up ahead. Making the choice to exercise discretion in this moment, Paul walked over and pushed the button to take him to a top floor. Seconds later, an elevator arrived. The doors opened and Paul could see that no one was in it, no surprise as he'd expected almost everyone else to be sleeping, which had made Harriett's earlier appearance even more unexpected.

He pushed the button to the seventh floor, where he knew most of the shops and restaurants were located. As he reached Deck 7, Paul stepped out to an empty hallway. His feet tapped on the hard floor, echoing down the long corridor, emphasizing how alone he was on the massive ship in that moment.

Up ahead, he spotted the lights of a gift shop that was still open. Although not a full service breakfast place, Paul guessed that it would at least likely have something to snack on. Inside the otherwise empty store, there was a clerk at the counter. She smiled at him, lifting her eyes up from a book she'd been reading to pass the time.

After placing the book down, the clerk watched from behind a small counter in case Paul found anything and needed her to ring the purchase up. He eventually did, locating a bottle of red wine, choosing a vintage Pinot Noir from the region of Burgundy, which had been carefully stored in a display cabinet. It was the most expensive option and he showed no hesitation choosing it, seemingly undaunted by the lofty price.

"You have good taste," the clerk smiled.

"Oh yes." Paul glanced down at the bottle in his hand, almost as if only just noticing the prized brand he'd chosen.

"I take it you must be something of a wine connoisseur?" the clerk asked, interested in small talk to pass the time.

"I mean, sort of," Paul replied, almost embarrassingly. "I'm sure this is a good one."

"Um, the *best* we carry on the ship," the clerk chuckled. "I'd love to sample a glass of it one day."

"Oh well, I don't usually splurge like this either, but it isn't often you get to go on a cruise. Still," Paul seized on his opportunity to ask a pressing question. "It's disappointing that the captain is turning the ship around. Must be quite an emergency."

"You noticed that too, huh," the clerk answered, confusion in her eyes, betraying that she wasn't going to be able to answer Paul's next question even before he asked it.

"You know why?"

"No clue," the clerk shook her head. "They don't tell me much. I'm small potatoes," she laughed.

Paul didn't reply. Instead, he proceeded to hand over a room card, which the clerk used to bill for the bottle of wine. She then handed it back to Paul and was about to make more small talk when she noticed Paul had already turned to leave, seemingly done with their conversation.

As it would turn out, Paul would polish off half off the bottle before finally falling asleep, the Burgundy an expensive but *effective* sedative. Meanwhile, when he woke the next morning, he'd get a better understanding of what exactly was going on. All he needed to do was exercise a measure of (alcohol-assisted) patience until then.

CHAPTER FOURTEEN
Dance With Lots Of People, Not Just Your Partner

The sun was already cresting high in the sky by the time the captain made his announcement over the loudspeaker, which was even piped into the cabins. Rumors had already been running rampant, as many of the passengers had long-since figured out that they weren't on their way to Cabo, after all.

In fact, per the ship's itinerary, they were supposed to have docked in the port of Cabo San Lucas around 5:30 AM, with passengers *expecting* to wake up to see that they'd arrived and could disembark on their various excursions. So no surprise that there would be endless questions about why the cruise ship was instead still far out to sea even as they neared midday.

Victoria had planned on surprising Myrick, secretly booking the two of them a private ATV tour. The excursion was all-inclusive, with an itinerary that included lunch near the Arch, a boat excursion to observe a sea lion colony and even a scenic camel ride along the crystalline waters of *Playa del Amor*. So when she got wind of the rumors, she was instantly disappointed, having really been looking forward to some time alone with Myrick. She knew it was going to be a one-of-a-kind experience, and *particularly* romantic given their kiss up on the bow of the ship the previous night.

Of course, the beauty of having someone like Myrick around was that she could turn to him for his insight on what was going on and be relatively certain that he would have a decent take on things. So while the other passengers threw out wild theories: that there had been a pandemic outbreak in Cabo or mechanical issues with the ship's engine, Myrick had a more accurate supposition. And it was one that he *only* felt comfortable sharing with Victoria at the moment.

"The crew member that went missing - Tempest Greylock... she must've been found," Myrick opined to Victoria, confident in his assessment of the situation.

"How can you be so sure? You haven't heard a word from security updating you."

"That's part of the reason I know it must have something to do with the search for her. I haven't heard or seen from Shev since last night when she told me that she needed my help. And there are only so many reasons to turn around a ship with no notice to the passengers."

"Maybe she's been working directly with her boss and that's why she stopped coming to consult you."

"Oh, I'm pretty sure that *is* the case also. I think they've told her not to talk to any of the passengers. They don't want to create a panic, which tells me it must be something serious. Interesting that the crew doesn't seem to know much either. It'd take a pretty stern order to keep something like this under wrap."

Victoria understood instantly what this meant, their vacation together was coming to an abrupt end. Worse, she could see in Myrick's softening eyes that the realization was hitting him particularly hard, doing his best to stay strong and focused in the event his investigative expertise was still needed at some point, but undeniably disheartened that his time with Victoria had been cut short.

Knowing what she needed to do, Victoria reached over and took Myrick's hand, gently leaning in and kissing him, as if to let him know that this was just the beginning of *their* adventure together. When she leaned back again, she could see he instantly seemed a different man, happy simply to be in her presence, distracted from the developing situation that was weighing heavily on his mind.

"I didn't mean to ruin our trip," Myrick's eyes had a sadness in them, his hand was in Victoria's and it was almost as if he didn't want to let go, worried that the bond between them could be stolen away if he did. "Maybe the less you know the better."

"Don't do that to me," Victoria clutched Myrick's hand a little tighter. "I don't want it to work that way between us."

"You want my honest opinion always."

"*Always.*"

"Be careful what you ask for," replied Myrick, suddenly pausing, but he could see in Victoria's eyes that she was pleading for the *entire* truth so he proceeded to tell her his deduction of things. "We sail under a Panamanian flag. You may have seen it hanging along the aft of the ship."

"I did. Not sure I recall which country it was though. But I do remember seeing a flag."

"Cruise ships sail on international waters. While at sea, it's subject to the laws of whatever country's flag it sails under. Many ships choose countries like Italy and Panama for tax implications. But of course, we're nowhere near Panama so if a serious incident happened onboard... perhaps even one that required police presence... Panamanian authorities aren't going to be nearby to assist."

"Then why not simply dock in Cabo San Lucas?"

"I'd venture to guess that the captain knows he'd be immersed in a potentially serious investigation. I doubt he'd want to be caught in Mexico, subject to their jurisdiction and whims."

"You think he'd be concerned they wouldn't take it seriously?"

"I'm pretty certain of just the opposite actually. If he gets the ship back to California, it'll be much simpler to ensure the investigation into any incident is kept low-key. Passengers would be able to disembark, subject to potential questioning, but still in their home country. That's a big factor, allowing law enforcement to follow up without a complete sense of urgency. And if it turns out that something really bad *has* happened, it'd also be simpler for the cruise line to conduct damage control.

"You think Greylock's been murdered, don't you?" Victoria wisely threw out.

"I do."

"By whom?"

Myrick shrugged his shoulders, indicating he wasn't entirely sure yet. He did have a general theory, although nothing more than a best guess at this point, and he certainly wasn't going to scare Victoria with it, given she was likely to come into contact with that exact person again on the sail back to San Diego.

"By whom?" Victoria pressed once more. "I know you've got an idea. You were with that security guard late into the night going over things."

"Could be a fellow crew member," Myrick gave one possible explanation. He then hesitated before continuing, "*Could* be a dancer also."

There was a lasting silence, Victoria taking in the import of what Myrick said. She knew he wouldn't have specified "dancer" - as opposed to passenger - if he didn't think that was a strong possibility. He also clearly suspected foul play and that led Victoria to a more pressing concern.

"Then we aren't safe. None of us are."

"I think we should assume at this point that there is a real danger to everyone aboard this ship."

"You need to address this with the captain."

"And what? Prance into the ship's wheelhouse and announce I'm Evann Myrick... a former detective... and I believe there's a murderer aboard this ship?"

"Something along the lines of that," Victoria replied undaunted. "They must already know about the crime and might actually *welcome* the help."

"Or they suspect it, but there's dissension on what to make of Greylock's death. Keep in mind, there's been very few details provided as to what has taken place necessitating the sudden turn around. There's also been *no* directive that passengers are to remain quartered in their cabins for the duration of the voyage. We're no longer headed to Cabo San Lucas obviously, but passengers are still free to roam around and enjoy the ship's amenities. If you knew for certain you had a murderer roaming the ship, would you take that risk?"

"No."

"And the captain calls the shots ultimately. He must either believe that the manner of Greylock's death is uncertain, or at least have convinced himself as such for career reasons. Either way, he isn't going to want to hear from a *has-been* detective who might throw cold water on his plans. He's not going to talk to me, Victoria."

"Then what about the security guard? She could help."

"That's putting her in an impossible spot. She'd reach out to me if she could. I think I have to wait until she initiates further contact."

"So what do we do?"

"*You* do nothing. I'm going to start snooping around and see if I can piece things together on my own."

"So I'm just supposed to lock myself up in my room?" Victoria wasn't happy with Myrick's answer.

Immediately, he became regretful, realizing he hadn't handled the situation well. His intentions might have been noble, but his delivery had left something to be desired.

"No, of course not. Honestly, I think we're all safer out in public areas anyway. Nothing is going to happen as long as we're in groups. But you can do me one big favor… you can be my eyes and ears. No one is as in-the-know and is as trusted as you in the dance community. If a dancer has concerns, you'll likely be one of the first to hear about it."

Victoria's body posture changed, so that she was leaning forward, grateful that Myrick did understand what an asset she could be to him. She didn't mind freeing him up to do his thing, she didn't want to be a distraction. There were better ways she could help him and she was looking forward to using her own connections to find out what she could.

"Please be careful," Victoria urged Myrick. She leaned in to kiss him, wanting to emphasize how important he was to her.

The kiss was different this time, less sensual but still affectionate, an intense bond now existing between the two, neither wanting the other to get caught up in unnecessary dangers. Both coming to realize their skills together were quite formidable when combined.

Standing up from the table, Myrick took one last sip of his coffee, then purposefully made eye contact with Victoria, wanting her to know that he took what she said to heart. He then turned to head out the door, making his way to the exterior of the ship and toward the promenade.

Almost immediately, he was hit with a cold gust of wind, starkly different than conditions had been the entire cruise up to that point. They were clearly heading back toward the California coast. Myrick could tell that the mighty ship had also sped up and he guessed they'd be back in port within a day. Unfortunately, it also appeared that there was a daunting obstacle in their path, not originally considered, as the storm that was brewing wasn't an issue when they were heading toward Cabo San Lucas. Now, though, it appeared to be directly ahead.

Myrick could see menacing clouds forming in the sky above. The seas appeared rougher as they crashed against the ship's hull as well. He decided to walk over to where Shev had taken him earlier, noticing the same lifeboats as before, although it was simpler to search for clues in daylight. Then Myrick noticed a heavy duty padlock had been placed on the door of one of the larger lifeboats, which he was almost certain *hadn't* been on it the previous night.

Finding the addition of the padlock unusual, he next decided to check the other mega-size lifeboat to see if it had one also. It did *not*. To Myrick, it seemed odd to add a larger padlock - which would require a specific set of keys - on a lifeboat door, as access to it would be hindered if the boat needed to be deployed in an emergency.

Pressing his face up against the tinted windows of the vessel, he could make out very little of the darkened interior, mostly just rows and rows of bench seating. He did, however, notice that there were two stretchers attached to the back wall of the boat, and that one of the two stretchers had been extended outward, as if recently put to use.

Stepping back from the boat, Myrick tapped on its plastic surface with the knuckles of his fingers, making three distinct knocks, as if it represented something important to him, which it did.

This was a crime scene now, Myrick surmised. *They've sealed it up so that no one will tamper with it.*

Still, it was obvious that something had been discovered inside and Myrick knew that *something* had to have been the missing crew member - Tempest Greylock. The question now was - *what had happened to her that was so terrible that the captain felt a need to conceal the situation from even his own crew, turn the ship around and make a hasty return to port?*

*****

Troubled by the way things were unfolding, Shev decided she needed to find some way to get information to Myrick without calling attention to herself. That was going to be near impossible though. Moretti was incredibly disappointed that she'd confided in Myrick to begin with, a serious breach in protocol. He felt betrayed and Shev regretted that she hadn't kept him more informed.

The captain, meanwhile, had made his orders clear and Moretti wasn't going to take any more chances, especially not with Shev. And so, his complete attention was on her, loading Shev up with menial tasks to keep her busy and from causing any more avoidable headaches.

"I can conduct the safety walkthrough on Deck 14," Shev volunteered, a job that Moretti ordinarily would've gladly turned over to her before.

"No, that won't be necessary. I'd prefer you here. We're sailing into a storm. I want you on the monitor surveying cams to ensure that all guests are safe."

In front of Shev was an array of video screens, depicting various areas of the ship, allowing security to keep eyes on most of the massive cruise vessel. Really the only places not equipped with surveillance cams were the passenger cabins and restroom facilities. All of the common and public areas had at least one camera within the facility.

Shev had the ability to activate the cameras remotely and even zoom in tight on anything if needed. The surveillance system was cutting-edge technology. But even as advanced as it was, incorporating a line crossing analytic, the system didn't always operate properly in maritime conditions. The majority of the ship's cameras were focused on decks where most people gathered, leaving them somewhat ineffective at guarding the nooks and crannies of the ship without human assistance.

And of course, it didn't help that the motion-activated system caused endless false alarms, sometimes triggered simply because a passenger had thrown an item overboard, leaving already tired and overworked crew members completely fatigued. Oftentimes, the line crossing system was ignored entirely, disregarded until there was cause for real concern (*which unbeknownst to the crew, this just happened to be that exact moment.*)

Glancing at the various monitors, Shev spotted a familiar face, not surprised at all to see him on the outdoor platform and near the lifeboats. She also guessed that Myrick had already pieced together *most* of what had occurred overnight, watching as he tapped three times on the exterior of the boat, then noticing as an expression of grave concern came over his face.

Just knowing Myrick was out there doing his own digging boosted Shev's spirits. Eventually, Myrick left the promenade area, leaving Shev to hope that she'd run into him soon and could get his direct take on the situation.

It appeared that the captain's surprise announcement had had a curious effect on the passengers as well. Given there wasn't any evident cause for alarm, most were simply trying to make the most of the shortened trip, getting in as many activities as possible. Shev found it surreal that all of the ship's recreations were geared up, despite the gruesome death of a crew member.

She could see that the casino area was practically buzzing with excitement, people gathered all around the various poker and craps tables. The slot machines were lit up as well, gamblers occupying almost every available chair. And the pool area was another hot spot. The crew had set up games and music was blaring loudly, passengers oblivious to the serious situation.

Those weren't the only crowded locations at the moment, the restaurants were teeming with people as well. In fact, it was difficult for Shev to continuously track all of the venues on the monitors, people going in and out of them in every direction, and she couldn't remember a time when she'd ever seen the ship quite this busy. She did, however, spot a *few* familiar faces in the crowd, as she'd interviewed them during her original investigation into the disappearance of Tempest Greylock.

Talon and Soriya were sitting at a table in a breakfast venue, neither really talking. Soriya was sipping coffee, steadily massaging her forehead with her fingers, as if suffering from a hangover of sorts. Talon was more alert, his eyes scanning all around the restaurant, apparently bored with his company.

Eventually, it seemed Talon spotted someone he wanted to talk to and Shev watched curiously as Talon got up and walked over to a table where Victoria was sitting *alone*. Shev couldn't make out the conversation, there was no audio piping through the monitors, but the interaction seemed cordial enough. Indeed, to Shev, the more interesting part was the evolving expression on Soriya's face, daggers in her eyes as she stared in Victoria's direction, as if to warn her to get her claws off Soriya's catch.

The situation kept Shev's attention only until she spotted Harriett, who had been the witness to the original cries that night. Shev still hadn't found enough evidence to link the two, but she was relatively certain that Harriett was lying about the sound coming from the port side of the ship. It dawned on Shev that Harriett might even have manufactured the convenient ruse simply to get Shev's attention elsewhere, searching the wrong side of the ship, and coming to the conclusion that Tempest must've fallen overboard.

Shev watched curiously as Harriett continued down a long hallway, the sea life woven into the carpeting on the floor of the ship all traveling in the opposite direction, which was a common theme on cruise liners, using decor to show which direction the bow of the ship was located, so that one could simply glance down at the fish on the carpeting and know that they all swam toward the front of the vessel.

She followed Harriett's movements as they traveled from camera angle to camera angle. Eventually, Harriett made her way into a dead end corridor, where Shev knew the workout room was located. Harriett had on yoga pants and a form-fitted tank top, and it was evident now to Shev that she was on her way to get some exercise in.

Continuing to watch, Shev observed Harriett go straight toward a treadmill, which had an immense glass window in front of it, affording a breathtaking view of the entire ocean outside. Harriett got on the treadmill and began slowly walking. The series of events seemed rather unremarkable until Shev realized that the treadmill Harriett had chosen provided an unobstructed view of the mega-size lifeboats positioned along the promenade below.

Certainly it could be mere coincidence, but it didn't escape Shev that this would serve as an ideal place for Harriett to survey the scene without calling suspicion to herself.

Seeing that Harriett had chosen a lengthy session on the treadmill, Shev turned her attention elsewhere and just in time to catch a lone individual (and another familiar face from her earlier interviews) walking into a below deck movie theater - Paul. The showtimes were posted on the exterior wall of the theater, indicating that the movie wouldn't be starting for another thirty minutes. Paul had the *entire* theater to himself at the moment.

While there were security cams situated inside the theater, the clarity wasn't as good in the low-light setting. Fortunately the theater was empty and Shev eventually located Paul, although she was surprised by the seat he'd chosen in a far back row. More curiously, Shev was certain that Paul was talking to himself.

Sure enough, zooming in for a closer look, Shev could see that Paul was muttering something under his breath. She could even almost make out the intonations of his mouth, doing her best to attempt lip reading, which was not something she did often or really *ever*.

It appeared as though he was upset, at one point even banging his hand against the arm rest next to him. The flickering of the movie projector above, which was currently set on a continuous loop of previews, only added to the dramatic feel of the situation, creating an ominous glow around Paul's silhouette. To Shev, it was a little like watching the making of a stop motion film, each frame coming into view with the intermittent flashes of light; and with each flicker, the expressions on Paul's face seemed to transpose eerily.

In time, however, he did seem to calm down and gradually his attention turned to the screen in front of him; the demeanor on his face morphing into something more serene. His expression suddenly calm and relaxed, Paul crossed one leg over the other, leaned back in the reclining chair, placed his hands behind his head and allowed himself to enjoy the previews in relative seclusion.

"Anything interesting on there?" a voice asked from behind Shev, startling her.

"Huh?" She turned around to see a young man with a distinctly boyish face and grin staring over her shoulder at the monitors. "When did you get in here, Mike?" Shev asked.

"Been here for a good five minutes," Mike replied, his smile even wider. "Seems like a security guard would pick up on something like that."

"Okay, weirdo," Shev replied.

She'd known Mike only a short time, but that was long enough for her to develop an unfavorable opinion of him. Mike was a relatively new member of the crew, cocky with good looks that helped him get away with more than most. He'd quickly developed an affinity for Shev but the feeling *wasn't* mutual. Instead of getting the hint, it only had Mike trying even harder to win Shev over, as Mike tended to get the things *he* wanted in life.

"It's borderline creeper to sneak in on me like that. I keep the door closed for a reason," said Shev.

"Right, well *anyway*, I actually came here to deliver this," Mike handed over a white slip of paper to Shev. She then took it and began inspecting the writing on it, recognizing that the notepaper was used by the reception desk to record complaints and requests from passengers.

There wasn't much written, so that the entirety of the scribbled message read:

Occupant of I.S. 143 complains that his wallet was stolen earlier today. Previously reported to B. Rotem. Hasn't heard anything since. Wants Rotem to provide update... asap.

Immediately, Shev began shaking her head, completely perplexed. She'd not spoken to *any* passenger about an item being stolen, especially a wallet. The incident definitely didn't ring a bell.

"You take this message down?" she asked, her eyes now back on Mike, a quizzical expression in them.

"No, I'm just the errand boy. Guest Services Officer asked me to bring this to you. Said it sounded like a priority and that she wanted to make sure you handled it personally."

"This must be a mistake. I didn't speak to anyone about a missing wallet. Maybe they got me confused with someone else."

"There's not a lot of B. Rotems onboard the ship," Mike returned with a wry smile.

Shev found it hard to argue with Mike's logic, although conceding the point didn't do anything to provide better perspective on the mystery either. Shev started to worry that she was losing her mind, which was admittedly possible since she'd gotten almost *no* sleep ever since Tempest's disappearance.

"Well, good luck putting the fire out," Mike finally spoke, breaking the awkward silence. "I'm gonna head back downstairs. But I'll be around later if you want to grab dinner in the crew quarters after work."

"Sure," Shev replied, her voice drifting, as if she wasn't even paying attention to her words at the moment.

Mike didn't care. He seemed encouraged by her answer. He then winked at Shev, who made no effort to reciprocate. Then

Mike slipped out of the door, leaving Shev alone in the room, staring down blankly at the sheet of paper.

At least, she figured, Moretti would have to *finally* allow her to venture outside the confines of the monitoring area. He wouldn't want an irate passenger on his hands and he certainly wasn't going to volunteer to deal with it himself. Shev, meanwhile, would get answers as to who had sent the cryptic note soon enough.

CHAPTER FIFTEEN
Keep Notes On What You Learn & Revisit Them

Myrick had been wrong about Victoria's safety in a public place, as it turned out she'd become an easy target for an assailant. The sneak attack *completely* catching Victoria off guard.

She'd been speaking with Talon, who'd been mumbling something about how weird the cruise had been and recounting the complicated situation he'd found himself in with regards to Soriya. Victoria had done her best to give him wise counsel, Talon was her friend, even if she disagreed with his bizarre decision making. Their talk seemed to even work, as Talon eventually leaned over, gave Victoria a hug and then thanked her for always being there for him.

Ten minutes later, and while Victoria was finishing off the last remnants of her breakfast, lost in thought, a figure came up from behind her, unannounced, dropping down into a seat next to Victoria. In turn, snapped out of her stupor, Victoria glanced over to see Soriya, a peculiar grin pasted on her perfectly symmetrical face. Despite the faux show of friendliness, there was a look of detest in Soriya's eyes, betraying her sheer dislike of Victoria.

"Um, hey," Victoria fumbled out the words, not sure what to make of the unexpected encounter.

"Stay away from him."

"What?"

"You heard me, he's with me now. You didn't want him. You had your chance. Don't mess up mine."

"I don't know what you're talking about."

"Yes, you do. Talon told me everything. He said the two of you once dated. That there was even talk of marriage at one point. And then *you* just cut it off. He's never gotten over it."

"He told you all that?" Victoria replied, perplexed that Talon would share such intimate details with someone he couldn't possibly know all that well yet.

"He did."

The certainty in Soriya's voice told Victoria all she needed to know. Talon *had* confided in her, perhaps in a weak, drunken, love-blinded moment. The more Victoria considered the possibility, the more disappointed she was in Talon, troubled that a stranger knew such intimate details about her past.

"That's none of your business."

"Depends actually… *depends* on if you stay out of my relationship with him."

"He's just a friend. Nothing more."

"Good. Keep it that way. He deserves a chance to be with someone who appreciates him."

Now completely taken aback by Soriya's bluntness, Victoria was at a loss for words. She already had a bad impression of the woman, and this sudden confrontation wasn't helping.

Strangely, it did, however, make Victoria wonder if there was an underlying hint of truth to Soriya's words. *Was Talon still not over their breakup yet?* Deep down Victoria believed that might be true, but Soriya's words confirmed her long-held suspicions. It'd been years since they'd been together, but every encounter, every dance, she could sense it in Talon, he was still hurting and hadn't entirely moved on yet.

Given the situation, *maybe* the best thing Victoria could do was heed Soriya's poorly delivered advice. *Who am I to stop Talon from finding happiness?* Victoria wondered. *He should be free to find whatever it is he's looking for, even if that isn't someone I'd choose for him.*

"I won't bother him again for the rest of the cruise," said Victoria, the tone of her voice stern and somber.

"Do I have your word about that?"

"Yes."

"Thank you," Soriya's expression suddenly changed as well, becoming pleasant, almost angelic, allowing Victoria a glimpse into what Talon probably saw in Soriya, the second image of a two-sided coin.

Without saying more, Soriya got up from the table, reaching to pick up the strap of her shiny gold purse, which had tipped over slightly when she placed it on the table. Slinging the purse over her shoulder, she made no further attempt at pleasantries, simply slipping away as quickly as she'd earlier appeared. Victoria, in turn, was left shell-shocked by the encounter.

No longer hungry, Victoria pushed her plate out from in front of her and toward the middle of the table. She was about to get up and leave the restaurant when she noticed an object laying in front of where Soriya had just been. Victoria reached over and picked up the small paper, which appeared to be a winner's ticket receipt and which must've fallen out of her purse.

And she gambles at the dog tracks, Victoria mused to herself. *Weren't you the one, Talon, who once adopted a greyhound rescue? You can do so much better than this girl. But... that's ultimately your decision.*

Turning in her chair, Victoria looked around the crowded establishment, wondering if she could (*or should*) find Soriya and give her back the winner's receipt, which had a black and white image of a greyhound dog with the words, "Green Acres Kennel Club" as a logo and was stamped as cashed-in just a few days prior to the cruise departure. She didn't see the abrasive woman anywhere though. Victoria guessed that she'd hurried to go find Talon now that their conversation was over and the necessary message had been delivered.

Victoria had on a long-sleeve cable knit cardigan to fend off the chilly breeze in the air. The button down sweater had pockets and she slipped the receipt carefully inside one, then stood up from the table and made her way out of the restaurant. She decided it might be a good idea to go find Myrick, hoping that he'd uncovered more details as to why the ship had turned around mid-voyage. Despite her intent, though, it wasn't long before she ran into another dancer, and her thoughts were quickly redirected.

Duncan was his usually cheery and animated self as he spotted Victoria, beckoning her over with a wave of his hand.

With him was a group of four people, all of whom Victoria recognized and knew were considered the *inner circle* when it came to decision making at Duncan's events. Victoria guessed that Duncan was likely consulting with them now that the cruise had been shortened, perhaps trying to decide if there was any point in trying to hold further events and workshops.

"Hullo there," said Duncan, as Victoria walked over. "How're you doing?" He asked as he leaned in to give her a hug, his thick mustache grazing across her forehead, tickling it.

"I've been better. Disappointed that they've cut our trip short. You cancelling the rest of the Lindy events?"

"Never," Duncan replied, as much to assuage Victoria as to convince the others in his presence. "Wouldn't think of it. Aye, I promised these people a good time. They're gonna get it too."

"Good for you, Duncan," Victoria replied, and she could see that the other four from his inner circle seemed to agree as well.

"My only concern is the weather," an older woman, with silver hair and pale blue eyes spoke, her tone grave. "We're sailing right into bad weather."

"Captain woulda turned 'er around if it was anything to be worried about, Bev," Duncan quickly reasoned, calling Beverly by her nickname. "We'll be fine."

"I've already started getting the word out that the Solo Jazz Throwdown is being moved up to tonight. Everyone will enjoy that," Bev added.

"That's assuming we can get enough dancers to brave the competition in the midst of a storm." Victoria brought up a valid concern. "Given the timing of it, we'll probably be in rough waters by then."

"Nay bother, we can just enlist a few of the pros to compete," Duncan glanced over at Victoria mischievously as he spoke.

"Seriously, Duncan," Victoria replied, knowing *exactly* where he was going with this conversation. "I came on this cruise to vacation with Myrick."

"Then have the lad dance it with you," Duncan immediately threw out. "Cannot think of a better way to make the trip more memorable, ken."

"We'll see," Victoria laughed back.

"Speaking of your detective friend, where is he?" Bev asked. "I haven't seen him since the poker game. Is he out spending all his winnings in the casino?"

"No, nothing like that. He's just been busy this morning."

"Busy? Doing what?" Bev pressed again. "We're out at sea. He shouldn't have a care in the world. He should be with *you* right now."

Victoria wasn't sure how to respond. She didn't want to alarm Bev or Duncan or *anyone* else about why Myrick was off doing some investigating. As far as the passengers were aware, they were returning to San Diego due only to a minor emergency. Victoria was privy to information that the rest weren't, and she knew Myrick would be disappointed if she let anything out without him knowing first.

"If I know Evann, he's probably holed up somewhere reading a good book," Victoria lied convincingly. "I know he's been dying to read Nealis' book *One Man*."

"Well, fair enough," Bev replied. "I guess he has earned some downtime after the performance he put on last night."

"He really has."

"Since he's busy off reading, can I enlist you to help pull things together for the competition tonight?" asked Bev, taking advantage of Victoria's apparent availability.

Immediately, Victoria realized the consequences of her lie. She was stuck and couldn't even use Myrick as an excuse out of the jam.

You so owe me, Evann Myrick, Victoria thought to herself.

But of course, given how engrossed Myrick was in his investigation, putting herself to good use elsewhere wasn't the worst idea actually. At least it would keep her busy and distracted, freeing Myrick up to work his magic. And as the sun started to set in the sky... and the dark storm clouds grew closer... it signaled that they were growing closer to the port of San Diego... and, *more importantly,* that time was running out to catch a killer.

*****

Even before she'd reached Cabin 143, Shev could hear the sound of a thud echoing from just inside the room. Then another. And another. The repetition of the sound almost in perfect cadence.

As soon as she knocked on the cabin door, the peculiar sound ceased. Shev then heard the thump of swift but heavy footsteps approaching from inside. She was standing in the interior of the ship, the "I.S." on the note shorthand for Interior Stateroom. The number 143 on the door was in large black numerals.

Just below the black numerals was a drawing of a wave, which was cresting in one direction, Shev aware that this was another subtle clue on ships as to what direction to go while navigating the interior of it, given how easy it was for passengers to get confused. The direction of the cresting wave indicated that the bow of the ship was forward of room 143.

Finally, the door creaked open and a face appeared on the other side, that of the inimitable Evann Myrick.

"I assume this was sent by you," said Shev, holding up the piece of paper.

"It was indeed. Quick, come in so we can talk outside the view of cameras," Myrick replied, opening the door wider so that Shev could steal into the room.

"We found Tempest Greylock. Her body was in one of the lifeboats," Shev reported as she entered the cabin.

"I figured as much."

"They also told me not to speak with you anymore,"

"I figured that was the case as well."

"Then what do we do?"

"Sounds like it's going to be up to *you* to solve this case now."

Shev's eyebrows rose, betraying her concern, not expecting Myrick's response.

"I can't-"

"You can." Myrick cut her off mid-sentence. "But don't worry. I'll be here to help behind the scenes. Let's start with video. Did cameras record anything from that first night on the ship?"

"There's cameras out there, but only certain ones are set to record. It's all in high def and it takes up a lot of space on the hard drives. Unless a camera is automatically set to store and record footage, it doesn't."

"So which ones would've?"

"I believe all of the interior hallways do. We try to make sure all the cabins are secure in case of theft. And of course, the cameras inside most of the restaurants and clubs. I believe the pool area has cameras that automatically record as well. All of the elevators too. That's about it, at least for what might be relevant to us in the investigation."

"Can you get copies of any footage for me to look at?"

"If you can be specific, *maybe*."

"Let's start with the hallway footage, *starboard* side, from that night between the hours of 2:00 and 3:00 AM."

"You don't want anything from the port side of the ship? That's where Harriett says she heard the commotion."

"I know… but any interior hallway footage from the starboard side of the ship will likely answer my questions."

"Okay then, I'll work on that. But tell me first," Shev's eyes turned toward an object gripped tightly in Myrick's hand and which she'd just finally noticed. "What's that?"

"Oh, this?" Myrick lifted up a white ball with red-stitching all around it. It was dirty and well-worn, evidently tossed around often. "This helps me think." Myrick tossed the baseball up into the air then caught it again in his bare hand effortlessly.

"Where did you get that?" Shev was now full of questions.

"From my dad. I've had it since I was a kid."

"No, I mean what is it doing with you on the cruise ship."

"I take it with me everywhere," Myrick answered, as if that should've been the obvious response, although he could tell by the confused look on Shev's face that she'd not expected this particular answer.

"And is that what caused the thud sound earlier?"

"You mean from doing this?" Myrick tossed the ball so that it careened slightly off the wall next to him and then bounced back toward his hand. "I didn't realize you could hear that all the way out in the hallway."

"Oh, I could." Shev laughed.

Myrick appeared embarrassed, but ultimately joined in the amusement at his expense. He then decided that Shev had pried into enough of his background for now and so it was time for him to take the lead in the conversation again.

"So tell me about the body of Ms. Greylock. I take it she was found lying *on* the stretcher," he offered up his hypothesis, simultaneously tossing the baseball in the air, which did seem to help him narrow his thoughts.

"She was." Shev was impressed that Myrick had already figured out that interesting detail, and it made her more confident that she was right in trusting him to explain more. "Her body was lying face up on it. There were marks on her neck, slight bruising… but no cuts… her eyes though were blood red in color like the vessels had burst."

"Sounds like a case of strangulation to me. Any signs of a struggle?"

"No, in fact outside the trauma to her neck, she appeared oddly peaceful where she was found. Her eyes closed, her hands placed over her abdomen, her legs crossed. You could convince me she'd simply fallen asleep and not woken up, suicide by overdose or something, if not for the things I just described. Oh, and one more creepy detail. The captain asked Chief Moretti and me to get the body to the morgue as quickly and discreetly as possible. We called in a couple of others from the security detail and I assisted as well. When I was covering her up on the stretcher, her head tilted just slightly. I hadn't noticed it the first time, but she had dry blood on the side of her neck. It appeared to be a small knife incision."

Shev could see by Myrick's reaction that her explanation had him deep in thought, as if she'd revealed details he hadn't entirely expected.

"Did it look like an 'X' shape?" Myrick surprised Shev with his reply.

"Um, I believe so. It was hard to say with the dried blood. But, uh, I do think it could've been something like that."

Myrick was silent for a long moment. "This is bigger than I realized," he finally spoke, his hand rubbing the stubble on his chin, as he hadn't shaved at all since boarding the cruise liner.

"So you think this was murder, don't you?"

"Yes, the cold, calculated and premeditated type."

"That's what I was afraid of. Although the captain insists we can't rule out suicide."

"The captain has concerns *other* than just manner of death on his mind and which are likely - and unfortunately - influencing his decisions. He's got superiors to answer to, powerful ones that would frown upon any bad press attributed to events that occurred on the captain's watch. You're getting a taste of how politics can play into an investigation. It happens. It's maddening. But there's no sense in pretending it doesn't.

We'll have to work within the framework of what's been given to us. And-" Myrick paused in thought before continuing, "I don't believe this is the *first* murder."

"There's been no other reports of anyone going missing." Shev wrinkled her brow, confused.

"I know. I highly suspect, though, that our assailant *has* killed before. Ms. Greylock was positioned that way for a reason. Which brings to mind the other six victims reportedly found in the California area recently, all of whom were discovered in a posed-like manner... with markings indicative of strangulation or suffocation... and with a distinctive 'X' like marking carved into their neck."

"We're dealing with a serial killer?"

"Unfortunately, I believe so. There are too many similar facts to convince me otherwise."

"All the more reason I'm *not* the person to take the lead on this."

"Who else will, then?"

"*You!*" Shev emphasized the obvious. "This is *your* expertise."

"It is. And it's a stroke of great fortune that I happen to be here. I can be of help to you. But you said it yourself, you're not even supposed to be talking to me right now. The captain wants to keep things in-house, at least until we get back into port. I highly doubt it's going to end well if you and I walk into the wheelhouse with information that I've uncovered. He's not going to listen. Worse, he's going to orchestrate things to ensure you aren't in a position to interfere either. Better if I assist you behind the scenes at this point. You can do the heavy lifting for us. I wouldn't ask you to do so if I didn't believe you were capable of it."

This was the *last* thing Shev had expected, and she was visibly shaken by Myrick's words, even if she appreciated the trust he'd placed in her. His logic was admittedly irrefutable, though. The captain would be absolutely livid if he found out Shev was talking with Myrick. His orders had been crystal clear. She was not to talk to any passengers about the discovery of Greylock's body.

The seas were the captain's domain and his orders were unassailable. She might even be confined to her quarters for the remainder of the voyage if she was found to have disobeyed her superior. The risk was certainly not worth it. Of course, that didn't mean there was any other option either, even if Shev *wasn't* up to the task. *Myrick was grasping at straws*, in her estimation.

"You're going to have to do more than just wait for me to do the impossible and track down a killer," Shev contended, unflappable in her position.

"Oh, I will. In fact, I've already begun doing so. I've done us a favor and whittled down our potential suspects to a limited few. I just have a few questions of each of them."

"Then interview them yourself."

"I wish I had the authority to do so. That, it seems, is something only you have the power to do."

"I've never conducted a formal interview in my *entire* life," Shev replied, incredulous.

"You've never spoken to someone after a drunken fight broke out between passengers on the ship?"

"Of course, I have."

"And you were able to figure out who the aggressor was."

"Half the time it's the fault of both sides, over-stimulated egos."

"Fair enough," Myrick laughed heartily. Shev's answer also proved his point. "Well put. So you do have the instincts to sift through information and uncover the truth."

"Um, *huge* difference between a simple fist fight and a murder... a *serial* murder."

"True, but-" Myrick paused, a discerning look in his eyes, directing a stare right into Shev's, as if to emphasize just how much confidence he had in her. "You can do this. A seasoned detective can always spot someone with the same skill set. You have a lot of natural detective in you. Which is a good thing because I believe you really are the *only* hope now of catching the person responsible for this. We get back to port without having already solved the crime, passengers will scatter all around the country. And whoever is behind Tempest Greylock's death will be the first to completely disappear off the grid."

Shev wanted to protest. She still thought his confidence in her was entirely misplaced. On the other hand, Shev had a strong sense of justice. Myrick's theory of what would happen if they didn't do something now was spot on. That, Shev decided, was just enough to outweigh her concerns.

"Okay, I'm in," she finally offered back. "What do you want from me?"

"That's the spirit," Myrick smiled widely, like a proud father. "For starters," Myrick pushed a piece of paper over to Shev. She then glanced down at it to see a list of names and a brief set of questions next to each. "I'd like you to talk to these four. Ask *whatever* you deem necessary, but make sure to get answers to what I've written below as well. I think once you do, we'll be relatively certain who the murderer is."

"I would," Shev replied, wanting to help but wisely aware of the parameters within which she worked, "But the minute my supervisor - Moretti - finds out I'm rounding up passengers to be interviewed, he's going to put an end to it."

"I figured as much. Fortunately, I have a friend who I think can help. A very boisterous - but intensely likable - Scottish fellow with a great deal of sway. I think I can convince him to help. Meet me down at the poker room, *Lucky Seven*, in exactly one hour. I should have everything arranged for you by then."

"And in the meantime?"

"Start pulling those surveillance videos. Once you have that downloaded, I'll do my part working through the footage while you simultaneously elicit crucial information from our suspects in the interviews," Myrick winked.

"And what if Moretti asks what I'm doing?"

"That's easy enough," Myrick smiled. "You haven't found my wallet yet have you? It's *very* valuable to me. I'd like to know who stole it. I can be quite a headache over something like this if not taken seriously. The squeaky wheel *always* gets the grease. Moretti has enough to manage without having someone like me stirring up problems."

Shev smiled back. Myrick was a quick thinker, an attribute in him that she was growing to appreciate more and more each time she chose to confide in him. Myrick's unassailable confidence in her also meant volumes, even if she had insisted otherwise. Something about the way he spoke had a powerful impact, instilling a sudden belief in herself.

Shev had *no* business trying to solve a homicide. Still, if Myrick was convinced she could, then maybe - *just maybe* - she could pull off a miracle. Or more possibly, die trying.

CHAPTER SIXTEEN
<u>Never</u> Attempt Aerials Before You're Ready

For the next part of his plan, Myrick was going to need to bring in the big guns, and so he wisely tracked down Victoria, explaining what had happened and what his idea was. Victoria was all too willing to help, especially after hearing who Myrick wanted to track down next.

"So are we going to find him or not?" Victoria asked, a look of self-satisfaction in her eyes, aware that her help was *definitely* needed at the moment.

"Yes, any thoughts on where he might be?"

"Last I saw Duncan, he was heading to the bar with friends. I'm pretty sure he'll still be there. Duncan can spend an entire day drinking and telling stories."

"I knew I liked the guy. He's quite a character."

"And an even better friend. He'll want to help. He just needs a little nudge in the right direction."

"Well then, let's go talk to the man."

Following Victoria, she led Myrick to a small bar, which was located on the West side of the ship and which provided a perfect view of the setting sun. Even before entering it though,

Myrick could hear the sounds of loud talking and laughter. One voice in particular stood out, the distinctive sound of a Scotsman recanting tales from his past adventures.

There was a huge smile on Duncan's face as he spotted Victoria walking over to him, and Myrick knew instantly how wise he'd been to enlist her to help getting Duncan on board with his idea. The man was surrounded by a good dozen other faces at a large table, all of whom seemed to be enamored with his stories. Even the bartender was listening out one ear, which was good as it kept him close by in case Duncan needed his glass of Scotch topped off.

"What would the two of you like to drink? Tis on me," said Duncan, once again proving he was a gracious host.

"I'll take a vodka tonic," Victoria smiled, grateful.

"Aye, and you?" Duncan turned to Myrick.

"Well, if I'll be drinking with a Scotsman... then I think any single malt from Bruichladdich would do."

"Braw, tis a fine choice indeed."

"Can't go wrong with a whisky from that distillery."

Myrick's response had Duncan's attention, as he was immediately impressed with both Myrick's knowledge and refined palate.

"A fan of Jim McEwan, are you?"

"I am. He's a good man."

"Makes a might fine whisky. 'Ere," Duncan pushed a freshly poured drink over to Myrick, "try this."

In turn, Myrick lifted the crystal glass to his nose, taking a sniff to savor the aroma, which had a strong peaty smell to it. He then placed the glass to his lips, allowing the liquor to sit on his tongue for a brief second before eventually downing it.

"Goes down smooth, ken."

"It does."

"Octomore-" Duncan began explaining.

"6.1 is my guess," Myrick completed his sentence.

Duncan sat back in his stool, arms crossed, chest puffed out, a content expression on his face. "Well, I'm not gonna lie, detective. You continue to impress me. Glad I've gotten to know you."

"The feeling is mutual. Thanks for the drink," replied Myrick. "I may need an even bigger favor from you though," he added, getting quickly to the point of why they were there.

"We," Victoria interjected for emphasis. "*We* need to ask an important favor of you."

"Alright then, let's hear it," Duncan's eyes blinked repeatedly, as he was fascinated by the sudden change in subject.

"We need you to reserve us the room *Lucky Seven* again," Myrick began.

"Well, that's simple enough," said Duncan.

"And-" Myrick started to explain, only to be cut off by Victoria.

"*And* we need you to make sure four specific members of our group are there to be interviewed by ship security," said Victoria, knowing that this cryptic request would be received better coming from her.

Now they really had Duncan's attention. The bartender had just slid over a new glass of scotch, and so Duncan took a swig from it, sizing up both the vague request and the two people asking him to assist.

There was a quiet pause before Duncan finished his sip and then decided to speak again. "What four guests?"

"Harriett Cribbs... Paul Granger... Soriya Danes," Myrick began listing the names.

"You would've picked a name there that I don't know - Soriya Danes. I have a braw memory for things, but that name doesn't ring a bell."

"Well, that's because she wasn't *with* our group originally. She's sort of tagged along thanks to Talon."

"Which brings me to my fourth name - Talon Andilet," said Myrick.

Duncan's bushy eyebrows narrowed as Talon's name was spoken, surprised and concerned that one of his pros was needed to be interviewed by security.

"If you ask Talon, perhaps he'll ensure Soriya comes with him," Myrick continued.

"Well," Duncan leaned forward, both of his hands massaging the entirety of his face, clearly deep in thought. "Haven't ever actually been asked to do such a favor before. But, if it's Victoria asking," Duncan glanced over to see that Victoria was nodding that it indeed was. "I'll do what I can."

"Thank you," Myrick replied.

"Yes, thank you," Victoria emphasized, Duncan still looking at her to make clear that this favor was more for her than anyone, which Victoria instantly understood and appreciated.

"Will either of you be there also?" Duncan suddenly had a few questions of his own.

"No," Myrick replied. "Just a security guard. Her name is Batsheva Rotem. Sharp girl. She'll be the one conducting the interview."

Duncan shrugged his shoulders, as if surrendering to the madness of the request, trusting that Victoria and Myrick knew what they were doing.

"Eh," Duncan finally spoke, allowing his accent to flow as he raised his glass, "Am trusting you on this one," he directed over to Myrick. "Hoping you're a wee bit wiser than the rest of us."

"We're a' Jack Tomson's bairns," Myrick replied a Scottish phrase to indicate his complete agreement, tapping the side of Duncan's glass, a look of gratitude on his face.

Duncan simply shook his head and chuckled to himself, amused by Myrick's botched Scottish accent. He then went immediately to work, making arrangements for the interviews to be conducted. All the while, dark skies were brewing in the distance.

*****

"I can't discuss this with you now," Paul exclaimed, pausing for a minute at the doorway of the cabin, "We've got bigger problems on our hands. They want me upstairs for some reason," he continued with frustration in his voice, closing the door behind him as he walked out into the empty hallway.

"Don't do this to us again-" a voice echoed back, but Paul dismissed it; the conversation over as the door the cabin clicked shut.

The phone call had been unexpected, coming from the director of the event, Duncan Campbell. Paul didn't know Duncan very well, only having come to meet him for the first time on the cruise. But he did seem to be an amiable fellow, and more importantly this was Duncan's event, so Paul thought it judicious to follow through with the odd request.

The timing wasn't great either. Paul had been in the midst of a frustrating, unnecessary argument. One that wasn't going to result in resolution anytime soon either. *She* wasn't going to stop pestering him, insisting that he shouldn't have even come on the cruise to begin with. Paul was a stubborn one though, oftentimes digging his feet in during an argument, and *his* opinion was that she should stay back and allow him to have a little fun also.

"Thank you for coming on such short notice," Duncan was there to greet Paul as he reached the entrance to the *Lucky Seven* ballroom. "I'm sorry to have pulled you away from your affairs."

"No worries," Paul replied. "What's up?"

"I'd like to introduce you to Ms. Rotem here," Duncan turned to a uniformed member of the crew standing just to the side of him. "She's with the ship's security. She has a few questions about an incident that happened the other night.

If Paul was caught off guard by the statement, he showed no signs of it, simply shrugging his shoulders, then pleasantly turning his attention to Shev before speaking, "Sure, what would you like to know?"

"I'm hoping you can be of assistance to me in an investigation. Nothing to be alarmed over," Shev then extended a hand out in greeting. "I'm Batsheva by the way. Most people just call me Shev."

Paul was immediately surprised by the security guard's informality. She appeared young, *maybe mid-20s?* Her handshake lacked confidence, and Paul guessed that the matter must not be *too* significant if this was the security guard the ship had sent to address the situation.

"Let me guess, someone felt cheated at last night's poker game. If so," Paul laughed. "I promise, it wasn't me. I'm more victim than suspect... especially after what that Myrick guy did to me."

"No, that's um-" Shev stopped. "There's something else actually. But I'd prefer not to talk out in the hallway. Could we please discuss this inside." Shev pointed to a table just on the other side of the open doorway.

"I'll keep reaching out to the others and let you know if anyone else shows up," Duncan offered, stepping aside so that Shev and Paul could proceed into the room alone.

"There's others, huh?" Paul asked.

"Yes, hoping maybe someone can help us with an incident that took place after the dance social the other night... the one at the dueling piano bar. I should've followed up on things more quickly. Unfortunately, I'm behind the eight ball and playing catch up."

"Oh, okay, well *again*, whatever I can do to help," Paul agreed, sitting down at the table.

Shev then took a seat across from him, her hands clasped in front of her, fidgeting her fingers, elbows on the table as she leaned forward. Meanwhile, Paul tried hard not to laugh at her amateur-ish mannerisms.

"You mind if I record this conversation?" Shev asked, pulling out her phone and selecting an app that had audio recording ability.

"That's fine," Paul replied, staring down at her phone, confused as to why this was necessary.

"Thanks, I'm new to this and it helps jog my memory later to be able to refer to the recording. So, for starters," Shev began, pushing the circular record button on the app, "My understanding is that you were there with someone... a woman named Harriett Cribbs." Shev was now tapping her index finger on the table in rhythmic fashion, as if that was helping her get into the flow of questioning. "Can you tell me about her?"

"Well, first of all I wasn't *with* her that night. In fact, I didn't even know her name until she told me it at the end of the evening. We just did some dancing together. We both didn't know many people at the event, we sort of had that in common, so we got along quickly. But I wasn't with her. She's actually kind of a strange girl if you want my honest opinion. Besides, I have a significant other. She wouldn't take too kindly to me flirting with anyone else."

"Oh, you have a girlfriend. Is she here on the cruise?"

"Well, no. But I'm not the type to do anything behind her back. She'd probably find out anyway," he laughed. "But to, um, answer your question, she didn't come on the cruise with me."

"I saw on the crew manifest that you have a single-occupancy room."

"Yes, that's right. Small too, even for one person. I guess that's what I get for being cheap originally. I tried to upgrade last minute, but they said that wasn't an option. I struggle a little with claustrophobia. *Not* fun. There's not even a porthole window."

"There aren't any in the crew quarters either," Shev volunteered, hoping to establish some commonality between them. "You get used to it... *eventually.*"

"Doesn't seem like I'm going to have much time to do that. My understanding is that we'll be back in port by tomorrow morning."

"Yes, that's the hope."

Shev could see that Paul seemed visibly affected by her response, as if he'd still not come to complete grips with the change in plans. After a moment to process things, Paul's expression slowly changed, becoming serious, and he finally asked, almost intuitively, "You want to get to the heart of why you've brought me here? I'm sure it wasn't just to ask me about other passengers. And I'm starting to get the feeling that you think I've done something wrong, myself."

"I'm sorry, that's not the impression I was wanting to convey at all. If anything, I'm more trying to piece together some of the missing details from that night. Ms. Cribbs, you've probably guessed, has provided her account of things. She mentioned that I should talk to you... and a woman by the name of Soriya as well."

"I have no idea who that is."

"Maybe you know the gentleman she was with - Talon Andilet."

"Yes," Paul smiled. "*Him*, I've met. But only in passing. Seemed like a preoccupied guy if you asked me."

Shev paused to scribble a few initial thoughts, as Myrick had suggested she jot down any gut feelings she had in the moment, a good detective knowing that sometimes the demeanor of a witnesses was just as important - *maybe more so* - than what they said.

Meanwhile, on that same piece of paper, Myrick had written down a few questions of his own and so Shev made sure to scan over and ask those as well. He wanted to know if Paul had visited the aft of the ship after leaving *The Phoenix & Dragon* that night. Myrick also strangely wanted to know specific details of the dance with Harriett - what music was playing, if anyone had attempted to interrupt Paul's dance with her, who was lead versus follow, etcetera.

Finally, finishing her interview with Paul, Shev felt as though it'd gone quite well. Paul had been entirely straight forward throughout it, answering all her questions candidly, even if at times some of his comments appeared less than helpful in solving the actual murder.

Shev was able to elicit the fact that someone had indeed interrupted Paul's dance with Harriett, although he couldn't remember who exactly it was. He did though admit to Shev that he'd been drinking heavily that night and his intoxicated state likely accounted for the gap in his recollection of events. Otherwise, he'd done a thorough job recounting the evening, allowing Shev to complete the interview in approximately twenty minutes, which was perfect as there was a knock on the door as soon as Shev got an answer to her last question.

"Sorry, to interrupt," Duncan poked his head in the room. "Ms. Cribbs is here."

"Oh perfect," Shev replied. She then stood to shake Paul's hand, and he did the same, notably not gripping too tight, almost like a dancer who was taking another dancer's hand and attempting to feel for a connection.

As Harriett entered the room, Paul was turning to go. Their eyes met, and while Shev could no longer see Paul's expression, as he was facing away from her, Harriett's seemed distrusting, as if she wasn't sure what to make of the conversation Paul had just had with a member of security.

By the time Paul had left the room, Harriett was seated across from Shev and the next round of questioning could begin. Unlike Paul though, it was quickly clear how reserved Harriett was. She seemed to sense that there was something more serious going on, and she remained guarded in her answers throughout the interview, despite Shev's insistence that it was simply a routine matter.

Interestingly, many of the questions Myrick wanted asked of Harriett revolved around how she'd met Paul and whether or not the two of them had developed feelings for each other. Harriett seemed to laugh the last part off, insisting that they weren't even really friends, just two people that enjoyed dancing with each other.

In fact, Harriett *volunteered* that she didn't actually know much about Paul, and that he'd asked even less about her. They liked to dance together, that was the extent of it. A funny nuance of dance, where it wasn't uncommon to sometimes form a bond with someone that you knew very little about but developed a quick connection with on the dance floor.

There was, however, one additional question that Myrick had written down and underlined to emphasis that he wanted to make sure Shev asked. It was a curious one, and Shev noted to herself that she wanted to follow up later with Myrick as to why he'd even insisted upon it, as Shev could've easily been the one to answer it herself. Still, she posed it dutifully to Harriett, asking Harriett if her room was located on the port or starboard side of the ship, with Harriett replying "port."

"I guess my last question is," Shev decided to bring things to a close, deviating off script on a curious whim to finish the interview off, "You seem really observant... Can you tell me anything about Soriya Danes? She's coming to meet with me next and she's something of an enigma as far as I can tell."

"Is that the tall brunette who stayed dancing at the piano bar with us till closing time that night?"

"I believe so. What can you tell me about her?"

"Not much. I'd never seen her before this weekend. It's not like I actually know her. But if you're asking for my *opinion*, then I'll tell you she gives off a bad vibe. I'm a good read of people and I'm pretty sure she's just looking for someone to leech off. And if I'm right about that, then she's got her nails dug into one of the pros already."

"My understanding is that she's spending most of her time on the cruise with a guy name Talon Andilet."

"Yes, that'd be the one. She's totally got him wrapped around her finger already. Doesn't seem like the brightest bulb."

"He's coming in to meet with me also."

"Then he'd be the one to tell you about her. It'll be through rose colored glasses of course. Hopefully you're a good study of people and can read between the lines. If so, I'm sure you'll come to the same conclusion about the woman as I have."

"Appreciate the heads up," said Shev, having asked the last of her questions.

With that, she smiled and let Harriett know that she was free to leave, which Harriett took advantage of and quickly did.

Duncan poked his head back in the room again, letting Shev know that the other two she'd requested to interview - Soriya Danes and Talon Andilet - hadn't arrived yet. He then promised to put out an APB for them, which Shev let him know that she appreciated.

Sitting back down at the table alone, Shev began thumbing through the notes she'd taken. And then she began to wonder if there might be someone *else* responsible for the murders and that they were overlooking. She even considered, given the answers so far, if Myrick hadn't known that and was only trying to eliminate those suspects he knew couldn't have committed the crime. Shev wrote down one final note as a reminder to ask Myrick about that very real possibility.

CHAPTER SEVENTEEN
When Following, Don't Anticipate The Next Move

The waves hammered against the bow of the ship, increasing with intensity as they headed toward the inclement weather. Captain Salazar had expected the seas to get increasingly turbulent, but the storm was proving to be even more formidable than he'd expected.

"Should we chart a course due West," the first navigation officer asked, "Try to deviate around the storm?"

"No, that'd add a good half day to our voyage. We can't afford a lengthy delay," Salazar replied, steadfast. He had a dead body on the ship and while the rest of the crew didn't know the extent of the emergency, Salazar *did* and wanted to get to port as quickly as possible.

He'd already radioed the situation in to his superiors in San Diego, who'd instructed him that a team would be waiting to extract the body as soon as he docked at port. Salazar, in turn, had promised that all necessary precautions would be taken not to alarm any customers in the interim. If Tempest's death truly was a suicide, the situation could be dealt with in-house. If not, authorities could proceed with due diligence at that point.

The last thing management wanted, however, was a rush to judgment. And the junior captain in the fleet, whose career seemed to be on the rise, didn't need to create that kind of bad press for the higher-ups in the organization, particularly those in the revenue-earning department, which had particular influence and autonomy in decision making.

"Captain, you summoned me?" Moretti asked as he entered the navigation room of the huge cruise liner. He rarely got up to the wheelhouse, his responsibilities taking place mostly below deck. But when he did come up to the bridge, he couldn't help but marvel at how vast the ocean looked from this vantage point.

Unlike previous occasions, however, where he'd been fortunate to do so on crystal clear days, this time was markedly different. There was a dark storm on the horizon, completely concealing the moon and the stars above. And he could see that the ocean swells ahead were immense and becoming increasingly foreboding.

"Oh good," replied Salazar, "I appreciate your prompt response, Moretti. As you can see we've hit a patch of bad weather."

"It does appear so, Captain."

"I know passengers won't be happy, but I plan on cancelling *all* outdoor activities set for tonight. Pool is closed early as well. I've already instructed the crew to get the word out. I'd like you to please do me a favor and have your team conduct a *thorough* security check of all points to ensure there's no one out and about against orders."

"Of course. I'll get right on it."

Moretti turned to leave only to be stopped in his tracks by the captain's next words.

"I trust you made sure that Rotem doesn't stir up any more trouble, correct?" The captain's voice had a hint of warning to it.

"Yes sir. Yes, I *did*. I've placed her on monitor duty. Well, at least until a passenger issue arose. Seems she'd been requested earlier today to follow up on a theft. Must've been so preoccupied with the situation with locating Greylock that she'd forgotten to properly investigate the matter. We received an irate note from the passenger requesting an update. Not like Shev at all to be derelict in her duties. She's gone to handle that, but I'd imagine she's back by now. She's great at keeping the passengers happy. She's an asset in that regard. They like how diligent she is. I'm sure she's handled it appropriately."

"What passenger?" Salazar asked.

"Don't remember actually. I believe she did give me a room number though… an interior stateroom… I want to say 143 was the number. Yes, Cabin 143."

The captain immediately turned and snapped his fingers at the first mate, pointing to a thick logbook nearby. The first mate quickly fetched it and handed it to the captain, who instantly began thumbing through it.

"Could I ask what you're looking for, sir?" Moretti pressed.

"I want to know who is listed as the occupant of that particular room on the manifest."

There was a moment of dead air as the captain continued his search through the ledger, an eerie stillness present, which was only broken by the howling of the wind as it traversed the bow of the vessel.

"Ah, just as I suspected. You told me that fellow... the former detective... his name was Myrick, right?"

"I believe so."

The captain spun the book around so that Moretti could see it, his finger pressed up next to the recording as to "Cabin 143" and the particular occupant's name.

"Oh no," Moretti immediately understood his mistake. "She's gone to talk to him, hasn't she?"

"You tell me."

Moretti didn't answer back. He didn't need to, understanding all too well the new problems Shev's disobedience had caused. *She was going to lose her job over this.* Moretti didn't relish the thought of having to be the one to fire her, although that was the least of his concerns at the moment, wondering if his *own* job might be on the line, the captain's original orders had been directed for him to carry out. Moretti had clearly failed in that regard.

"Find her now," Salazar demanded.

"I apol-" Moretti attempted, only to be immediately cut off.

"I said *find* her. You're dismissed, Chief Moretti."

"Yes sir," Moretti dutifully replied, quickly turning to leave, ambling down a flight of steps faster than his aged body had moved in some time.

Now standing outside, on the exterior deck of the ship, and out of the captain's sight, Moretti allowed his own frustration to take over, pounding his fist against a railing. He then glanced over the side, able to see many of the decks below him. It was a good vantage point to search for his disobedient employee, but Shev was nowhere to be seen.

Instead, Moretti caught sight of crew members wrangling up the last of the passengers, sending them toward the interior of the ship. It was well-timed too, as the first rain bands were starting to hit, pelting against Moretti's face and body, like tiny pin-prick darts.

He paused for reflection momentarily, thoroughly humiliated and ruminating on where Shev might be found. It was then that Moretti noticed a lone figure dart through the darkness on a deck far below. From this height, he couldn't make out much of the person - not even if it was a man or a woman - but it clearly *wasn't* a member of the crew, as the clothing was very casual, the attire a passenger would wear. Unlike the other customers who were scurrying toward the interior of the ship, this particular person was going the opposite direction, and unspotted by the crew.

Moretti briefly considered proceeding down to that level to find out who the person was, but then - thinking wisely - decided he first needed to take care of the specific order of the captain, finding Shev and dealing with her *shocking* insubordination. Meanwhile, he was certain the crew would do a thorough job clearing the deck, trusting that they would ultimately locate any stragglers and usher them safely inside the ship's interior.

*****

Shev was just finishing up the last of her interview with Talon, who'd appeared for the interview a good twenty minutes late. Despite his tardiness, however, she was still grateful that she'd gotten to speak with him, as Talon had provided the most compelling answers of anyone yet. Nearing the end of her questioning, Duncan suddenly poked his head in the room yet again, his voice noticeably distressed.

"Captain's given a heads up... we're heading toward a wee bit gale, ken. It's a might dreich out there already. Turning into a night for snuggling under the covers," Duncan laughed. "Gonna go check on my volunteers. You may want to wrap up things in here also," Duncan explained.

"Sure," Shev replied, not surprised to hear the news. She'd seen the radar screens earlier, including the foreboding red bands that they were sailing directly toward. Even without the aid of technology, she'd been at sea long enough to recognize the long, wispy shape of the clouds in the sky, the changing direction of the winds which were now blowing due north, the stronger scents prevalent in the air and what that all meant - they were approaching unsettled waters. "We're actually done here anyway."

"Aye, that's good," Duncan ducked back out of the room, his hands more animated than ever.

"You're telling me you *definitely* haven't seen her since breakfast," Shev turned to Talon one last time, making sure he wasn't holding back anything.

"She said something came up... didn't offer any details... and I haven't seen her for a good 2-3 hours."

"Okay, well if you do run into Ms. Danes again, please tell her that I *need* to speak to her as soon as possible."

"You gonna tell me what this is all about?"

"Unfortunately that's not something I can do at this point. But there's no cause for you to be concerned."

"I'm sorry, but I don't buy that. You've asked me some personal questions, most of them about this girl I've just met. Obviously she must be in some sort of trouble. I think you owe it to me to explain what's going on."

"I honestly can't yet," Shev replied, concerned about how much hot water she was already in for continuing to investigate Greylock's death. "Although, I can say that it's *always* wise to be aware of the company you keep."

"This conversation just gets weirder by the moment. But okay," Talon started to get up from the table, but then paused momentarily. "By the way, tell *Myrick* that I said hello," he added, artfully.

"Huh?"

"Come on, I know some of these questions came from him. They are way too personal. Only he - and Victoria - would know to ask me those things about Soriya. And I doubt Victoria would stab me in the back like that… there's only one person on this cruise that I think might stoop that low."

Shev didn't respond, caught off guard by how quickly Talon had seen through her. She'd evidently underestimated him. She then watched as he smirked and stood up, signaling that he was done with their conversation, not even waiting for a reply from her.

As he walked out, Shev remarked to herself just how bizarre it was that someone capable of being so discerning could also be easily manipulated by a cunning woman at the same time. It then dawned on her that perhaps she - *and maybe even Myrick* - had misread things.

Perhaps, Shev considered, *it's actually Talon putting on an act and playing us all for fools. If so, he's doing so masterfully.*

Turning off the recorder on her cellphone and then packing up a few items, Shev left the room as well. She could see that Duncan was already gone, likely hurrying to assist his volunteers in preparing for the storm. She'd expected Talon to have disappeared as well, perhaps to go find Soriya and confide in her about the interview.

Instead, a quick glance around the casino and she spotted Talon plopped down at a slot machine, inserting a solitary coin in the slot and pulling the lever, as if he didn't have a care in the world. It was certainly possible that this was simply Talon's way to de-stress. It was also equally possible, in Shev's estimation, that he harbored a soulless quality to him, unaffected by the concerns of the people around him. *Maybe even as a result of a painful event from his past - and which Shev wasn't aware of - that was creating a void and a buried hate in his heart.*

Talon's odd behavior only made Shev more disappointed that she'd not been able to speak to Soriya. It seemed that she'd learned a great deal from the other three interviews, and she could see why Myrick felt they were necessary. Still, the motives of Soriya (and her current whereabouts) remained a mystery and that gnawed at Shev. And much like Myrick had predicted, it was bringing out the inherent detective in Shev, instilling in her a need to develop answers.

Standing in the hallway, Shev pulled out her phone one more time, checking to make sure she'd secured a connection through the ship's wifi. She could see that the signal was strong inside the casino area and so she clicked on an audio file entitled

T_Andilet.wav, selected Myrick's number as the recipient and then typed in a quick text to go with it, which read simply:

```
"Interview 3 of 4. Still looking for Soriya
Danes. Will send that as soon as I locate &
talk to her. Wish me luck."
```

After hastily drafting the message, Shev pressed send and then waited for confirmation that the text had been "delivered".

"Not where I was hoping to find you," a gruff voice spoke, catching Shev by complete surprise. Startled, she fumbled with the phone in her hand, slipping it quickly into her pocket as she looked up to see Moretti, an angry expression on his face.

"I'm sorry, Chief. I've just been conducting follow up on the theft of a passenger's wallet and-"

"*Don't* lie to me," Moretti cut her off, more upset than ever. "You're in enough trouble as is. Captain told you not to talk to that Myrick fellow. Unfortunately, you've already disobeyed that order. To what extent, I don't know."

"I had no choice. There's a murderer on the ship."

"Quiet," Moretti immediately spit back, wagging a bony index finger to silence her. "This is not the place to talk about things like that." He glanced around nervously to see if any passengers had been in earshot. Fortunately, none seemed to have heard or noticed Shev's imprudently voiced concerns. "Come with me," he demanded with a wave of his hand, "*Now!*"

Shev had never actually seen the old man angry. She was startled, a deer in headlights, not sure what else to say or do. Wisely eschewing a scene, she followed as Moretti led her down to the artery of the ship, as it was the private corridor traveled by crew to take care of many of the behind-the-scenes needs of the vessel.

As they continued on, Moretti not uttering a single word regarding where Shev was being taken, they passed completely by the security office, Moretti making no effort to enter it. Shev quickly became alarmed, realizing there were only two other rooms up ahead - the morgue... and the brig.

Seldom used, the ship did have a small jail. There were only two cells in it. Frightened, it suddenly dawned on Shev that she was going to be securely detained, the situation far more serious than she'd originally understood.

"You're not going to place me in a cell, are you, Chief?" Shev broke the silence, her voice cracking.

"I'm sorry, Captain's orders. Failure to abide by a direct order is insubordination. He's furious and wants you to remain here for the duration of the cruise. I'll do my *best* to smooth things over in the meantime."

Moretti broke out a key card and then scanned it on the outside of a steel-framed door, which then opened up to a small detention area. On one side of the room were two heavily-barred cells. On the other was a desk, chair and cot-sized bed, which was set up for a security guard to oversee prisoners. Moretti led Shev over to the observation area and indicated for her to take a seat on the cot.

"This will be your quarters until we reach port. Remain in here until I come to get you."

Shev was relieved that she wasn't being placed in an actual cell, but that didn't completely assuage the nauseating pit in her stomach, as she knew things had grown serious and she was in more trouble than she'd realized initially.

"I had to do something. I couldn't just turn a blind eye to the safety of the passengers. You have to believe me," Shev finally spoke, her words broken (*much like her heart*), aware that she'd done irreparable harm to her direct supervisor's trust in her.

"I don't know *what* to think. We'll talk more about this later. I'm going to go offer my apologies to the captain. I have a lot of work smoothing things over ahead of me. Do *not* leave this area under any circumstance, you understand?"

"Yes, sir."

Moretti watched as Shev took a seat on the edge of the single bed, her body slumped over, her face buried in her hands, hiding the extreme shame she felt. He then reached out his hand as he spoke, open palm facing upward, "I'll need any security cards you have-"

Looking up, her eyes sunken, Shev reached inside her pocket and turned over the universal access card she'd been issued. "That's all I have on me," she said.

"And your phone," Moretti continued, hand still extended out.

Shev hesitantly turned over the cellphone, Moretti seizing it and placing it in the interior pocket of his jacket. Without saying another word, Moretti turned and walked out of the room, his hard soled shoes hammering the solid floor of the brig's holding area until the plodding sound eventually faded away into the distance.

The last thing Shev heard was a distinct *click*, which she understood was the lock being secured. She was now a prisoner on her own ship, destined to remain confined until they'd reached shore again and corporate management could deal with the situation, doling out a punishment commensurate with the level of her gross insubordination.

CHAPTER EIGHTEEN
Step With The Balls (<u>not</u> heels) of Your Feet

After each statement was taken, Shev had forwarded the audio file to Myrick for his review. He'd already listened to the interviews of both Paul and Harriett when a notification text popped up that Shev had sent him Talon's interview as well. Myrick couldn't help but be particularly curious as to what Talon would tell them, his relationship with Soriya something of an enigma, and also one that came with serious risk. Since Shev hadn't located Soriya yet, Myrick figured he might have to be the one to do so.

Before heading out, he listened to the entirety of what Talon had to say. Most of it was predictable, including the auspicious circumstances of meeting Soriya. She was clearly using him. That much was obvious.

Talon though didn't have much of an explanation for what he'd been doing between the hours of 2:30 AM when he left the company of Soriya and dawn that same morning when Myrick and Victoria encountered him at the pool deck. Talon's explanation was that he'd simply found a lounge chair to rest in, lost in thought until the buzz of the alcohol finally wore off. It wasn't until the sun rose that he decided to head inside, running into Myrick and Victoria at that point.

Paul and Harriett's interviews were more revealing, and included far more conceivable explanations of their whereabouts after leaving the dueling piano bar that evening. Harriett reiterated the story about how she'd gone to the serenity deck, eventually hearing the screams. Most of the information she provided matched up with what she'd provided earlier.

She did, however, try to wriggle out of one concerning detail. Shev mentioned that they'd found something *of concern* on board one of the mega lifeboats, although she purposefully didn't go into any details about what exactly it was. In turn, Harriett suddenly disclosed - for the first time so far - that the larger lifeboats were nearby when she'd heard the commotion that night.

Myrick picked up on a change in Shev's tone at this point in the recording, as if she'd realized how quick Harriett was to twist her story to fit the facts. And in an apparent attempt to get to the truth, Shev next asked why Harriett hadn't revealed such an important detail before. Harriett's reply, which Myrick noted *sounded* sincere, was to insist that she had done so - or at least *meant* to anyway.

Shev continued to press Harriett, clearly not convinced of her innocence, questioning as to whether anyone could confirm her version of events. Harriett replied that she hadn't run into anyone between the timeframe of overhearing the commotion and reporting it to security. As such, Shev - and Myrick - only had Harriett's word to go by.

Next Paul provided some context on where he and Harriett had gone after the dueling piano bar, volunteering that he'd gone straight back to his room, thinking Harriett had done the same. When Shev explained that Harriett had gone to the serenity deck, Paul seemed instantly surprised. He did, however, admit that it might be possible given the two had parted ways before returning to their rooms.

The simplest way to figure out who was telling the truth would be to watch the surveillance tapes from that night. The exterior of the ship hadn't been saved to recording, but all of the interior hallway footage had. Shev, meanwhile, had sent Myrick those files to review, as he'd earlier requested.

He'd decided to start by queuing up the file entitled *P&D.mpeg* and then scrolling back to the timestamp around which he knew the dueling piano bar had closed up for that evening. Quickly, he spotted himself and Victoria on it, noting that he'd put on a few pounds and it *might* be wise to avoid the all you can eat dining for the duration of the trip. He also watched as his most likely suspect in the case left the bar, literally walking right past where he and Victoria had been sitting.

Next up, Myrick turned his attention to a file entitled *HallwayCams301-349.mpeg*. On this footage, he eventually spotted Paul walking down a corridor with odd-numbered rooms along the starboard side of the ship, passing by Stateroom 329 and then placing his key up to a door marked 331, confirming that Paul *had* gone back to his room after the social that night. Myrick zoomed in on the footage of Paul, hoping to study his facial expressions, knowing that sometimes those were the best clues about a suspect. Paul's demeanor, however, appeared quite calm, not exhibiting any outward signs of distress, such as having been in an altercation.

The high def footage was so clear Myrick could even see the eyes of the sea creatures stitched into the carpeted floor beneath Paul's feet. With each step he took, he seemed to be going in the same direction of the fish and other ocean life. Paul, it seemed, *had garnered an aquatic escort to his room*, Myrick chuckled to himself. In fact, even the wave artwork beneath the number 331 on Paul's door was pointing forward of the direction he'd just come from, as if nature was leading him to his particular cabin.

Shortly thereafter that, Myrick viewed video that made it seem as though Talon's story added up as well, footage marked *HallwayCams351-399.mpeg* catching him walking Soriya to her room, Cabin 365, although there was clearly an awkward, almost comedic, moment caught on film as he attempted to follow her into the room and she rebuffed him. It was a detail that Talon had *conveniently* left out of his story and Myrick could see why. And Myrick even found himself feeling a tinge of sympathy for Talon in that moment, although it only lasted for a brief second.

From the signs on the wall, Myrick noted that Soriya had an exterior stateroom. He also remembered that those rooms each had balconies, as he'd wanted one himself, although Victoria explained that the only rooms with the incredibly discounted dancer-rate were interior cabins. Still, Myrick was kicking himself for not splurging on a room with a better view, especially since he'd not had an opportunity to even step out onto one of the balconies. It also made him wonder if it was possible to hop from one balcony to another; which would be admittedly risky but perhaps still manageable if someone was desperate to pull it off undetected.

Meanwhile, Harriett didn't show up on the interior hallway footage or any of the other video files that Shev had provided and which would've recorded events around that time frame. That fact certainly didn't disprove her story, but it did confound Myrick's efforts that he couldn't rely on surveillance video to check Harriett's version of events, unlike he'd been able to do with the other three potential suspects.

While still lost in deep contemplation, and staring at a paused frame of Talon just passing by Stateroom 359 on his way back to the elevators, Myrick was startled by the sound of knocking. He quickly minimized the video footage, worried about who might be outside his cabin door. Once certain it was no longer visible, he went to go answer the knock. Fortunately, as soon as he did, he spotted the smiling face of Victoria on the other side.

"It's nearly 6:30," said Victoria, glancing down at her watch, hopeful that her words might coax Myrick out of his room. "This is our last night out on the ocean. Do you want to have dinner with me? Maybe I could even be a good person to bounce theories off. It worked once before, you know."

Myrick remembered back to his first real conversation with Victoria, which had taken place at a West Coast Swing event nearly a year earlier. It was then, sitting at a cozy hotel bar, that he'd realized how discerning she could be. And interestingly, that conversation *did* end up being crucial to the case, revealing important clues to solving the West Coast Swing murders. Maybe Victoria's take on things would prove helpful yet again. It didn't hurt, of course, that Myrick preferred to be in her company, and so he was more than willing to give that suggestion a chance.

"Dinner's on me tonight," replied Myrick, grabbing his coat and cap from off a nearby shelf.

"Um, *all* the meals on the ship are free," Victoria giggled back.

"In that case, order *anything* your heart desires."

"I love when you spoil me like that," Victoria smiled seductively.

"Of course." Myrick winked.

"So anything in particular you wanted to run by me before we put all that aside and just enjoy being together for this last night on the cruise?"

"Good question. Did you find it as odd as I did that Duncan didn't already know who Soriya was, especially given she was at the poker game? Makes me wonder if that's really her name. Maybe she's just using it as an alias during the cruise."

"Oh no, it's definitely her real name," Victoria replied, confidently. She then began fishing around in her pocket, pulling out a single slip of paper and handing it over to Myrick. "This fell out of her purse earlier today. Her name's printed right there on the ticket - Soriya Danes."

Inspecting the winner's ticket in his hand, Myrick came to the same conclusion as Victoria, agreeing that Soriya wouldn't go by an alias while gambling, as she'd want her identification to match up if or when she collected her winnings.

"Mind if I hold onto this?"

"Not at all. It's of no use to me," Victoria replied, then changed the subject. "So now that I've helped you *once again*, can we please go get that drink?"

"Yes. Yes, I think that's a splendid idea."

With that, Myrick and Victoria found themselves a quaint restaurant for one last meal aboard the ship. They laughed as they recounted all the adventures they'd experienced in the short time they'd been together. Then they discussed the logistics of how they were going navigate visiting each other going forward, Myrick noting that he was pretty sure he'd stored up thousands of points on his credit card that he believed could be converted to frequent flier miles.

All the while, a killer somewhere on the ship was sizing up the next victim in the series of murders.

*****

The rain was coming down hard now, tapping on the fiberglass overhang just above where Harriett had taken cover from the storm. She needed a place of solitude after the questioning that she'd undergone with the security officer, which had understandably rattled her nerves and put her on edge.

From her sheltered alcove, Harriett had a perfect vantage point to watch the seas, which had become as volatile as her emotions. She didn't necessarily like when she got like this. To others, Harriett always seemed to be the epitome of reserve, but deep inside she suffered from severe anxiety attacks, many times practically disabled by them. The episode she was going through at the moment was particularly jarring.

It was clearly attributable to the way Shev had spoken to Harriett, treating her almost like the suspect in a crime. In their original encounter, Shev's questions were open-ended, simply trying to find out what Harriett thought she'd heard that night. This time Shev was far less cordial, pressing for details, as if she was convinced Harriett had withheld facts during the original interview.

It didn't help that Harriett was already on edge from the strange behavior she'd witnessed from Myrick, Victoria and some of the other dancers, and now she was convinced that her original hunch had been right and something terrible had taken place that first night of the cruise. Her suspicions were confirmed when Shev no longer seemed to believe it was possible that Harriett had been mistaken about hearing the screams, instead her focus had changed to *where* they'd come from. In fact, that was what had Harriett really worried at the moment. Harriett, it seemed, had made a mistake talking to security and she was just now starting to come to grips with how significant that error in judgment had been.

"This isn't a safe place to be," a chilling voice cut through the darkness, startling Harriett.

Looking up, she spotted the silhouette of a shadowy character walking toward her, as if materializing out of the wind and rain. But as soon as the person reached the protection of the overhang and removed the hood from off the thick raincoat, Harriett recognized the face immediately.

"Oh hey, I-I was just trying to find a place to collect my thoughts. How did... how did you know I'd be here?"

"Just a hunch."

"You're not stalking me are you?" Harriett laughed, not actually meaning her words, but more so to make light of the situation. It was probably good to have some company, even if from someone she'd only just recently met. For Harriett, friends had *always* been hard to come by.

"Maybe."

Harriett got a chuckle out of the dry humored reply, expecting to see a smile in response. Instead, the edges of her mouth fell as she finally noticed the coldness of the menacing eyes staring at her.

"What do you mean *maybe*?"

"I mean, I do know you talked to that security officer."

"Of course I did. Wouldn't you if you thought someone was in danger?"

"If you hadn't said anything, none of these problems would be happening now. You caused this."

"I don't understand. We discussed this already."

"And I told you to let it go. That you'd obviously been mistaken."

"If that was so, they wouldn't have called me back in to talk. They must have some reason to be concerned."

"And they do."

There was an eerie stillness, the only sounds remaining: the steady drone of heavy rainfall and the stir of the howling winds, which seemed to funnel furiously underneath the overhang. Harriett gripped her jacket tighter as a sudden burst of air hit her, but the goosebumps on her arms weren't caused by the chilling wind, instead fear was rising up inside her as she started to understand that the person she was talking to might have a more sinister intent.

That feeling was only amplified as the dark figure pulled out a cloth bag from out of a pocket of the raincoat, stepping deliberately toward Harriett in the process. Realizing she was in serious danger, Harriett turned to run, although as she spun around, it occurred to her that the spot she'd chosen had her cornered. Her eyes darted furiously around, seeing a door, but as she reached for the handle, she realized instantly that it was securely locked.

Turning around again, the attacker was already on Harriett, a firm hand grasping her arm and the bag being swung over her head with the other. Harriett let out a bloodcurdling scream, which was immediately drowned out by the intense storm. Now that the decks had long since been cleared, there was no one even remotely close by enough to hear or come to Harriett's aid. She was going to have to fight for her own life.

Instead of making a fruitless attempt to thwart the bag being placed over her head, Harriett instinctively reached down to her belt line, fumbling for the dagger that was attached to the buckle of her belt. Securing it, she then swung the small blade backwards. Its edge swiped along the thigh of her attacker, who let out of a bellowing cry of pain, simultaneously doubling over and creating a chance for Harriett to escape. She didn't hesitate, immediately making her getaway, darting out from underneath the overhang, her face getting pelted by the hard rain instantly.

The winds were now incredibly fierce as Harriett desperately attempted to navigate the ship's slippery deck. She'd unwisely chosen a spot that was tucked away along a narrow walkway with only the nearby railing to steady herself. As she cut across the precarious ledge, she was hit with a sudden gust of wind, her feet slipping on the wet surface, causing her to fall violently to the deck.

The collision dislodged the dagger from her hand, sending it spiraling overboard and into the sea. At the same time, a severe pain shot up her leg. Harriett trembled as she reached for her ankle, realizing instantly that she must have fractured it. Using the railing for support, she pulled herself back up to her feet, limping forward gingerly, the entire side of her body supported by the steel bar running along the side of the vessel.

She'd gotten no more than a few yards when she felt a forceful hand on her shoulder, jerking her violently backwards. Then a second hand slipped a wet bag over her head, squeezing the drawstring on it so intensely that Harriett thought her head would burst from compressed blood flow. She struggled but the instant she let go of the railing to reach for the bag, she lost all ability to stand, her ankle shattered and the ground beneath her feet slick from rain.

Harriett suddenly felt her body being lifted off the ground, the stranglehold her attacker had on the bag so strong that it was keeping her upright. She kicked and flailed, unwilling to quit fighting until the last bit of life was gone from her body. Eventually, Harriett went completely limp. There was a stillness in the air as her body dangled beneath the killer's hands. Finally, Harriett was dropped to the ground, her body hitting with a thud as she collapsed in a motionless heap.

The menacing figure stood over Harriett, simply staring down at her for a long moment, as if trying to process the moment. Then a bizarre change came over the killer's face, much like before, as if remorseful to see the lifeless body lying dead on the boat deck.

"Not again," a stuttering voice breathed, just as Harriett's attacker started to bend over to pick her up. "I can't fix them all."

There was a pause, the attacker's expression changing once again, and then Harriett's body was lifted up along the nearby railing. Down below, the waves were hitting the veseel fiercely, seemingly pounding out a slow, steady funeral dirge. It was then that Harriett's body was tossed overboard, dropping down into the dark abyss. As her body hit the violent waters, she slowly sank to the depths of the sea; this time ensuring that the killer's latest victim would never be found.

CHAPTER NINETEEN
Even If Painful To Do, Study Yourself On Video

Shev had lost track of time sitting alone in the makeshift jail. She wasn't confined in a cell, but she still felt like a prisoner. The room was practically barren, save for the bed she was sitting on and the nearby security table which held a computer monitor displaying images from the cameras that captured the interiors of the two empty jail cells.

Moretti had gone to the extraordinary step of even locking the door, which was unnecessary at the moment, as Shev was completely defeated and there was nowhere for her to go anyway. She'd remain confined in the quarters until they finally came to port the next morning and the captain sent for her.

There would be a thorough review of her actions; not so much to get down to the bottom of Tempest's death, but more so to decide what to do about Shev's unthinkable disobedience. And much like before, there would be no one coming to her defense either. She'd already become acutely aware of that fact after her only supposed ally - Chief Moretti - turned his back on her the minute he risked Captain Salazar's wrath. She was going to have to fall on the sword and hope that the career ramifications wouldn't be too severe.

The computer in the room wasn't hooked up for any purpose other than to survey and record inmates inside the jail cells. Sitting practically zombie-like, Shev stared blankly at the flickering dull blue screens, which seemed to serve no real purpose at the moment, much like Shev felt about herself, leaving her with nothing to do but think back on the mistakes she'd made and whatever consequences lay ahead for her.

Out of nowhere, Shev sat upright on the cot, as if hit with a sudden realization. She then quickly slid over to the nearby computer, clicking on an icon that brought her to a screen that gave access to several video cameras.

Shev had used this workstation before, usually when she'd had to detain a passenger for an incident and was assigned to sit watch in the jail cell for extended periods of time. The server had very limited access. It lacked internet connectivity and it couldn't be used to send emails or attempt any other type of communication. But it was patched into the network's camera system. Clicking on one in particular, Shev pulled up live surveillance footage from an interior corridor.

Several passengers were currently walking in the hallway, crossing in and out of the camera's range, as they scurried toward their cabins during the storm. These cameras had a limited viewpoint, but more than enough for Shev to answer her own question. The bold numbers were visible on at least five of the cabin doors, so that Shev could read them in ascending order - 341, 343, 345, 347 and 349, the sea life - as it did on all the levels - following the flow toward the bow of the vessel in the same direction as the rising cabin numbers. Next to the number 349 was a sign that pointed the direction to the elevators, which were just a few feet away. That same sign also pointed to an emergency stairwell, which would've been in the exact opposite direction, and which Shev remembered was near Stateroom 301.

It was clear, Shev had overlooked a critical detail and one that proved she'd been lied to by one of the primary suspects in the case. She couldn't believe it had taken her so long to figure it out. The only question now was why try to deceive her about such a seemingly inconsequential fact?

The answer to that, however, was becoming slowly evident as well, the killer had used the stairwell - *not* the elevators - as an escape route after the crime. The same back stairwell that just so happened to be one of the few used by crew to go down to Deck 0 and which also accessed Deck 7 not far from where the larger lifeboats (and Tempest's body) were located.

Trapped inside the room, Shev knew it was critical to relay this information to Myrick somehow. Unfortunately, as she scanned through the different drives of the computer, it was clear it had been repurposed only as a monitor for the various cameras. She didn't even have access to the master drives where the video was being stored. The computer wasn't going to help her get word to Myrick.

Even though she already knew that things were hopeless, Shev got up from the table and hurried over to the door, desperately fiddling with the key lock, trying any security codes that she remembered. They'd all either expired or been disabled. She wasn't going to be able to get out that way.

She considered banging on the door, knowing that the security room was only a few doors down and that Moretti would eventually hear her and come to find out what the commotion was. She also knew that he wouldn't be interested in any of her theories, dismissing them immediately. It would only make matters worse if she tried turning to him again. Her discovery, it seemed, would have to remain with her until they got back to port and she could inform authorities, who would at least take that information seriously.

One of the things that Shev hated most about brig duty was that the jail cell was positioned along the slanted aft of the shift and she could literally hear the propeller as it churned in the water. It was almost impossible to tune out, and made sleep near impossible for the person assigned to guard a prisoner in a cell. The assignment to that duty was pure torture.

But then it dawned on Shev, however, that this section of the ship also had a watertight escape door. It was rather hard to distinguish, obscured between the large pipes of the wall, but Shev had been privy to the schematics of the vessel as part of her security training and was tasked with knowing *every* square inch of the massive cruise liner. With that in mind, it didn't take long for her to remember where the security hatch was located.

She'd seen the hatch opened before, but only from the outside and *only* when the craft was safely docked. Crews accessed it when working on the aft of the ship, sometimes for safety checks or routine maintenance work. Shev also was aware that the door was near the metal ladders affixed to the far end of the cruise ship and which reached seven levels up, coming to an apex just at the railing of the promenade.

Scaling it in calm waters in total darkness sounded absolutely terrifying. Doing so during a storm was beyond comprehension.

Myrick could be in danger though, especially if he wasn't aware of the unique clues that were all over the vessel and which proved that only one person would have had the opportunity to commit the crime. Yet, in contrast, all of the notes she'd recorded and had given to Myrick only bolstered the killer's alibi. Shev suddenly realized that she'd played right into the hands of the murderer and led Myrick away from solving the case, leaving her frustrated with herself for not catching the obvious discrepancy earlier.

There was a thick metal handle on the interior of the heavy door that sealed it tight. It wasn't easy to undo the latch, but Shev pulled down hard on it, eventually hearing the distinct click that indicated it had unlocked. She then placed her hand around a second handle, red in color, which she could turn while pushing on the door, giving her the ability to open it.

As soon as she'd pried the door open, Shev was hit with an immediate glimpse of the nightmarish conditions outside. The storm winds flung sheets of torrential rain into the interior of the ship, pelting Shev's face repeatedly until she could barely keep her eyes open. Despite that, she continued to push open the door wider, fully exposing the violent skies and churning water of the ocean in front of her, so that she could even see the propeller kicking up a heavy wake in its path.

To steady herself, Shev held tightly to a metal pipe, gripping it so tight that the edges of her fingers turned pale, then cautiously stuck her head through the opening, exposing herself to the elements. It was hard to see in the driving rain, but turning her eyes to the side, Shev tried desperately to size up the distance between the now-open door and the affixed metal ladder.

Eventually, Shev came to the conclusion that it was *possible* to swing her body toward the attached ladder and grasp onto it with one hand, while still holding onto the door for safety and support. Of course if she miscalculated, she could easily go plunging into the dark waters below, no rescue even possible, as no one was even aware of the foolish maneuver she was attempting. The thought of that type of death - being left hopelessly adrift in a vast freezing cold ocean - made Shev's legs go weak, forcing her to doubt that she had the courage to try something so risky.

The only other alternative was to leave Myrick to fend for himself. She'd gotten to know him well enough to understand he was a brilliant mind, and she guessed he'd have likely solved the crime if not for the misinformation she'd provided him from the recorded notes in the interviews. It was highly unlikely he'd debunk the alibi without Shev's input. She was Myrick's best - and possibly *only* - chance to solve the murders. And Shev's biggest flaw was that she was protective to a fault, even if it came at incredible risk to herself.

Before allowing more time to reflect on the danger involved, Shev leaned further outside the porthole, instantly battered by the ferocious winds, then bladed her body so that one hand gripped the door tightly while the other fumbled for the ladder. Eventually, she caught ahold of it, only to realize that the situation was even more frightening now, having compromised her stability.

The ground beneath her feet had become slick from the hammering rain. Her weight was split between the safety of the hull's interior and the metal ladder attached to the ship's exposed exterior. Even if she changed her mind and let go of the ladder, there was a good chance she'd fall. There was clearly no turning back at this point.

As she let go of the door, Shev simultaneously swung her entire body toward the ladder, her one hand already clutching it in a vice-like grip, the other flailing for some sort of hold along it as well. Her free hand had just made contact with one of the vertical bars right as her feet searched desperately for the bottom rung. Unfortunately, she'd underestimated just how slippery the soles of her shoes had become and her feet slipped out from underneath her before her second hand could establish any sort of secure hold.

Shev's body flung violently from side to side, fierce storm winds making it near impossible to maintain a grip. Now on the verge of plunging into the churning ocean, Shev's eyes grew wide in terror as her fingers on the one hand still clinging to the steel bar slowly lost contact with it. Miraculously - and seconds from falling - she felt one foot plant onto the last rung of the ladder. As it did, she used all of her strength to pull herself up and then pressed the entire weight of her body up against the aft of the vessel, too petrified to move.

Remaining in place for what felt like an eternity, Shev tried desperately to compose herself, completely aware that she'd been mere seconds from dying. Finally, she summoned the courage to glance upward, taking in the dark sky above and the impossible distance she'd have to climb in order to reach the safety of the ship's promenade level.

The ladder was pressed up along the exterior of the slanted aft. The howling winds had a suction effect so that it almost felt as if the violent air was pulling her away from the safety of the ladder, not yet willing to let go of its potential victim. Somehow, she found the strength to reach her hand up to the next rung, pulling herself upward as she did. Then she reached another step and yet another. Slowly she ascended it until she was at the highest point, allowing her access to the railing of the promenade, her arms weak and trembling at this point and with almost no might left in them.

As she finally pulled herself onto the safety of the deck, Shev collapsed to the ground in exhaustion, doing nothing to protect herself from the raindrops that were coming down hard and pelting her unprotected body. There, in the eeriness of her surroundings, Shev lay in disbelief of what had just happened and how close she'd come to death.

Her breathing heavy, she eventually sighed in relief and then decided it was time to pull herself together and go find Myrick. Shev opened her eyes slowly, using the back of her hand to fend off the fierce raindrops from above. Yet, almost as soon as she did - and once she could finally see again - she noticed a shadowy figure standing over her... and with what appeared to be an axe in hand.

*****

Myrick had been relatively certain who the killer *had* to be, but as he'd listened to the recorded interviews taken by Shev, he was beginning to second guess himself. There were also aspects of the investigation that differed from any other case he had worked, as his feelings for Victoria were coming into play and impacting his ability to judge the character of potential suspects, especially Talon. And Myrick wondered to himself to what, if any, degree that these factors had affected his overall reasoning. Regardless, it was wise to take a conscious step back and reassess things, his original theory potentially now disproven.

The one person Shev hadn't been able to interview was Soriya. Myrick began to wonder if she might just be his main suspect. If so, he was going to have to track her down, as she'd done an excellent job of keeping her private life a secret. The cruise ship was massive and people were milling all about. Myrick knew his best chance to find Soriya was Talon. Unfortunately, finding him would be tough. His fortunes, however, turned when he headed into the casino, aware that Talon had an affinity for gambling.

Sure enough, he eventually spotted Talon packed in at a long craps table. Almost as soon as he spotted him, Myrick could see that he was on a losing streak, evident by the way Talon pounded his hand on the table after losing a round and the small stack of chips immediately in front of him. Myrick watched as Talon then took a heavy swig out of a half-empty beer bottle.

As Myrick continued to make his way over, Talon looked up and saw him, seemingly possessing an uncanny ability to sense the approach of his rival. Almost immediately, Talon tapped on the table to indicate to the dealer that he was cashing out and then he stood up from his stool, deciding to confront Myrick, setting an aggressive tone.

"What do you want?" Talon growled, making no attempt to hide his disdain for the man.

"I need to find Soriya," Myrick replied, urgently.

"I have no clue where she is."

"Listen, I know we've had our differences… I'm sorry about that… but I could really use your help right now," pleaded Myrick. "I think she might present a danger to some of the passengers, maybe even you."

"Oh, that's rich," Talon rolled his eyes. "Now, you're going to warn me. I'll bet you're loving this, aren't you? Right about me yet again… I'm the sucker. Well, don't worry, man… I figured her out already. She was just using me. Lost all interest as soon as she heard we were heading back to port."

"It's better off that she's out of your life now."

"Is it?"

"Yes, Talon."

"And it's better that Victoria moved on from me as well, I take it."

Myrick understood that the tenor of the conversation had taken a confrontational turn and he was getting a glimpse of a side of Talon that he hadn't fully experienced yet, likely amplified by his liquored-up state. Myrick wondered if they weren't on the verge of a fight. He paused for a moment, suddenly realizing that Talon's shoes were still wet; apparently having been caught outside in the storm recently, perhaps having to do with his confrontation with Soriya.

"The breakup with you and Soriya really hurt you didn't it?" Myrick poked at Talon, aware that this was the only way he'd be able to keep Talon talking, as he wasn't likely to volunteer information otherwise.

"No. If you want to know the truth, we said a few last words to each other out on the pool deck, then she got all emotional just as the rain started coming down so we went our own ways. You must be getting a whole lot of self-righteous pleasure out of hearing all this."

Ignoring Talon's sarcasm, Myrick began to worry that Soriya was getting desperate, escalating the potential for something tragic to take place.

"Which direction did she go?"

"Pretty sure she took off toward the back of the ship, last I saw of her. Probably best if we never cross paths again," said Talon, angered. "It won't end up well for her if we do."

Myrick was surprised by Talon's sinister words, but he also was convinced that the threat was an empty one, incited by the pain in his heart and the alcohol in his system. More importantly, there wasn't time to deal with Talon's emotions at the moment and so Myrick turned to walk away, the conversation over as abruptly as it had begun.

"I know you're gonna go try finding her," said Talon, his voice surprisingly emotionless and cold, stopping Myrick in his tracks. "Don't make things worse than they already are."

Myrick's back was to Talon so he couldn't see his face, but the chilling change in the man's tone was unmistakable, making Myrick suddenly consider what Talon might be capable of if the warning wasn't heeded. There was a brief moment of tension as Myrick considered what he wanted to do next, his body slowly turning to confront Talon, ready to put an end to this once and for all. Fortunately, Myrick got a grip on himself, biting his tongue before answering back, his silence a powerful response.

Deciding to be the bigger man, and respecting his earlier promise to Victoria, Myrick continued walking, making his way down the length of the casino and eventually out the door so that

Talon was no longer in sight. Meanwhile, Myrick could tell that he wasn't being followed, confirming the wisdom in his decision to walk away before things got out of hand.

"I could really use some inspiration about now, God?" Myrick whispered quietly, now out of earshot of Talon or anyone else. *"I'm not going to be able to solve this one without You. Maybe You could just send someone of Your choosing to help me,"* Myrick shrugged his shoulders, an amused expression on his face, aware that God tended to do the unexpected in his life and it was wise to be purposeful in what he asked for in prayer.

Turning his attention back to the events where he felt he could at least control himself, Myrick decided he needed to find Soriya and he had a general of idea of where she had likely run off to. In truth, Myrick had originally - perhaps hastily - written Soriya off as the killer. She just didn't fit the prototype in his estimation. Years of police work and he'd seen just about *everything*. He'd met plenty of Soriyas in that time as well, although often they were suspects in financial-type crimes, prone to preying on the elderly, who often had the most wealth to steal. Those types didn't tend to draw further attention to themselves. It didn't add up. Then again, *nothing* really had so far in this case.

So, by process of elimination, he began to reconsider her potential involvement in the crime, maybe even just as a co-conspirator in them. After all, she'd been the most evasive of the suspects, not even showing up for the interviews, which was certainly dubious. And of course Myrick had been away from law enforcement for a good year, his skills as a detective, it seemed, growing a tad rusty over that time. It was entirely possible he just didn't have that same instinct for solving cases anymore.

It didn't help either that Shev had gone MIA. She'd made an ideal partner, despite her inexperience. Myrick also had a sinking feeling that she'd been disciplined once again for trying to assist in the investigation. If so, it was undeniably Myrick's fault for dragging her back into it, making him even more determined to solve the crime, proving that Shev's instincts had been right all along. She deserved *at least* that much from him after she'd put her own career on the line in an attempt to do the right thing.

Eventually, Myrick reached the doors that led outside and toward the aft of the ship. The conditions on the exterior of the craft had only worsened, causing his stomach to churn. This was Myrick's first time out on the rough waters and he was starting to experience sea sickness, which could easily take him out of commission at any moment.

Despite the sensation, and while clenching his coat tight, Myrick proceeded out into the storm, the elements working against him - almost as if to warn him to turn back. But Myrick was stubborn and he'd become determined to find Soriya, *wherever* she might be hiding.

CHAPTER TWENTY
Give The Song's Final Verse Dramatic Emphasis

Shev couldn't make out the face of the figure standing menacingly over her, but she *did* recognize the voice that called out from the darkness, grateful for the perfect timing of the person there to rescue her.

"Step away from her, Paul! It's over!"

The ominous figure crept back slightly, axe still clutched tightly, pulling the hoodie off his face so that Shev had a better look at him, Paul's eyes cold and soulless. He appeared nothing like the man she'd interviewed earlier, now seemingly almost possessed.

"Drop the axe too!" Myrick continued, stepping out of the darkness and further into visibility under the glow of a hanging light.

There was a tense stillness as Paul glanced down at the weapon in his hand. He was still mere inches away from Shev, who was sprawled out on the deck of the ship, and unable to defend herself if Paul decided to swing its sharp edge down on her. Instead, he slowly twisted the handle, so that eventually the blade turned in a new direction, now pointed at Myrick.

"She deserves to die. They all did. *She,* of course, tried to talk me out of it, but I knew what needed to be done."

Listening to Paul's words only scared Shev even more. They were completely irrational and made no sense. He was evidently delusional, capable of anything at the moment, and *certainly* willing to kill. Even though the axe wasn't pointed in her direction, the fact that he still clutched it in his hand terrified her.

"I can help you. I just need you to trust me, Paul," Myrick replied.

"Stop calling me that. Stop calling me *Paul.*"

Again, Shev was surprised and frightened by Paul's crazed behavior. She had a clear view of his face. It was *definitely* him and he was beyond rationalizing with if he wouldn't respond to his own name. She became even more confused as she heard Myrick's next reply.

"How about I call you by your real name then?" Myrick asked. "I know you're not really Paul Granger. So who exactly am I dealing with? Maybe I can help."

"Oh, good, we can finally end the charade. You can call me Frank. I hated the whole idea behind assuming someone else's identity. That was entirely Raven's idea. She's a trickster of sorts. Gets a perverse thrill out of deceiving people, I guess. Me, I'm the honest one. I'm even honest with Raven... let her know the women who I like... and those I don't." Frank panned the axe back in Shev's direction to make clear who he was referring to.

"Then you know you can trust me also," replied Myrick, immediately, wanting to keep Frank's attention on him and away from Shev. "I believe in being straightforward as well. The two of us can talk this out."

Listening, Frank stood stone-faced in the rain, seemingly intrigued by Myrick's words. A cruel grin then spread across his face as the corners of his mouth inched upward. "Oh, I can't trust you. I can't trust anyone. Not even *Raven*. As soon as she betrayed me, I knew I could never trust anyone ever again."

"Then it's Raven that should be held responsible," Myrick offered, wanting to make it clear that he did understand Frank. Hoping that his words might even distract Frank long enough that Myrick could get a drop on him. Seizing on his chance, Myrick took a cautious step forward. As soon as he did, however, Frank lifted up the axe threateningly, causing Myrick to pause in his tracks.

"*We* were a team. That's what I believed. Then she started to blame everything on me. Even felt bad for the people *we* killed. But don't listen to her lies, she's just as guilty as I am. She was the one who understood them. She was the one who warned me not to trust women to begin with."

"And Raven wields a great deal of influence over you, doesn't she?" Myrick replied, knowing exactly what he was doing.

"Finally, someone who has figured it out. She's the liar. The deceiver in this. You'll lock me up for the obvious. But the real mastermind... the one who hides behind the curtain, manipulates me like a puppet. She'll have a clear conscience. Well, I'm not going to allow that."

"Do you want me to speak to her?" Myrick asked. "Do you want me to confront Raven first? Because I will, Frank. I'll make sure she answers for what she's done. I *do* believe you."

As Frank's expression seemed to calm, Myrick understood that he was on the verge of convincing him to *finally* listen. Meanwhile, Shev was about to seize on the moment also, slowly twisting her body, putting herself in a position so that she'd have enough force to sweep Frank's feet out from underneath him.

Myrick watched, unable to do anything, as Shev made the mistaken decision to act, kicking her foot out at Frank. She'd assumed he hadn't seen her. She was wrong. Out of the corner of his eye, he'd caught Shev's motion, sidestepping her kick. As soon as he was out of harm's way, his grip on the axe tightened.

"Stop Frank!" Myrick bellowed out, rushing toward him.

It was too late. Frank came down with the flat base of the axe right across Shev's forehead. Despite Shev using her arm to blunt some of the force, it was still a crushing blow. Instantly, her world went black.

Myrick hit Frank with the full force of his body, the two of them tumbling to the ground, sliding across the slick, wet deck. The axe flew out of Frank's hand, clanking against the railing, teetering on the edge of falling into the cold waters below. Immediately, Myrick felt a blow across his face, Frank's knuckles crushing into his cheek. The blow was so intense that Myrick flailed in the air and a circular object that had been concealed inside his coat went flying to the ground, rolling off into the distance.

The two fought back and forth, Myrick eventually starting to get the upper hand, years of combat training at the police academy coming back to him instantly, as if ingrained into his being. He leveled a punch right into Frank's gut, knocking the air out of him. Myrick didn't hesitate, grabbing ahold of both of Frank's arms, forcing them downward so that he had him subdued for the moment.

Had the wind and elements not been a factor, the fight would've been over, Frank finally captured. Instead, the rain was coming in horizontally now, pelting Myrick right in the face, blinding his vision. Frank seized on the opportunity, head-butting Myrick with unbridled strength, causing Myrick to go tumbling backwards, completely dazed. The ship already tilted in that direction, the ground beneath his feet slippery and the force of the blow and the wind around him all working against Myrick, he careened against the railing, then - inevitably - went over it.

With a desperate grab, he wrapped his arm around the top metal bar, saving him from the fall to his death. His relief, though, was short lived as he saw Frank pull himself up into a standing position, searching for the axe with his eyes, then finding it and picking it up.

Myrick's eyes were mere inches above the railing, but high enough so that he could see that Shev was still knocked out cold. He was going to have to act fast to pull himself back up onto the safety of the deck before Frank was upon him. With all his strength Myrick struggled until he had a second hand on the railing, quickly pulling himself above it so that his entire torso was above the highest rung. One more lurch and he'd be able to throw himself back onto the flat surface of the promenade.

It was then that his arm slipped, the metal bar slick from rain, and he fell backwards again, barely holding on as he looked fearfully down at the churning dark waters below, his feet dangling with nothing to stabilize them. *Death* was coming for Myrick.

Frank, in turn, slowly came to the edge of the railing and then glared down at him, the axe wielded high in his hands. His eyes were full of evil intent and Myrick understood there was no help coming; he *was* going to die. It was just a matter of whether he would let go and fall to the consuming waves below or wait for Frank to level the heavy blade at him.

Summoning up the last of his strength, Myrick whispered a defiant prayer, making it clear even in the end where his faith resided. He then watched as Frank lifted the axe ready to come down with a blow that Myrick had no chance of defending himself against. As Frank's arm moved downward, an object collided with the side of his face, causing his head to jerk violently and then sending him stumbling away from the railing until he disappeared from Myrick's line of sight.

The sounds of a vicious struggle then appeared to take place. Myrick couldn't see what was happening, but he *could hear* the fight that ensued, at one point the metal of the axe even colliding against the deck, as if it had been swung. The fight seemed to go on for an eternity; meanwhile, Myrick was losing the last of his grip, unable to summon up the strength to swing his second hand up to the railing.

His fingers loosened one by one, until there were only the tips of three on the slick railing. Then, he lost all contact with the bar entirely, feeling weightless as he began to fall into the dark void. As death tugged at Myrick, someone else's strong grip was doing the same. Somehow the person who had taken out Frank had also come to Myrick's rescue at the last possible opportunity as well.

"I've got you!" Talon cried out.

Dangling precariously, Myrick didn't feel like Talon had him at all. In fact, he felt relatively certain that he was about to pull Talon overboard as well. It suddenly dawned on Myrick that Talon should let go of him before the two of them fell to their deaths. Myrick could also tell by the grip on his wrist that Talon was not going to let go. He watched in disbelief as Talon summoned up every ounce of strength in him, his face contorted in a tortured expression, as if for some reason he was in excruciating pain as he pulled.

Incredibly, Myrick's arm was finally close enough that he could grab for the railing. He did so, determined to do everything he could to assist as he'd figured out why Talon was in such incredible agony and the sacrifice he was making to save Myrick, using the same arm to save Myrick as had just undergone the reconstructive surgery.

Once Myrick had a solid hold on the bar with one hand, he used the leverage and Talon's help to pull himself up and over the railing, going tumbling to the safety of the deck. Completely spent, Talon fell to the ground also, unmoving from sheer exhaustion. Myrick, though, understood there was no time to rest, his attention spanning the area around him, waiting for Frank's next attack. Instead, when he did spot Frank, he found that Frank was still crouched over, hands over his face as if in complete shock.

Myrick spun quickly to his feet, locating the axe and racing over to pick it up while he had the brief chance to do so. As soon as he had the weapon in hand, Myrick turned his attention back to the Frank, still convinced the man was an extreme danger.

"It's over, Frank."

Myrick watched as the defeated figure on the ground finally lifted his head, surprising Myrick that there seemed to be tears in his eyes and they were full of immense remorse.

"He's done it again, hasn't he?"

"You have, Frank," said Myrick.

"Frank?" the broken man spoke, sheer bewilderment in his eyes. "Frank's not here."

Myrick had been expecting this moment, although the suddenness of it still shocked him. He'd developed his suspicions during the poker game, as if he was dealing with two completely different personalities. The bizarre dance with Victoria only furthered his beliefs, her insistence that he kept switching from lead and follow roles with little to know warning. What Myrick couldn't figure out was the seemingly airtight alibi, as the video footage confirmed what Paul had insisted in his interview with Shev - that he'd come straight from the piano bar to his room after the dance social that night. Still, it was clear now that Myrick's original suspicions had been right all along.

"Can you tell me who I'm talking to now?" Myrick asked, certain that he'd get a surprising answer.

"Raven. Well, Paul too. You know me as Paul also. I'm good with becoming other people."

"Then where is the real Paul?" Myrick asked, although relatively certain he already knew what the answer would be.

"Frank killed him. Frank killed his girlfriend also. Which is why I had to get away. He wouldn't stop. Paul was already dead so there was no harm in taking his name and identity. I couldn't undo what Frank had done. But I could try to protect myself."

"I understand," Myrick replied, aware there was no sense trying to explain things to Raven at the moment, as she clearly believed what she was saying. "I'll need you to come with me though."

Entirely despondent, Raven did as told, methodically walking over to Myrick; and Myrick struggled with the bizarre realization that he was arresting someone for murder who had no clue of the horrible things she'd done, her alter-ego Frank committing all the killings while assuming control of their multiple personalities. It was a surreal encounter. And it got even stranger as Myrick watched the expression in Raven's eyes morph, going wide then becoming consumed with rage.

Frank was back.

There wasn't enough time to react, Myrick had let his guard down thinking that he was still dealing with Raven. Frank was an imposing figure and the element of surprise was working in his favor. He was on Myrick before Myrick even had a chance to react. Fortunately, Talon reached out at the last possible second, catching the edge of Frank's foot, just enough so that it caused Frank to stumble. Myrick lowered his shoulder and Frank spun off of it, his feet sliding across the slick deck, into the rail and tumbling overboard.

Frank reached desperately for the security of the metal bar, missing it completely. He then disappeared into the waves below, Myrick was just able to reach the side of the vessel in time to see what appeared to be Frank's tormented face go underwater for the final time. There was no possible way to save him.

Collapsing to the ground, Myrick was spent and caught in disbelief. Eventually, Talon pulled himself up next to him, the two former adversaries with their backs up to the railing, not saying a word. It was then that Myrick spotted the worn baseball lodged against a corner wall, realizing that it had fallen out of his coat pocket and it must've been used by Talon to hit Frank in the side of the head just as Frank was coming down with the axe. It was an impressive throw... and Talon's swift thinking had undoubtedly saved Myrick's life.

Shev was still lying on the ground, unconscious. Myrick could see that she was steadily breathing, but he also knew she needed medical attention. He started to pull himself to a standing position when he noticed Talon massaging his arm, as if the prior injury had been seriously re-aggravated.

"Bum arm, eh?" said Talon, seeing that Myrick was looking directly at it. "I told you it was good."

Myrick chuckled at Talon's words, aware that they were muttered in jest and that the desperate act had left Talon in excruciating pain. It was a bravery like Myrick had rarely witnessed. And it proved that Victoria had been right to place so much faith in Talon all along.

"First time I've ever been wrong about someone," Myrick offered with a smirk. "I owe you my life. I can't thank you enough."

"You can't," said Talon, the right edge of his mouth inching upward in cocky fashion.

"Still, I'm pretty sure I'd clock that fastball at no more than 70 miles an hour," Myrick's shrugged his shoulders as he spoke. "I probably throw 80 on a bad day," he laughed.

"Sure you do old man," Talon began to laugh, only to wince from the shooting pain radiating down his arm. "You think you could help me up? I should probably track down medical attention."

Myrick reached over a hand to Talon, helping him to his feet by his good arm. The two then hurried over to Shev; Myrick confirming by her pulse that her vitals were steady, then insisting on staying with her while Talon rushed off to find a medic to assist.

Their motley crew of a team had worked a miracle together. The killing spree had mercifully come to an end.

EPILOGUE

This was Myrick's first ever trip to Scotland, enamored immediately by the quaint little island that Islay was, but also equally aware that it held tremendous historical value. Sitting at a stool at the Ballygrant Inn, he found himself amazed by the tradition preserved and on display all around him. He also couldn't believe that he was finding himself in this spot only a few short months after the eventful cruise. Still, he'd made a promise and Myrick always made good on his word.

After a few minutes, a gentleman sat down on an empty stool next to Myrick, the two the only people at the bar at the moment. Without saying a word, Myrick pushed a glass with a caramel color liquid in it over to the individual sitting beside him. The man then picked up the glass, placing it just beneath his nose as if to savor the aroma, then took a slow deliberate sip, moving the liquor around on his tongue before swallowing. Finally, he placed the glass back down on the bar, a warm expression on his face.

"This is a dram from Jim's private cask, isn't it?" the man asked, his hands moving wildly as he spoke.

"It is. Only the finest for a Scotsman like you, Duncan," Myrick slid over the rest of the Port Charlotte bottle for Duncan to inspect and relish.

"Well, I can't rightly say I've ever been given a gift more suited to my tastes," Duncan replied, turning his attention back to the liquor and taking an additional sip.

The whisky had been the most expensive Myrick had ever purchased and he couldn't have been happier to see his friend enjoying it. It did help the budget for Duncan to have insisted on putting Myrick up at the Ballygrant, making sure that the room was comped long before Myrick arrived; and of course Myrick had fortuitously come into *hefty* winnings at a recent poker game as well.

"You know, I read the papers. They gave a wee bit more credit to that Rotem girl than you in 'em. Seems she's been treated as some sort a hero."

"You mean Shev?"

"Aye right, do believe you referred to her by that name before," Duncan noted, wisely.

"Well, in my opinion, she deserves *all* the credit. She's sharp. Figured out on her own that the inner workings of the ship completely disproved Frank's alibi that he'd returned straight to his room after the social at the piano bar. He would've had to have gone the long way around the ship to have gotten to that back stairwell... which you can see on the surveillance video was the direction he came from before returning to his room... and just so happens to have been the same back stairwell where I found the red blood smear on the handrail and which has since been confirmed as Greylock's DNA."

"Did you always know that that fella Paul... er, Frank... was the murderer?"

"I admit, I waffled a bit. Poor Ms. Cribbs was an early suspect of mine. That was until I made the exact same mistake she had and confused the port side of the ship with the starboard side. It's a common issue with passengers out on the water for any extended period of time, confusing the left and right side of a vessel. And of course, she reiterated her confusion when she told Shev that she thought her cabin was on the port side of the craft, even though odd numbered rooms on a cruise ship indicate their location starboard side."

"And why not Ms. Danes? She's quite a peculiar girl. I wasn't much a fan of hers from the get-go."

"And neither was I. But she clearly wasn't involved in the murders. That in itself was easy enough to conclude from the winning greyhound track ticket Ms. Danes had left behind at the breakfast table."

"You deduced that all from one slip of paper?"

"Well, there were several other clues as well, but the receipt was a pretty solid alibi, even if Ms. Danes' had never intended it to be. Only a handful of states still permit dog racing. California isn't one of them. In fact, if I recall correctly, the closest would be Texas. Given the date stamp on the ticket, it would've been impossible for Ms. Danes to have pulled off the murders in the Oakland area. She couldn't have been our serial killer."

"I read that the real the real Paul Granger's body was eventually located too. Found both him and his girlfriend together. Although I thought it quite bizarre how only she had that strange 'X' shape carved into her."

"Frank suffered from a dissociative disorder. When his alter-ego, *Raven*, took over she acted quite differently than him. In fact, I've since found out that only Paul's girlfriend - Carrie - had been positioned post-homicide and that Paul's body was left exactly in the same location and position as where Frank murdered him. I'd surmise that Raven felt a sort of kinship with the female victims. Her personality detested Frank's. I'm assuming that was Raven's way of doing something for the victims post-death - *or at least the female ones.* As for the 'X' shape, a closer inspection during autopsy revealed the carvings appeared more like crossed spears, a common symbol for protection from evil, which Raven must have added each time as secure passage for the victims in the afterlife."

"Aye, aye, explains a lot that that Frank was bit of a rocket, eh?"

"Actually, just the opposite. You have to know about dissociative disorders to really understand why I was skeptical of that likelihood. A case like that of Frank/Raven's is *extremely* rare. Most split personalities are so subtle that you can barely tell if someone has that type disorder. Multiple personality disorders don't make a person violent, which is why my original reaction was actually to dismiss that possibility. But of course, every person is different. Unfortunately, Frank had an inner hate inside him, much like killers often do. It goes back to the days of Cane and Abel… and the dangers of allowing evil into your heart."

"Fascinating. So then, what happened to that dear lassie… Shev? I saw a quote from the captain that he wanted her promoted to chief of security on his vessel. Aye, he was quoted as saying she was his finest crew member. How's she doing since?"

"Well, for starters, she's moved on from the cruise line industry," Myrick couldn't help but shake his head and laugh. "She's found herself in a better spot though. Turns out the Colorado Springs Police Department still had a huge hole to fill without me there." Myrick winked. "I placed a couple of calls and let them know they needed to get in touch with her asap before some other sheriff's agency got wise and snatched her up."

"Well that's tidy and all, but enrollment in a police academy will cost a pretty penny," Duncan noted. "You think maybe she needs a sponsor? If so, I'd be glad to help, ken."

"Oh, I think she'll be just fine," Myrick winked back.

Duncan didn't need Myrick to explain for him to know that Myrick had covered everything himself. It seemed the two of them were cut from the same *noble* cloth. Aware now that Shev was going to be just fine, Duncan turned his attention to another question he had, and one in which he unfortunately was aware more about than perhaps even Myrick was.

"And how are things with Victoria?"

"They're good."

"Are they, though?"

"Best they can be. She's back in New York. That's her home."

"Talon's hometown too," Duncan added, wisely.

Myrick didn't reply, but his eyebrows rose in an equal measure, and his forehead creased in evident concern, telling Duncan everything he needed to know.

"It'll work out in the end, lad. Life has a way of doing that."

"I'm in for the adventure of finding out. What's meant to be will happen."

"To adventures," Duncan lifted his whisky tumbler to toast Myrick, then added a well-traveled Scottish saying, "Might as well be happy while you're living, for you're a long time dead."

"To adventures," said Myrick, tapping the top of Duncan's glass. "May we both have many more to come."

"Dance adventures," Duncan added.

"Perhaps. Although hopefully next time around, I'll choose a style that doesn't come with so much inherent risk of death."

Myrick laughed. Duncan, in turn, joined in with him. Then Duncan's face became more serious, as if he had a revelation.

"You know," he said, "You might want to give Country 2-Step a chance. And I believe that was part of the winner's prize at the poker tournament, if I remember correctly."

"It unfortunately was," Myrick simply replied, not saying more.

He did like country music though. Just not nearly enough to convince him that he wanted to learn an entirely new type of dance… at least - *if* he could help it - not anytime soon.

A WORD FROM THE AUTHOR: Thanks for reading *Rock-Step, Triple-Homicide*! I would love to hear your input on the novel. Please send me an email (ddorsey@Studio15inc.com) or connect with me online (Facebook, Instagram, Twitter or LinkedIn). In addition, if you're in the Florida area and want to get some Lindy dancing in, here are some of the groups/locations I highly recommend: Bold City Swing, Monarch Ballroom and Jacksonville Country & Swing Dancing. And of course, there's also my absolute favorite place to dance - The Dance Shack (www.TheDanceShack.com). Save some dances for me!!!

ABOUT THE AUTHOR

DOUG DORSEY** is the author of seven novels - *Never Alone, Broken Hero, The Deception, The Red Ledger, Kick Ball Slay: An Introduction to West Coast Swing... And A Murder Mystery, The Betrayal,* and *Rock Step, Triple Homicide: An Introduction To Lindy Hop... And A Murder Mystery.* For more information on his books, visit him at www.Studio15inc.com.